The Beaumonts

—THE BEAUMONT SERIES—

BOOKS 6&7

ANGIE DANIELS

Caramel Kisses
Publishing

For questions and comments about the book please contact angie@angiedaniels.com.

ISBN-13: 978-1-941342-01-5

Caramel Kisses
Publishing

Caramel Kisses Publishing
PO Box 2313
Chesterfield, VA 23832
www.caramelkissespublishing.com

Every Second Counts

— THE BEAUMONT SERIES —

BOOK #6

ANGIE DANIELS

Chapter 1

Jabarie Beaumont cradled Brenna in his arms and gently planted light kisses to her hair and temple. She responded with a sleeper's sigh, a delicate sound that spoke to his heart and his sex-deprived libido. God, he wanted this woman! He wanted her so bad the hard-on he'd had from the moment he'd awakened to her voluptuous ass rubbing up against him threatened the seams of his boxers.

For a long mesmerizing moment he lay there holding her close, captivated by the delicious smell that was all Brenna. As he listened to her sleeping peacefully the soft exhalation of her breathing filled his heart with joy. Within seconds he began to feel that sensation only she had the power to make him feel—a hot physical flood that engulfed him each and every time he held her in his arms.

Propping himself up with one elbow, his gaze raked her beautiful caramel face, admiring her high cheekbones, small round nose and full rosy lips. After nine years of marriage, he still possessed an insatiable craving for Brenna Gathers Beaumont that had him yearning to slide between her legs and forget about everything except the fire that burned between them.

Brenna rolled toward him, dragging the sheet away and revealing the curves of her round succulent breasts that had nursed their children. Memories of the hours they'd spent making love and creating the Fabulous Five filled Jabarie's mind and caused his erection to stretch a few more agonizing inches.

His eyes traveled along her abdomen that was firm and flat. The only signs of having given birth were a few faint stretch marks and lush childbearing hips he loved to grip tightly while he pumped deep inside her welcoming body. Reaching out, he ran his fingertips along the contours of her body, traveling across her neck and shoulders downward to the firm curves of her breasts, where he teased a finger around her chocolate nipples in small circles, feeling them hardening in response.

Brenna stirred slightly. Her toned legs stretched out, sliding along his as Jabarie brushed the pad of his thumb across the tightening flesh.

"Hmmm," she moaned, and he felt her body quiver beneath his touch. In a matter of seconds her nipples were rock hard, and when he lightly squeezed she made a sound low in her throat, an echo of intense pleasure.

"Good morning, baby," he whispered, drawing her attention.

Brenna opened and shut her eyelids several times before she was able to focus on the face only inches from hers. Her hazel gaze held him for a long intense moment, causing his pulse to kick in while his dick jutted against his thigh.

"Morning," she mumbled drowsily, her word a mere breath of air on his skin.

He was mesmerized. Her rich beauty was hypnotic as she lay there, a mass of honey-brown hair spread loosely around her pillow, and her soft hazel eyes staring up at him hungrily.

Reaching out, Brenna ran her manicured fingernails along the muscles of his back that flexed beneath her heated touch. She traveled down over his hip, then slipped her hand between his legs and rubbed the bulge in his boxers. "What do we have here?" she asked in a soft sleepy voice.

Jabarie's breath left his chest in a rush. "A hard dick," he replied, and hissed as she ran her long slender fingers along its length.

"Mmmm, I can see that," she purred playfully, then grazed her thumb over the sensitive tip in small circles, causing Jabarie to flinch.

"Don't start anything you can't finish," he warned while his hand slipped between her thighs, stroking soft brown curls and drawing a whimper from her lips.

"I didn't start this, you did," Brenna moaned, and spread her legs, giving him full access.

His mouth hovered over hers as he growled, "And I have every intention of finishing."

Leaning forward he threaded his fingers through her hair, then brought his lips to her, kissing her passionately while his heart burst with desire. Never had he loved a woman the way he loved Brenna. She was his soul mate, the mother of his children, and the woman with whom he had pledged to share his life.

Jabarie listened to her breathless sighs as his lips traveled across to her cheek, savoring her soft whimpers when he dragged his tongue down along her neck, between her breasts, then curled around a hardened nipple.

"Ooh yesss," she whimpered, pushing her nipple

deeper into his mouth. His hand slid along her ribs, then traveled downward before sliding around to her belly. Her thighs parted and she lifted her hips from the bed in anticipation. When his fingers traveled to the V between her legs and slipped inside, cries of ecstasy tore from her throat while her fists clenched the bunched sheets beneath her.

"I gotta have you," Jabarie said huskily as he pushed his boxers down over his hips, and immediately lowered his weight on top of her. Her hands opened across his back and he groaned at the feel of her body, delicate and soft beneath him. He lifted himself onto his palms, with no thought except burying himself deep. Gently he pushed her thighs further apart and was prepared to slide inside her sweet heat when he heard something that caused him to arch his head back and whisper, "Bren, did you hear that?"

Brenna gazed up at him, paused, then shook her head. "Hear what?"

"Someone's laughing. Shhh, listen." Sure enough, in a matter of seconds he heard it again. He gave Brenna a knowing look, then slid over toward the edge of the bed. Gazing underneath, he was met by two pairs of identical sable eyes. Upon finding out their hiding place had been discovered, his three-year-old twin sons burst out with laughter.

"What are the two of you doing under there?"

"Hiding from Bree," Julian explained.

"Daddy ... Are you and Mommy wrestling again?" Justice asked.

The question caused Brenna to giggle softly while Jabarie struggled to keep a straight face. "Yes, we're wrestling," he replied, then quickly changed the subject. "Why are you hiding from Bree?"

"'Cause she wants us to play Barbie."

"Yuck!" Justice screeched.

Jabarie glanced over his shoulder at his wife, who was slipping a blue nightgown over her head, and groaned. *I guess I won't be getting any this morning.*

"Come out from under there," he ordered, then rolled onto his back and secured the sheets up over his waist. He waited as the twins slid out from under the king-size bed and immediately started bouncing around.

"Mommy, Mommy, can we have pancakes?" Julian begged.

Justice nodded his head vigorously. "Yes, puh-leeze."

Brenna gazed adoringly at her toddlers and nodded. "Yes, *if* you go and watch television while I make breakfast."

"Okay!"

"Yeah!" they answered in unison, then went racing out of the room and down the hall toward the family room.

"Ask Bree to turn on the television for you!" Brenna called after them. As soon as they were gone she collapsed back onto her pillow and groaned. "Goodness, it isn't even seven o'clock. Where do they get all that energy?"

Jabarie chuckled as he rolled over and planted a gentle kiss on his wife's lips. "They get it from their old man. You know I've always been your energizer bunny."

"Is that so?" she grinned playfully.

"Yes, and if the kids weren't up I could show you better than I can tell you." He kissed her again and was quickly reminded of his hard-on thrusting anxiously against the sheets. As if he needed to be reminded they weren't alone, he heard Bree in the family room ordering the twins to stop jumping on the couch. "I guess we'll have to finish this later," he said with a playful grumble.

Brenna gave him one of those smiles that took his

breath away as she stroked his erection. "I promise I won't fall asleep on you tonight," she purred in a voice that left him throbbing even more. They started kissing and petting again and his body started burning with desire. He was seconds away from finishing where they'd left off when he heard his oldest, Arianna, screaming at the top of her lungs for the twins to get out of her room.

Brenna pushed gently against his chest. "Baby, I better get up before she wakes Lil' Jay."

Reluctantly, Jabarie kissed Brenna once more before allowing her to slide out from underneath him. Rolling onto his side, he admired the enticing sway of her lush hips as she sashayed her petite frame across the thick carpeting toward the adjoining bathroom. He was tempted to follow her into the bathroom and secure the door for a quickie, because as horny as he was it would definitely be quick. He'd had every intention of making love to his wife last night, but by the time Lil Jay had become a victim of the sandman, Brenna was already fast asleep.

From the baby monitor on the nightstand he heard soft whimpering, indicating their two-year-old was waking up.

"I guess it's time for me to get up, too." A few seconds later, Jabarie tossed the sheets away and rose, ready to start another fast-paced week.

Chapter 2

After making the children breakfast and sending her sexy husband out the door for a nine o'clock meeting, Brenna hurried to her room so she could get dressed and get to the gym for an hour of cardio before arriving at the independent bookstore she owned. She glanced briefly at the slender watch on her arm. Their nanny, Francine, was scheduled to arrive at any moment.

Brenna slipped into the massive master suite that was well over two thousand square feet, with large picture windows, a cathedral ceiling, and French doors that led out onto a private beach. Their bedroom was her oasis. Rich dark brown furnishings captured the elegant beauty of great traditional European design, with ornate appliqués and corbels accented by the flowing leaf and scroll detailing. Stone columns led into a spacious sitting room where she used to spend hours curled up on a plush chaise lounge in front of a gas-burning fireplace reading romance novels by her favorite authors. Brenna couldn't remember the last time she'd had time to enjoy a good book.

She returned a long red robe to the door of her personal walk-in closet, then moved past a king-size bed that sat high off the floor over to a large dresser drawer and removed a sports bra and matching panties. Humming softly, she padded across plush cinnamon-colored carpet into the adjoining bathroom that was designed to resemble a spa retreat, with a large Jacuzzi tub, a spacious glass-encased shower and a magnificent view out onto the Atlantic Ocean. As soon as she walked over to the double sink Brenna's eyes traveled up the mirror and she gasped.

I plan on finishing where we left off was written in pink lipstick across the glass.

A smiled curled her lips and her nipples tightened at the thought of what would have occurred if the twins hadn't been under the bed. One thing about her husband, he had an insatiable appetite for sex and always managed to make her feel like the most desirable woman alive.

As she splashed warm water onto her face, Brenna thought about how much she loved that man. They had met when she was in the fourth grade. Although they had both been innocent at the time, he had been her first love. Friends had asked how she'd managed to spend her life loving only one man. That was simple. Jabarie was all she had ever wanted. Even though she had been born of more humble beginnings, he never made her feel beneath him.

If only she could say the same about everyone else.

The Beaumont Hotel of Sheraton Beach was one of the most prestigious five-star hotels on the East coast, with breathtaking views and access to every amenity imaginable. Growing up, she'd had the luxury of being in every corner of the hotel, and it wasn't because her family could afford the daily rate. It was because her mother had been the housekeeping supervisor.

She and Jabarie had been friends since he'd spotted her running through the main lobby of the hotel. Heir to the Beaumont fortune, all the Beaumont children were required to spend their summers working at the hotel. When Jabarie started cleaning the guest rooms Brenna was certain that wasn't what his father Roger Beaumont had meant at all by learning the business from the ground up, but Jabarie hadn't seemed to mind, and neither had she. While her mother daydreamed, flirted and tried on clothing that belonged to the hotel's wealthy guests, the two of them would clean the rooms.

Then on her thirteenth birthday Jabarie gave her a plastic ring from a Cracker Jack box and promised that someday they would marry and run the Beaumont Corporation together. That was before her mother had run off with a high-powered politician and had become the topic of a small-town scandal. Jabarie's parents, who from the beginning never thought she was good enough, looked down on Brenna more than ever. She was no longer allowed at the hotel, and even worse, Jabarie was forbidden to see her again.

But that didn't stop them. For years they'd had to sneak around, and by the time Jabarie had turned eighteen he'd let the world know they were in love and that he had every intention of someday marrying her. Despite the gossip he'd proposed, and they were to be married shortly after Brenna's twenty-first birthday.

Brenna shuddered as she recalled the lies and all the effort his parents had gone through to finally break them up the day before their wedding. Devastated, she had moved to Dallas, where she had opened her own bookstore. It wasn't until five years later, after her aunt Nellie had sprained her ankle that she'd finally returned to Sheraton Beach to run the store while her aunt mended. Jabarie then pursued her with relentless determination, and in the end she and him discovered that love was even better the second time around. They'd recently celebrated nine wonderful years together and were the proud parents of Arianna, Bree, Julian and Justice, and two year-old Jabarie Jr., a.k.a, Lil Jay.

Speaking of children...

The house was way too quiet. Brenna quickly brushed her teeth, then walked across the bedroom and stuck her head out into the hall. She didn't hear a sound. Sure, the house had more than seven thousand square feet and the master suite was on the first level, but with five kids the house was *never* quiet unless they were asleep or up to something, and it was way too early for nap time.

She slipped her feet inside her Nike tennis shoes and stepped from the room, across Brazilian cherry wood flooring into a wide two-story foyer with a massive chandelier hanging overhead. She paused at the bottom of the grand staircase, listened again, and heard faint sounds coming from upstairs, where the children occupied four of the five bedrooms.

As soon as Brenna reached the top, she sniffed. Something smelled fishy. She'd always had one of those super-sensitive noses. When others couldn't smell something she could, and something clearly didn't smell right.

She walked down the hall and past the twins' room, which was empty, and paused outside Bree's room. Pressing her ears against the door she heard soft whispering coming from inside. She knocked and the whispering stopped. The door opened just enough for her six-year-old daughter to stick her head out.

"Yes?" she asked.

Yes? Brenna's brow arched. "What are you doing?"

"Nothing," Bree mumbled, but her round walnut-colored eyes said otherwise.

Brenna sniffed again and scrunched up her nose. "Why does your room smell like sour laundry?" She glanced over Bree's head into her room with increasing curiosity. "Young lady, what do you have in there?"

"Nothing, Mommy," she groaned.

"It doesn't smell like nothing," she declared, then signaled for Bree to step aside as she pushed the door open and walked into the room. Her eyes traveled around the room looking for the stinky culprit. "What is that smell?" she asked again impatiently.

Bree shrugged a bony shoulder. "I don't know."

Brenna gazed down at her daughter's smooth cinnamon face and long honey brown ponytail. She was wearing a t-shirt and shorts that were too big for her slender body, which meant she had been in her big sister's drawer again. Her eyes traveled all the way down to her pink painted toes before returning to her face. "Where are your gym shoes? It smells like you've been playing in the ocean again."

Bree hesitated before pointing toward the closet. "They're in there."

The moment Brenna pivoted on her heels she heard something moving on the other side of the door. Abruptly, she swung open the closet and gasped at what she saw. Julian, Justice, and a dog that was so big he had to be related to Beethoven, were huddled in the corner. She turned up her nose as the stink radiated through the room. "What's going on in here?"

The twins opened their eyes and grinned when they finally noticed their mother standing over them. The second the dog realized he was free to leave he barreled out of the closet before Brenna was able to jump out of the way. He knocked her onto her butt and started licking her face.

"Hey, quit it!" she cried as she tried to dodge his slimy wet tongue.

"No! Bad dog!" Bree cried as she hurried over and tried to get the St. Bernard off her mother, but he was too big for her to manage. The twins joined in, and before long they were all rolling around on the bedroom floor laughing as they were covered in dog drool.

Eight-year-old Arianna stepped into her sister's bedroom with Lil Jay right behind her. "What in the world...?" Stunned, her voice trailed off at the sight while the youngest scrambled over on his short legs and dove right in, giggling and laughing along with the others.

Brenna tickled Lil Jay for a few seconds, then all four decided to start tickling her. Between all the chuckles she glanced over at Arianna, who was leaning against the door jamb with a hand at her hip, shaking her head.

Okay, so maybe I do look a bit ridiculous.

"Enough!" Brenna finally cried, then pushed the dog away and rose to her feet, breathing heavily as she spoke. "Somebody has some explaining to do."

Silence fell like a sledgehammer, and all eyes were on her. Even the dog was sitting at attention.

"Where did this dog come from?" Brenna asked as her eyes traveled to her oldest.

Arianna shook her head, sending her French braid whipping across her shoulder blades. "Why are you looking at me? I didn't do it. Ask those three!" she replied, pointing an accusing finger in the direction of Julian, Justice and Bree.

Brenna's gaze shifted to the twins, with their round angelic faces. She had been their mother long enough to know double-trouble was far from innocent. "Julian ... Justice, who brought that dog in the house?"

As if he knew she was talking about him, the brown dog whimpered and flashed her with his big puppy-dog eyes. She sighed because she had a soft spot for animals, even though this one was filthy and smelled like he had been swimming in the sewer.

"Not me," shouted Justice.

"Me, neither," Julian added.

Brenna's gaze traveled over to her second oldest and paused. Bree wrung her hands and looked guilty as she blinked her wide eyes with a silent plea for forgiveness.

"Bree ..."

"Mommy, he was all alone! If I hadn't brought him home he could have died!" Bree cried.

Brenna gazed at her little drama queen as a single tear rolled down the child's smooth cheek.

"Mommy, can we keep him?" Julian asked.

"Yes, puh-leeeze!" Justice begged, hugging the dog tight.

"Peeeeeze," Lil Jay chimed in.

Seeing the anguish on their little faces, Brenna looked over at the mangy beast and sighed before saying, "C'mere, boy." Obediently he hurried over to her, wagging his tail. Crouching down, she checked his neck for a collar and muttered under her breath when she discovered there wasn't one. *So much for wishful thinking.* "This dog probably has a home with a little girl or boy your age who's waiting for him to come home." *One could only hope.*

"But what if he's alone in the world?" Julian asked with a slight lisp.

"Yeah, Mommy," Justice echoed.

Brenna groaned inwardly because she knew what they were getting at. She didn't like being put on the spot. "Then we'll ... we'll talk to your father about it when he gets home tonight and see what he says."

"Yeah!" The twins cried in unison. They started jumping up and down and hugging the dog like they had just won the lottery. Even Lil Jay looked excited.

"Hold on. I didn't say we're going to keep him."

"But if we can't find his mommy we can," Bree added as she swiped the tears away.

"You're the bestest mommy," Justice announced as he hugged her leg.

Woof Woof. Even the dog agreed.

Brenna rolled her eyes toward the ceiling, then looked

over at Arianna, who was still standing in the doorway with her nose turned up. "He stinks," she snorted.

The doorbell rang and Arianna dashed off to answer it. It was almost ten and the nanny was due any second. *Wait until she sees what we have.* Brenna looked down at her clothes and groaned. She smelled and was covered in doggy drool. There was no way she was going to the gym this morning.

"Before I leave, why don't I make an appointment with the groomer, because somebody needs a bath." She scooped Lil Jay up into her arms and headed toward the hall. The other three followed.

"Come on, Norman," Justice called.

Norman? Oh, brother.

Chapter 3

Jabarie hung up the phone, then swung around in his chair and stared out the executive office of the prestigious Beaumont Hotel. Located high on a hill, he had a magnificent view of Sheraton Beach, Delaware. The small oceanfront town overlooking the Atlantic Ocean had been home his entire life, and he couldn't imagine living anywhere else. From where he was sitting he could pinpoint Main Street with its cobblestone streets and mom-and-pop stores. And across from a sandwich shop, right on the corner, was the Cornerstone Bookstore that Brenna managed.

He glanced briefly down at his watch and scowled when he noticed it was barely eleven o'clock. Brenna didn't close the store until five, and then there were swimming lessons and whatever else she had scheduled for the children. Like most Mondays, the evening would end with pepperoni pizza. A smile curled his lips at the thought of his pride and joys. He couldn't trade them for anything in the world. Although if they barged into his bedroom one more time he just might seriously consider putting them up on the auction block!

He and Brenna had barely been married a year when Arianna came along, and after that they followed consistently: Bree, then the twins Julian and Justice, and Jabarie Jr. Although he adored his family, there were days when he missed the spontaneity he and Brenna had once shared, sneaking off to enjoy one of the hotel suites during lunch, or even spending the entire weekend in bed. He blew out a deep breath. Those were definitely the good old days. Now, between careers and raising a family, the two of them were so busy that there was barely time for sleep, let alone sex.

Jabarie groaned for even allowing his mind to go there, while his loins stirred with frustration. They had been so busy lately that sex had become less of a priority, and he needed to find a way to fix that quick, fast and in a hurry. He had already called the nanny this morning to let her know a locksmith was scheduled to come out to the house around noon. No more kids hiding under the bed, he thought with a hearty chuckle. Somehow he and his wife were going to have to coordinate their calendars and pencil in a few sexual rendezvous. Besides the hotel's future, keeping the spice in his marriage was a top priority.

Jabarie dragged a frustrated hand across his face as he recalled the meeting he'd had with his staff. The Beaumont Hotels were a chain of full-service five-star hotels managed by the Beaumont Corporation. They currently had forty-eight hotels in cities and vacation destinations across the country. Customer satisfaction was their mission, and the corporation's customer loyalty program was one of the largest of its kind. They were also proud of their corporate culture that was designed to fill positions with local residents. Unfortunately, the hotels had been feeling the effects of the economic crisis over the last few years, and also unfortunate was the fact that the Sheraton Beach hotel had taken the hardest hit. What was even more heartbreaking was that it was the original hotel and was the home of the corporate offices.

As the CEO, Jabarie felt as if he carried the weight of the corporation on his shoulders. It was his job to keep the hotels operating and their thousands of staff employed. When his CFO, Katharine King, had first mentioned the hotel's significant drop in revenues around the Christmas holiday, Jabarie had hoped profits would have increased after the summer season. However, to his dismay, Katharine announced at the staff meeting that they had not increased. In order to cut costs by a million dollars they were now in the position of having to lay off ten percent of their staff. As far as Jabarie was concerned it was ten too many. In Sheraton Beach, everyone was family.

"You're thinking way too hard."

Jabarie swiveled around in the chair and glared at the wide grin on his older brother's face as he leaned against the doorjamb with his hands buried inside the front pockets of his slacks.

"Just thinking about the layoffs," Jabarie replied with a scowl and leaned back in the large executive chair.

Nodding, Jace strolled across the oak flooring. He was dressed in a sharp black Brooks Brothers suit that looked tailor-made for his six-two frame. He moved over to one of the wingback chairs in front of Jabarie's desk and took a seat. "Yeah, I can't stop thinking about it, either. But I don't know what else we can do. I've gone over the numbers, and Katharine is right. We don't have much of a choice," he replied as honestly as he could.

Jace was President of Human Resources. He knew first-hand the cost of benefits, salaries and training programs for the thousands of employees the corporation employed across the country.

As a five-star hotel their hiring ratio was eight employees for every guest room to insure excellent customer satisfaction. Jace had suggested lowering the ratio to six, which would eventually get the hotel out of the red.

Annoyance rose as Jabarie thought about the economic hardship the layoffs would bring to their town. "We're going to have to think of something. Those men and women greet me in the lobby every morning with smiles and gratitude. There's no way in hell I'm going to slap them in the face at the end of the month with a pink slip," Jabarie barked, and slammed his hand against the desk.

"Bro, I know how you feel. I'm sure between the two of us we'll be able to think of something," Jace said, stroking his neatly trimmed goatee. "Otherwise we'll just have to find ways to deal with the problem. Maybe even possibly some extended leave to the workers to try and soften this as much as possible. I have my staff already working on possible severance packages."

Jabarie's eyes narrowed. "Let's focus our energy on finding a solution."

Jace's brow quirked. "Relax, man. You know I'm on your side. All of us are. But we have to be realistic here."

Jabarie knew his brother was right. He just wasn't ready to admit it. Letting people go would be like failing, and failure just wasn't an option. They had been in business for more than fifty years, and not once had they laid off a single employee. That was something his father was quite proud of, and had every right to be. Roger Beaumont had left him in charge, and even though he was the CEO, he, Jace, and their younger sister Bianca ran the corporation.

"We've still got a few weeks to come up with a plan before we meet with the board. I advise we use that time wisely," Jabarie suggested with a heavy breath.

Jace stared at his brother, a gamut of emotions crossing his face. "What's gotten into you? I know this whole thing has you upset, but I get the feeling something else is going on."

"Nothing you can solve." He tossed him a glance. "Why you so damn happy, anyway?"

"I had a fabulous weekend. Sheyna's brother, Scott

and his fiancé Zanaa, kept Jace Jr. while she and I headed up to Atlantic City."

"You win anything?"

"Hell, yeah. I won big," Jace replied and gave a suggestive laugh.

"At least someone is getting some. Romance is hard to come by when you've got five little kids running around the house," Jabarie added with a hearty chuckle.

Jace shook his head. "You know I love my nieces and nephews, but having one six-year-old is more than enough. I'm starting to think you and Brenna are trying to catch up with Uncle Patrick and Aunt Gwen."

Patrick Beaumont was their father's younger brother and the father of seven children, two girls and five sons, otherwise known as the Force MD.

Jabarie shrugged. "Brenna and I had always wanted a big family. I just didn't realize all I'd have to sacrifice to get it," he said with a laugh. "I love my little rascals, but damn, can Big Daddy have five minutes to make love to Mama?"

"Sounds like the two of you just need a vacation."

Jabarie scratched his head thoughtfully. "A vacation would be wonderful."

"Who's taking a vacation?" Bianca Beaumont Brown asked as she sashayed her petite frame into her big brother's office, carrying her morning latte. She was elegantly draped in a crisp mustard brown suit.

Turning towards his sister, Jace flashed a wide grin. "Jabarie and Brenna need a vacation to rekindle their flame."

Bianca looked skeptical as she eased into one of the empty chairs across from his desk. "That's easy. Go down to Florida and check out the new condo Mother just bought," she suggested.

Jabarie thought about it and shook his head. "No, I

need something away from telephones, Internet, and people."

Bianca shifted a delicately arched eyebrow in his direction. "Am I missing something?"

"He ain't gettin' none," Jace offered.

"Oh." She laughed and crossed her slender legs, showcasing chocolate leather pumps. "I feel your pain. London and I had the same problem when Sierra was younger, but now that she's getting older I am getting plenty of—"

Jabarie held up a hand. "That is way too much information," he scowled. The last thing he wanted to do was think about his little sister having sex.

His clear gaze swept over his sister's delicate features. She had their mother's beauty, with slanted walnut-brown eyes, a short round nose and a rich, nutmeg complexion.

There were four of them. All the brothers had inherited their father's sable brown eyes and chocolate brown skin. Jace was the tallest and the oldest. He preferred dealing with the employee relations side of the business and gladly let Jabarie take over the head of the corporation. Bianca, the baby of the family, was the creative one of the bunch and the VP of Marketing. Jaden, the youngest brother, was the black sheep of the family and the silent partner. Although he owned an equal share in the corporation, he preferred screwdrivers to corporate headaches, and had opened a span of auto body shops from here to Los Angeles.

Unable to sit another moment, Jabarie got up and paced back and forth behind his desk. "I don't know why I'm sitting here discussing my sex life with either of you."

"Because you need our help," Bianca commented between sips.

"She's right," Jace agreed. "Plan a weekend getaway and leave."

"That's easier said than done. Our nanny only works during the week. With Mother and Father in Barbados until Labor Day, Brenna refuses to leave the kids with just anyone."

"London and I can come over and spend the weekend with them," Bianca offered.

A crooked smiled claimed Jabarie's lips. "Yeah, I remember the last time the two of you *watched* my kids. We came home to find a fire truck parked in the driveway."

Bianca shook her head and brown curls danced softly around her neck. "How was I supposed to know Bree likes to burn candles in front of the smoke detectors?"

He chuckled. The thought of being able to get away for a weekend sounded almost worth a revisit from the fire department.

Jace shifted in the chair. "Sheyna and I would be more than happy to take the boys. You know JJ loves hanging out with his cousins."

Bianca tossed a hand in the air. "See ...? And London and I can handle the girls."

Jabarie smiled to himself. "Well, I guess it's settled." Now all he had to do was figure out how to convince Brenna.

Lost in his thoughts, his eyes traveled to the numerous plaques adorning the wall. Several had been awarded by the mayor for their commitment to the community. Clearing his throat, Jabarie felt a wave of guilt for thinking about a vacation when so many people were depending on him to keep food on their table.

"Now, on to more important things ..." He stopped and lowered onto the end of his desk as the frown returned to his forehead. "How the hell are we going to save fifty jobs?"

Chapter 4

"Thank you for your business, and please come again." Brenna bid goodbye to the slender teenager who was too busy talking on her cell phone to hear her. *Teenagers.* She couldn't even put down the phone long enough to appreciate good customer service.

Reaching up, Brenna pushed a strand of hair from her face as she stepped from behind the counter. "Craig, I'll be in my office if you need me."

He looked up from unpacking a box of books long enough to nod. "No problem, Mrs. Beaumont."

Brenna groaned inwardly. The eighteen-year-old college-bound student had been working part-time for the summer and was truly a life saver. Now if only she could get him to call her Brenna instead of making her feel like she was sixty every time he referred to her as Mrs. Beaumont.

As she strolled across the small quaint bookstore, Brenna waved at Chelsea, who was working behind the counter of the small coffee shop to the far right of the store. Last year, when Delaney had retired and decided to close Delaney's Donuts, Brenna bought the space and had it converted into the Cornerstone Coffee. Once the wall had been removed, customers could browse books and read their purchases while enjoying a cup of coffee. The shop was an instant hit with the teenagers in the area.

Brenna stepped into her small office at the corner of the store, walked behind her desk, and dropped into her chair. Immediately, she checked her cell phone to make sure she didn't have any messages. She was waiting for a call from the groomer. Thank goodness she had been able to get Norman a last-minute appointment. On the drive over, with the window down on the minivan, she had been pleased to discover the dog was well trained. Now they just needed to figure out what to do with him, because in the meantime her children were quickly becoming attached.

After finding no messages, Brenna logged onto her computer and checked her calendar. Lil Jay had an appointment with his pediatrician on Wednesday. The twins had karate lessons tomorrow. Arianna was swimming tonight and had ballet practice Thursday. And Bree was invited to a birthday party over the weekend. Another busy week. Brenna ran a shaky hand through her hair as her eyes traveled over to the family portrait perched on the bookshelf beside her desk. Regardless of whether she liked it or not, her children were growing up right before her eyes.

And that's what scares me.

There were only so many hours in a day, and most of them she spent at the book store. By the time she scooped up the kids for their activities and finally returned home she was so tired she barely had the energy to get them ready for bed. One thing she'd vowed when she and Jabarie had decided to start a family was she would always be there for her children. And when Arianna asked her on Saturday why she was never home, the realization swept over Brenna that maybe Arianna was right. She was hardly ever there.

Last week she had flown to a book buyer's convention and had missed another one of Arianna's dance recitals. Although Jabarie had been present, it just wasn't the same. She wanted to be everywhere her children needed her to be. She never wanted them to wonder why she hadn't been there for them. And knowing that she hadn't been around when her children needed her most bothered her.

Brenna nibbled on her bottom lip as she remembered growing up with a mother who was hardly there because she was too busy trying to be something she wasn't. And when, without batting an eyelash, Shaunda had finally run off with some rich dude Brenna had been left to be raised by her aunt. Brenna adored Aunt Nellie, yet she'd never understood how her mother — how any mother — could choose a man over her own child.

Shifting slightly on the chair, she tried to push away the overwhelming emotion she felt every time she allowed herself to remember. She and her mother had since mended their relationship and Shaunda doted on her grandchildren whenever she was in town. However, every time Brenna watched her mother with the Fabulous Five, she still couldn't help wondering why her mother hadn't been there for her.

Once again she gazed at her beautiful family and couldn't resist a smile. It felt like just yesterday when she had found out she was pregnant with their first child. Now Arianna was eight and so opinionated, while Bree was determined to save all the animals of the world, one breed at a time. She was determined to teach her girls how to be amazing women, with dreams and goals. Brenna frowned at the irony. Owning a bookstore had always been her dream, and now she was seriously considering sacrificing her wants for something she loved even more: her children.

For the last couple of weeks she had been contemplating hiring someone full-time to manage the bookstore. Then she could focus on being a stay-at-home mom, going to PTA meetings and making cookies for book sales. As much as she dreaded those things and valued her independence, she wanted to be that mother who was actively involved in her children's lives. She still had plenty of time to run a bookstore, but she only had one opportunity to raise her children.

Brenna's personal line rang, cutting into her thoughts. She reached over and grabbed the receiver before the second ring. "Cornerstone Bookstore, Brenna Beaumont speaking."

"Brenna, guess what?"

"What?" she replied the second she heard the excitement in her sister-in-law Danica's voice.

"Kimora took her first step this morning!" she exclaimed.

Her mouth stretched into a wide smile. She could just see Danica's face glowing with pride as she saw her ten-month old daughter trying to walk. "That's wonderful! Was Jaden there?"

"No," she said in frustration. "He was already at the shop, so you know he about had a fit when I called and told him."

She was certain Jabarie's youngest brother wasn't too thrilled about missing his daughter's first step. The little redhead had her daddy wrapped around her little finger. "Trust me, once they start they never stop."

Danica sighed. "I know, right? They sure don't stay babies for long."

"No they don't. Look at your son. It seems like it was just yesterday when you were pregnant with Joshua."

"Now he's three." There was a brief pause. "My babies are growing up *sooo* fast."

Brenna's eyebrow arched suspiciously. "Are you crying?"

Danica laughed around a sob. "I'm just happy, that's all."

They chitchatted some more about the children and

school starting in three weeks before Brenna shifted the conversation. "Danica ... do you think I'm a good mother?"

She gasped. "Of course you are. Why would you ask something like that?"

Brenna swiveled on the chair as she spoke. "I've just been thinking about all the time I spend at the store and realized Francine spends more time with my kids than I do."

"So why don't you cut your hours like I did after Joshua was born?" Danica suggested.

"Because I don't think that's enough. I really feel that I need to focus on my family and try being a stay-at-home mom."

"Is that really what you want to do?" She didn't miss the disbelief in Danica's voice.

"No, but I feel it's what I *have* to do," Brenna said with a sigh of uncertainty. "I work because I want to, not because I have to, but lately it feels like that's a selfish choice."

"You work because that's the type of woman you are. I'm the same way. If I was sitting around twiddling my thumbs I'd pull my hair out."

"I know what you mean. The bookstore gives me a feeling of self-worth."

"Then what's the problem?"

"The problem is I feel guilty for wanting to be more than just Mrs. Jabarie Beaumont and the mother of the Fabulous Five."

Danica gave a gentle laugh. "Trust me ... You're a lot more than that. And there's nothing wrong with having a life outside of home. But I know how you feel. I felt the same way with Joshua, and again with Kimora. However, I would have thought after five kids ...."

It was Brenna's turn to laugh. "Yes, I should be used

to feeling like this by now. Which is why I think that if the feeling isn't going away then it's time I pay closer attention. Don't you miss modeling?"

There was a pregnant pause and she could just see the naturally redheaded beauty pondering her question. She had spent years as a runway model before marrying Jaden. "Sometimes I do, but modeling's long hours and hard work and I just couldn't see myself ever doing it again full-time. But I made that decision long before I married Jaden and started a family." Danica had moved to Sheraton Beach after retiring from modeling and opened Ujema Wear, a quaint swimsuit boutique on the boardwalk.

Brenna released a long frustrated breath. "I just feel like I should be able to have it all. You know?"

"You're not superwoman, although you've got *way* more energy than I ever had. But you're a good mother and there's nothing wrong with wanting something more. So quit beating yourself over the head. Have you talked to Jabarie about how you're feeling?"

Brenna released a heavy breath. "No, he worries too much."

"And so do you. Relax. I'm sure you'll make the right choice."

"Thanks, Danica."

"No problem. I'll see you at dinner on Thursday."

"We'll be there." The Beaumont family got together at Beaumont Manor for dinner every Thursday. Although her in-laws were on vacation and wouldn't be present, the sibling wanted to keep the family tradition. Brenna used to dread spending an entire evening with Jabarie's parents, but over the years they had grown fond of each other. Not to mention the fact that Roger and Jessica adored their grandchildren. As bougie as Jabarie's mother was, Brenna never thought she'd see the day a child would bring the royal highness to her knees.

Brenna hung up the receiver and took a few moments to think about their phone conversation. Maybe she was just going through a phase. She hoped so. Otherwise she would have to make a decision soon.

Hearing the bell over the main door jingle, Brenna looked through her large glass window onto the floor. The second she saw Jabarie stepping into the store she felt as if the air had been sucked out of her lungs. It didn't matter that they'd been married nine years or that she had known him since she was ten. One thing still hadn't changed. Jabarie had the power to make her lose her breath. Looking handsome in a double-breasted navy suit, every step he took caused heat to radiate through her body. *I'm a lucky woman*, she thought. And as he grew closer, her heart began to race in anticipation.

Grinning, Jabarie stopped right outside her open door and knocked. Brenna steepled her fingers and decided to play along.

"May I help you?" she asked.

"I'm here to see my beautiful wife," he announced with dimples prominent on both sides of his jaws. At six-two, he looked massive standing in the doorway.

She arched an eyebrow. "Really? And what does your *beautiful* wife look like?"

"Caramel … thick … with the sexiest legs."

The deep sensual tone of his voice vibrated through her body and settled down low. She couldn't resist a blush. "I don't think there is anyone here that matches that description."

"I beg to differ."

Without further ado he stepped into her small office, shutting the door with a click, and immediately the air crackled around her. Before Brenna could rise, Jabarie pulled her up from the chair and guided her to stand between his legs while he rested his hip on the edge of her desk.

"What are you doing here?" she asked with a grin.

"I missed my wife," Jabarie murmured as he curved an arm about her waist, then leaned forward and claimed her mouth in a kiss so filled with hunger she had to hold on to keep from buckling to her knees. When his tongue slipped inside her mouth she forgot all about the kids and her job, and instead focused on her amazing husband.

Brenna wrapped her arms around his neck, drawing closer. Her reward was his rumbling groan. Jabarie's skillful hands roamed over her lush curves before finally settling on top of her ass, where he gripped and squeezed before she pulled back and released a giggle.

"Nasty," she teased as he playfully nuzzled her neck. "You should have told me you were coming. I would have asked you to bring food."

Jabarie lifted a hand and caressed the side of her face. "The only thing I'm hungry for is you."

"Is that so?" she said gazing up adoringly into his sable eyes.

"Yeah, that's so." He turned his head slightly and she smiled at the sight of the scar above his right brow, an injury he had gotten at the age of twelve while skateboarding.

"How's your morning been?" she asked, raking her fingers through his thick curls.

"Stressful."

Brenna didn't miss the hint of despair in his voice. "What is it?"

"Budget cuts. I might have to let some employees go."

"Oh no! When did —?" she was cut off by a finger pressed against her lips.

Jabarie shook his head. "I didn't come to talk about

my problems. I came down here so I could finish where we left off this morning." And before she had a chance to respond, he dipped his head and captured her mouth again.

Finish? Her nipples puckered. When Brenna had read the note on the glass she had no idea he'd meant this afternoon ... behind the desk ... in her office.

Heat coursed through her breasts and pooled hotly between her thighs. His tongue eased into her mouth and danced with hers. She leaned forward, pressing her pelvis against his, desperate to feel very inch of him. And her husband had plenty.

His hands clutched at her hips, holding her to him so she could feel the evidence of what he wanted from her. "I plan to make love you," he hissed.

"Baby," she managed between kisses. "Craig will see us through the glass."

"Then unless your assistant is majoring in sex education, I advise you to close the blinds."

Between kisses, she reached over and twisted the wand. She had always loved the layout of the office, with its large glass window that looked directly out onto the floor, but after she and Jabarie had gotten married, Brenna had decided that with a husband as virile as Jabarie, having blinds installed was a good idea. Thank goodness she had followed her instincts!

Jabarie's lips moved to brush her nose, cheek and chin, planting soft kisses along the way, and when he reached her neck he lingered, sucking and teasing until a moan slipped from between her lips.

"Baby," she whispered as her eyelids lowered.

"I'm right here, Bren," he said. Her heart pounded so hard she thought it would collapse. Jabarie sucked and licked at her throat. Her breasts swelled and her nipples puckered, aching for his touch.

Brenna struggled to keep her voice down to a soft moan, which wasn't easy to do, considering how good he made her feel. She slid her hands across his massive shoulders and around to his back, then traveled down to knead his delicious ass. Damn, she wanted this man so bad she ached. He felt good. He'd feel a whole lot better, she thought, if she was at home lying on her back with Jabarie on top, pounding into her body. Hard. Fast. Deep.

Brenna was seconds away from unzipping her sundress, freeing her breasts and begging Jabarie to feast, but decided to follow his lead, Instead, she simply held on to him, loving the way he took his time licking, sucking and heating her body, sending her mind to some far-off place. Where? She didn't know. Hell, she didn't care. All that mattered was his lips, tongue, teeth, and his rock-hard penis jutting against her.

One of his hands left her hips and smoothed its way down over her curves and under the hem of her dress. As soon as she felt his warm touch, she shivered on contact.

"What's wrong?" he asked barely above whisper.

"Nothing. Absolutely nothing at all," she breathed. Except that touching her inner thigh was not enough. She wanted those long fingers to climb higher, where she needed to feel him most.

As if he could read her mind, Jabarie growled against the flesh at her throat. His fingers slid upward and the closer he got, the tighter her muscles clenched. Brenna held on to his shoulders, bracing herself, and the second he stroked her clit she gasped and her eyelids flew open. The intense look on his face was almost her undoing. Lust was blazing in his eyes while his hand cupped her mound possessively.

"Jabarie," she warned.

"What's wrong? You want me to stop?" he asked as he slipped a finger under the elastic band at her crotch and stroked.

"Yes … no." Brenna licked her lips trying to stifle a moan. "You're starting something."

He arched a brow at her. "That's the plan. No twins to stand in the way of touching you." He softly caressed her moist folds as he spoke. "You're wet, Bren. Seems to me I'm not the only one who's horny."

"Yes, God, yes," she whimpered. Jabarie always did have a way with words. He brought his lips to her ear and whispered intimate details, causing her body to tremble while his fingers drove deeper inside the crotch of her panties, drawing closer and closer until reached her swollen clit. Jabarie caressed the hood before moving underneath, like he had all the time in the world, as if he had forgotten they were tucked away inside her office. Outside the door Brenna heard the faint sound of customers in the store, but the more Jabarie played with her kitty the less she cared about anything except for her husband's magical fingers.

"You aren't playing fair," she moaned.

"Didn't you get the memo? All's fair in love and war."

She felt lost to everything but him as he touched her. With his thumb he applied additional pressure to her stimulated clit and Brenna gasped, then dropped her mouth to his shoulder to stifle a cry.

"You like that?" he whispered close to her ear.

Her voice was shaky. "You know I … *Ohhh* … you know I do."

"Good. For a moment there I thought I wasn't doing my job." He slid his finger along her moist folds and it took several seconds before Brenna realized she was rotating her hips, grinding her mound against his hand. Her whole body was hot, sensitized, as he fondled and teased, her juices coating his fingers.

"You're going to get us caught," she managed between breaths.

Jabarie dragged his mouth along her cheek, down across her jaw, and lower until he reached her neck. "Caught doing what? Satisfying my wife? There's no crime in that."

She disagreed, because what he was doing to her should have been outlawed. It was wicked and so damned unfair. She wanted to cry out in ecstasy, yet she couldn't. Instead, she was forced to hold it in or risk the entire bookstore hearing them.

"There's no crime in wanting to make love to my wife," he repeated.

"Yes—I mean no, there isn't." She placed her hand on his forearm, making sure she didn't lose her balance and risk him ending his tantalizing quest.

"I want you so bad my chest aches," he hissed.

Gazing into his powerfully dark eyes, she realized he had that look—powerful, determined and horny.

"I'm not leaving here until I make love to you," he warned.

His words nearly did her in. She was blazing with desire and wanted him too. Her body knew him, her body craved him. And her husband knew exactly how she liked it.

"Take them off," he ordered. He withdrew his hand from inside her panties and almost instantly she felt the loss. Quickly, she pulled the low-rise panties down over her hips and kicked them under her desk, then pressed her eager body against him again, rubbing her mound along his erection.

"Please touch me," she begged, and when his sable eyes heated wickedly at the exact moment his hand made contact, she whimpered with pleasure. Jabarie pressed his mouth to hers, muffling the sound in a kiss that was almost brutal, while his finger probed at her opening. Slowly he eased inside, thrusting in and out, as her walls squeezed around him.

"Why are you teasing me?" She enjoyed foreplay, but this was downright unfair.

"You begged for me to touch you, remember?"

She gave what sounded to her like a strangled cry as she replied, "Yes ... I guess I did."

"Besides, I'm not teasing ... just making sure you don't forget your husband has skills," he said and practically devoured her lips while his fingers drove deeper.

Goodness. How could she forget? Every time he walked into a room she was reminded of how good he was with his hands, among other things. Every time she gazed at their children she was remind how skillful he was in bed. Even now he was slowly driving her insane.

"If it makes you feel any better, you're not the only one aroused." Jabarie took her hand and flattened it against the fly of his trousers.

A flirtatious grin curved her lips. "I see."

She leaned forward, bringing her mouth to his, and immediately slipped her tongue inside to match his confident strokes. Brenna felt his penis pulsing against her fingers, making her increasingly wet and hot. She squeezed and stroked his length through the fabric, enjoying the sounds coming from his throat.

There was a soft knock at the door. Brenna startled and jumped away like the time she had been sixteen and had been caught kissing behind the bleachers.

"Uhhh, Mrs. Beaumont, sorry to bother you, but the groomer is on the line."

The timid voice through the door drew Jabarie out of his daze and he frowned. "The groomer?"

Oh boy. She had yet to mention Norman.

Brenna hurried over to the door and made sure the lock was firmly in place. "Craig, just put the call on hold and I'll pick it up."

"The hell you will," Jabarie growled as he came around the desk and stood behind her, making sure she felt his erection pulsing against her ass. On contact, she shuddered with desire.

"Craig ... can you take a message? I'm kinda, uh, busy."

"That's my girl," Jabarie whispered close to her ear. He then urged her to walk forward with his hands at her waist, guiding her toward the desk. "Is there something you need to tell me?" he asked.

Feeling Jabarie's dick thrusting against her, Brenna couldn't think straight. "Yes ... we have a shaggy new addition to the family."

"The more the merrier," he said in a voice low and smooth. "Now, where were we?"

When they reached the massive expanse of her desk, Brenna looked over her shoulder and was barely breathing when she saw the dark intensity on Jabarie's face.

"Bend over," he ordered, then gave her a slight push at the center of her back, drawing her down until she was flat against the mahogany wood. Without hesitation, Jabarie lifted her dress up over her hips and hissed softly under his breath. Brenna could just imagine how she looked leaning over the desk, with her ass in the air, thighs slightly parted, and his gaze devouring her from her head down to her feet in strappy sandals.

"Spread your legs for me, baby."

She did as he instructed, then wiggled around on the cool surface as Jabarie positioned himself between her thighs, covering her with his body. It wasn't the first time they had made love in her office, but today they were about to officially christen her new desk.

"You okay?" Jabarie asked as he brushed her honey brown hair away from her neck and planted light kisses.

"No," she purred, "But I will be in a few seconds."

"No doubt." He chuckled lightly. "Now, push that ass back and hold onto the desk."

She complied and heard Jabarie draw in another harsh breath. "You look so damned sexy like this." He took a step back then reached down, stroking a path from her feminine folds all the way up to her ass, and her breath hitched. "You're so wet," he whispered as he touched her butt cheeks, spreading them slightly apart, then traveled slowly down along her moistened folds again, delving slightly inside. Brenna squirmed and rocked her hips, urging his finger deeper. When he added a second finger, a long rush of air slipped from between her lips. She wiggled and moved with the rhythm of his thrusts, aching for him.

"Please," she begged, mouth open, cheek pressed against the cool desk.

"Please what?" Jabarie asked and drove deeper.

"Fuck me."

Jabarie removed his jacket and tossed it onto the desk beside her. Then Brenna heard a zipper and his slacks fell to the floor with a *whoosh*. In a matter of seconds he was wedged between her thighs, gripping her hips and spreading her wide. "Remember, we have an audience right outside the door," he reminded as he slowly eased inside her heat, a little at a time, and Brenna thought she was going to die from the pleasure.

"Thanks for the reminder," she said around a gasp as he slid further, then pulled out slightly before pushing forward again. Dammit, he was teasing her, reminding her who was in control. Jabarie knew just how to make her body ache for him.

Brenna squirmed, urging him further, and finally he pushed all the way in. Using the desk as leverage, she rocked her body back, matching the rhythm. Jabarie held on to her hips and penetrated hard and deep. With her mouth closed she moaned, trying to hold in what she was feeling, when what she wanted to do was scream at the top of her lungs. Thank goodness Jabarie eased back slightly on his thrusts. Otherwise, it would have been over before it had barely begun. She released a heavy sigh and slowed her hips.

"Shit, you feel good," Jabarie groaned and steadied his strokes. Reaching around, his thumb massaged her sensitized clit again. And when he pulled out and slammed back in again, Brenna cried out his name. "Shhh," he whispered as he begun to move faster, driving even deeper inside her. Within seconds he was fucking her harder and burying himself so deep she wasn't sure how much longer she could hold on. "Come for me, Bren," he coaxed, and that was all the encouragement she needed. Her inner walls squeezed his length as a long and powerful climax tore through her body. She clamped her teeth into her lower lip, suppressing Jabarie's name, screaming inside. Jabarie continued to pound her from behind, and shortly after she heard a loud moan, then his body slumped on top of her.

When their breathing finally slowed he removed his weight and collapsed onto the floor. Laughing, Brenna tumbled on top of him.

"Do you think anyone heard us?" she managed between giggles.

"I don't give a damn," Jabarie growled playfully as he pulled her in his arms and pressed his lips to hers. "Nothing is gonna stop me from making love to my wife."

"The twins did this morning," she reminded him.

"I called a locksmith," he whispered against her lips. "No more interruptions."

The couple laughed and he kissed her some more, then Brenna slowly rolled over and watched as Jabarie rose smoothly and started tucking his shirt back inside his slacks. As soon as they were zipped and his belt was buckled, he reached down for her hand and lifted her onto her feet. "Bren, how about we take a trip next weekend?"

As she straightened her dress her eyes sparkled. "That sounds nice. What do you have in mind? I think the kids would enjoy going to Sesame Place."

Jabarie shook his head at the mention of the children's amusement park. "The type of entertainment I'm looking for is clearly adults only. No kids. Just you, me and a king-size bed." His gaze skipped over her in places that if they weren't married would have been considering inappropriate before settling on her face.

Just the thought of being alone with her husband for an uninterrupted weekend caused her stomach to contract, but then that guilty feeling of not spending enough time with the kids returned. "I don't know if we should leave the kids. Arianna is already complaining I'm never home."

His eyes were smiling, but Brenna couldn't help but notice that there was a glimmer of concern there, too. "The kids will survive ... I won't. I need some time alone with my wife."

Brenna took a deep breath. How could she explain that she already felt guilty about not spending enough time with the kids?

Before she could explain further, Jabarie brought his lips down to hers again. "I'm late for a meeting. We'll talk about this some more this evening. *And* about our furry new houseguest."

She forced a nod. "I'll see you tonight."

He retrieved his suit jacket from the desk, then Jabarie leaned over and kissed her once more. "I love you, Mrs. Beaumont."

Brenna smiled. "I love you, too."

Chapter 5

Jabarie loved his cousins like they were his brothers, but there were days when he wished they'd call with advance warning before coming to Sheraton Beach.

"Dude, I'm married."

"Yeah, but you're not dead. Aw, c'mon man! I can't believe I'm in town for the week and none of y'all wanna kick it!" Remy Beaumont whined as he paced the length of the bar, sending his long hair swaying every which way.

Jabarie glanced over at his younger brother Jaden sitting on the stool beside him with his brow raised. Some things never changed.

The two brothers were sipping beer and eating hot wings at Spanky's, a popular Main Street bar and grill. Remy was the youngest boy of "The Force MD," as his seven cousins were dubbed back when they were teenagers, and the wildest, as far as he was concerned. With a mixed heritage of Samoan and African-American, Remy was popular with the females and a bona fide bachelor who did whatever he wanted, when he wanted. He was the kind of man who lived life with passion. Remy resided in Richmond, Virginia, but was likely to jet off anywhere in the world without a moment's notice. As a result, he loved meeting woman everywhere he went, and he lived for one-night stands.

Jabarie had to chuckle as he remembered the years he'd spent hanging out at the clubs, dating women with the intent of satisfying an immediate need, but that was long before Brenna had returned to Sheraton Beach and he had reclaimed her heart. From that day forward the only woman who mattered was Brenna, and after nine years of marriage nothing had changed. "Man, I'm past all that. I'd rather spend the evening curled up on the couch with Brenna." *Or preferably buried between her thighs.* Their afternoon rendezvous still had him smiling. It had relieved some of the sexual tension, but what he wanted was twenty-four hours of uninterrupted, mind-boggling sex.

"Aw … come on Jaden. I *know* you're not going to leave me hanging," Remy stated with annoyance.

Jaden brought the beer to his lips and sipped. "Naw, dude. I'll pass."

Remy dropped off the bar stool, flexed his biceps like a wrestler and growled. "Y'all killing me, yo! C'mon, my future wife might be out there waiting to meet me."

Jaden grinned. "Then it sounds like you don't need us."

"And since when are you interested in a wife?" Jabarie asked.

Remy chuckled. "I'm just tryna keep it boss."

"And I'm sure you wouldn't have it any other way," Jaden teased.

Remy was known as Dr. Feel. He loved the ladies as long as the situation made him "feel" good, but the second one tried to put on the chains he was off to the next beautiful honey.

He was the co-host of the nationally syndicated radio program, *He vs. She* that was heard by thousands of listeners across the country. The show offered a provocative point of view on men, women and relationships. Listening to him and his beautiful female co-host sparring night after night was hilarious.

"I was thinking about heading up to Philadelphia on Friday to hang out with Diamere. Y'all game?" Their cousin Diamere Redmond owned a string of popular nightclubs in central Philadelphia. Jabarie and his brothers frequented the popular hotspots whenever they were in the city.

Jaden shrugged. "Going clubbing doesn't sound like a bad idea. I'll see if Danica and I can get a baby sitter."

Remy just stared at him for a moment. "You're kidding, right?"

Keeping a straight face, Jaden said, "Nope, she and I could use a night out."

Their cousin scrubbed a large hand down his face, then shook his head. At his frown, Jabarie took one look at Jaden and the two burst out with laughter.

"Cuz, we're just kidding. A boys' night out doesn't sound that bad," Jabarie said, chuckling.

A smile tipped Remy's lips. "Oh, okay, I see y'all got jokes!"

"You know we like giving you a hard time," Jaden replied, smiling. "I'll see if Jace wants to join us."

"That's whassup! I'll check and see if Rance wants to meet us there."

The crease between Jabarie's brows deepened at the mention of one of Remy's older brothers. "I've been meaning to holla at him. How's he doing?" he asked.

The smile stripped from Remy's face as he shrugged. "It's been a long ride. Until his ankle heals he's got strict instructions to take it easy."

Jabarie nodded, remembering the televised NBA All-Star game. Their team had been up six points when Rance--also known as Dr. Dribble--stole the ball, dribbled, dunked, and came down hard on someone's foot and broke his ankle. He was out for the rest of the season.

"He'll be back on the court before you know it," Jaden replied confidently.

Remy leaned his back to the bar and reached for the frosty bottle of beer. "Yeah, that's what I've been telling him, but he's been pretty down lately. A night out with the boys is exactly what he needs."

"No doubt," Jaden agreed with a fist pound.

* * *

Jabarie crossed the wooden bridge that granted the only access to Beaumont Lane. He followed the long paved road surrounded by lush scenery past Beaumont Manor, where he had grown up and where his parents still lived. Traveling a mile up the road he came to a heavy wrought iron gate with a keypad and an intercom. He leaned out the window, typed in the code, and watched for the gate to open before he continued up the narrow path. As he eased around the curve the grand house came into view.

Home sweet home.

Up ahead was their seven-thousand square foot home with floor-to-ceiling windows exposing million-dollar views of the Atlantic Ocean and miles of private white sandy beach. Jabarie pulled into the four-car garage and killed the engine. Within seconds he climbed out, stuck the key into the door and stepped inside. He was instantly met by big brown eyes and a bark of a greeting from a huge brown St. Bernard.

"Hi Daddy!" Bree cried as she came racing toward the door.

Jabarie leaned down and kissed her cheek, then gave her curious look. "Where did this creature come from?" Although he didn't even have to ask to know which of his children was responsible.

Bree dropped down to her knees and hugged her furry friend. "I found him on the beach. Mommy said we can keep him if we don't find his home."

"Really?" he sputtered with laughter.

She nodded. "We made signs and put them up but nobody's called."

Lucky us.

Jabarie gazed over at the gigantic dog, then lowered his briefcase to the floor and whistled. "Come here, boy."

The dog happily trotted over to him with his tail wagging. He's a big homely thing, he thought, but at least he was soft and clean. "What's his name?"

"Norman," she announced.

"Norman?" he bellowed with laughter. "Who in the world came up with that name?"

"I did!" Julian announced as he came charging down the hall and launched into his father's arms.

Jabarie caught him with an exaggerated groan. "Umph! That's a wonderful name," he replied staring down at him adoringly then kissing his lips. He lowered him back to the floor. "Goodness, you're getting heavy."

Julian giggled.

He looked lovingly at Bree and smiled. She reminded him so much of Bianca when she was younger. "Where's Justice, Lil Jay, and Arianna?"

"Arianna's watching cartoons. Justice's sleep. Lil Jay's with Mommy. He's not feeling good."

Jabarie nodded, took one final look at the furry additional to his household, then moved down the large foyer to a turned staircase. As he passed the stairs, he stuck his head into the two-story family room and found his oldest lying on the couch watching *Phineas and Ferb*. "Hey, Arie."

"Hi, Daddy." Arianna waved without looking away from the screen. Chuckling, he shook his head and headed around the corner toward the master suite on the other side of the kitchen. As soon as he stepped into the room he heard running water coming from the bathroom. A smile curled his lips. Brenna was in the shower.

* * *

Brenna was wrapping a large white bath towel around her when she felt hands on her shoulders. Big strong hands that her body knew all too well.

"You should have waited for me," he said in a voice so low and sensual it made her stomach do a flip-flop.

Jabarie began to massage her shoulders, loosening the tension of another long and exhausting day. "I thought I'd better take advantage of the peace and quiet while I could," she replied as she dropped her head back against his chest and sighed. "How's Remy?"

Jabarie chuckled close to her ear. "Wild as ever. He wants me and the boys to play hooky for the rest of the week and roll up to Philadelphia with him."

Brenna felt his hot breath as Jabarie rested a kiss at her neck that sent tingling sensations under her skin. "Sounds like fun."

Jabarie turned Brenna around and she stared up at his gaze, his expression hot and suggestive. "I know something that's a whole helluva lot more fun," he whispered. Then his lips swooped down in a kiss so raw and hungry her legs almost slid out from under her. A warm shiver passed over her skin, but she was far from cold. Instead, she felt hot and aroused. The heat and strength of his body surrounded her like a warm cocoon.

Damn, he was a good kisser, she thought, but then he always had been. If anything, over the years he had perfected the technique. In fact, Jabarie had fire traveling to all those intimate areas of her body, igniting her with a desire for a whole lot more. Clinging to his shoulders, she struggled to maintain her balance.

Jabarie's lips parted and his tongue slipped inside

with passionate thrusts. Brenna stopped thinking about Lil Jay's teething and focused on Jabarie's tongue dancing around in her mouth, tasting, encouraging, and enticing. His hands slid across her hips, then moved down, squeezing and kneading her ass, pressing her firmly along the length of his erection. Her breath caught and she had to bite her lip to stop herself from moaning out loud, particularly because the family room was only a few feet away.

Opening her eyes, Brenna drew back slightly and gazed up into his handsome face. Their lips were barely touching, but it was enough to send tremors skipping across her skin. "You must have really missed me," she teased.

Jabarie's hands perused the length of her spine, then skimmed her shoulders before dropping to brush the outer curve of her breast with his fingers. "Always."

She stood unmoving beneath the onslaught of his touch, hands clenched, barely breathing. Her back arched and her breasts swelled in anticipation. She yearned for him to touch and squeeze her tingling nipples.

"You feel what you do to me?" His voice was gruff.

Brenna ground against him, feeling the evidence of his erection, and nodded. "Yes, I feel it," she moaned, then bit her lips to stop from laughing. "But didn't I just give you some for lunch?"

A devilish smile caught her attention. "Yes, and now I want some more."

And so do I. Her body still sang from their little afternoon snack, but as far as her husband was concerned there was no such thing as too much, and she agreed. Heat blossomed between her thighs and her knees weakened. Goodness, would she ever get enough of him making love to her? she wondered. She had friends who claimed the sparks fizzled after several years of married, but she had yet to experience that. If anything, the sex had gotten hotter and more erotic between them with each year they celebrated together.

Jabarie nipped at her earlobe while his tongue played with the diamond stud there. With every stroke her body came alive, heat surging through her like an electrical current.

Jabarie tugged at the towel and it fell to the floor, which she quickly kicked away. He then brought his hands up and massaged her breasts, squeezing and plucking at her aching nipples. All she could do was moan and rock against him. And when he captured a nipple between his thumb and index finger and fondled lightly, she gasped. Within seconds her nipples were erect and pleasure shot straight to her, causing her feminine core to pulsate.

"Yes!" she cried out.

"Shhh," he warned softly, then leaned forward and claimed her mouth in a kiss that was savage. Brenna lost herself in the kiss, leaping headfirst into it, offering her tongue, intensifying the sparks that ran through her body.

This was the man she had fallen in love with. The man who had given her five beautiful babies and who had set out to be everything she'd always believed a father should be. She'd never known her own father, yet she'd dreamed that he would have been as devoted and loving as Jabarie. Her husband was so male, so strong, that she loved him more with every passing second she shared with him.

Her body was so hot and hungry for him, she cried out when Jabarie released her. Opening her eyes, she watched as he took a step back, then reached up, loosening his tie and unfastening the buttons on his shirt. He stared at her, sable eyes transfixed, slowly taking in her naked body with male appreciation. He made her feel attractive and downright sexy. And when his tongue darted out and swept across his juicy lips, he turned desire into spiraling need.

"Bren," he murmured. "You're so damned beautiful."

Breathless, she had to force herself to speak. "Thank you," she replied as he stripped off his shirt and tossed it aside. Brenna stared at his bare, muscular chest and shook her head. Jabarie was sexy as all get-out. Washboard abs and hard pectorals, he put men half his age to shame. He stepped forward and brought his hands up to cup her full breasts, then buried his face in her cleavage.

"Yes," she murmured. She swayed toward him and closed her eyes while Jabarie placed light kisses along her skin, drawing closer to her aroused nipples that were screaming, *touch me!* She could barely breathe, and by the time he finally captured one with his hot mouth and sucked it deep between his lips, she gave a deep sigh of pleasure. "Oh … Jabarie …" Her head fell back, and her breath caught.

She moaned while he sucked her nipples, first one and then the other, drawing them farther into his mouth. Her breathing was ragged. Her body was burning up. It was one giant inferno.

Brenna cradled his head at her chest, threading her fingers through his curls, and held him against her, encouraging him to draw her nipple even deeper into his mouth. Then he pulled away and gazed down at her. As she stared into their depths there was no mistaking the hunger in his eyes as he lifted her off the travertine tile floor and carried her over to the double sink, lowering her onto the edge of the countertop.

Jabarie looked down at her with heavy-lidded eyes. "Damn, Bren," he muttered, and reclaimed her mouth.

While they kissed, his fingers glided across her breasts, down her belly, and through the patch of brown hair at her apex before stopping where she was dying for him to touch. "Open your legs," he growled.

She parted her trembling thighs and watched as Jabarie lowered onto one knee.

He placed a palm at the inside of her leg and the contact caused her skin to tingle. Jabarie slipped two fingers between her slippery folds and with one push he was deep inside. Brenna arched off the counter and drew in a long breath. What she was feeling she couldn't even bring to words. And when Jabarie pulled his fingers out to the tip then pushed in, she thought she would lose her mind. She was wet and so incredibly aroused that she was rapidly spiraling toward orgasm.

Brenna started rocking her hips, meeting each delicious stroke. "Yes, baby," she moaned. "*Yesss.*"

With his fingers still buried inside, Jabarie found her swollen bud, then leaned forward. Brenna sucked in air at the first touch of Jabarie's lips. And when he started licking hungrily, she was no longer able to contain herself.

"*Ohhh!*" Brenna cried out. He moaned his appreciation and licked again and again, then flicked his tongue against her clit, watching her response as pleasure vibrated through her entire body.

Soft whimpers slipped from her lips as he tasted and nibbled away at her, taking his sweet time. She was aroused and eager, her hips drawing closer and closer to his tongue, yet it was never close enough. Her husband took his time, knowing how to apply just the right amount of pressure before easing back. With every swipe of his tongue he teased and demanded, encouraging her to draw closer to an orgasm that was so close. With her eyelids lowered, Brenna leaned her back against the mirror, grateful for the cool glass against her heated flesh. Jabarie removed his fingers and continued kissing and teasing, tasting her essence with his tongue while sweeping over the surface with circular movement. She cried out and grabbed onto his shoulders, digging her nails into his flesh.

"Feel good?" he asked, his warm breath heating her tender flesh.

"*Yessss, yessss*," she whimpered, like he really had to ask.

Jabarie's tongue traveled along her folds, then he reached up and slid two fingers inside again, pushing deep, then out, and even deeper still, and then he twisted his fingers, driving her insane. Within seconds she clasped both hands over her mouth and muffled a scream. She shuddered and bucked and cried his name as an orgasm rocked her body, yet Jabarie didn't stop his pleasurable assault until he had drawn out every last moan from her.

As she struggled to find her breath, Jabarie took his mouth away and lowered onto the floor in front of her. Brenna slowly opened her eyes and swallowed deeply. Her husband was staring at her, quietly watching her with her legs spread, his eyelids hooded with pleasure.

"I could sit here all night staring at you sitting there naked on the counter," he said, then his gaze dipped down between her legs.

"Really?" she replied with a drowsy smirk, and spread her thighs even wider.

"Really," he groaned. Jabarie rose. His hands were on his belt, his eyes on her as released the buckle, unfastened his pants, and lowered his zipper. Her gaze traveled down to his crotch where his erection strained beneath the fabric, and her clit pulsed at the sight. It was crazy, but her body was obsessed with having him buried deep inside of her. He had a way of stirring something inside her that made each and every time they made love feel like a new erotic experience.

As he moved closer she inhaled deeply. Just the thought of him pounding into her right now until she milked him of every last drop had her kitty pulsing with heat.

Brenna slid forward on the counter until her legs were dangling over the edge. As soon as he was within arm's length she pulled him closer so that he was standing between her thighs. She reached down and touched him, sliding her hand over his long, thick penis, in slow, even strokes.

"I love it when you touch me that way." Jabarie stared at her, his eyes dark with lust.

"I know what else you love," she smirked, then dragged him closer until their lips touched.

"Mommy! Lil Jay's crying!" Bree called from the other side of the bedroom door.

Brenna jerked upright on the counter and heard Jabarie cuss under his breath. "Story of my life."

She gave him a sympathetic grin. "Sorry, baby. Lil Jay's teething and running a slight temperature. I'll make it up to you later." She pressed her lips to his once more.

"You know this is unfair, right?"

"I know." Smiling, she dropped off the counter and retrieved the bathrobe sitting on the bench in the corner, then hurried to see how their youngest was doing.

Jabarie's eyes followed the sway of her lush hips out of the room. Then he shook his head and muttered. "Damn."

* * *

Jabarie changed out of his suit into athletic shorts and a faded black wifebeater, then opened the tall French door and stepped out onto the terrace that looked out upon miles of private beach. Seagulls were flying directly over the shore, calling out to one another. He took a deep breath, drawing in the salty air, and allowed his eyes to drift over the water.

He had everything a man could possibly want. Five beautiful kids, a gorgeous wife who was the best mother any man could possible hope his family to have, a big home, and financial security. And now a dog, he added with a chuckle.

The only thing missing was more time to spend with his wife. In fact, if his calculations were correct it had been three years since they'd last gone away, just the two of them. They needed another vacation. He just needed to get Brenna to realize it as well.

Jabarie stepped out of the bedroom and climbed the stairs toward Lil Jay's room. Brenna had been at it non-stop since she'd left the bookstore. It was his turn to take over for the rest of the evening.

He moved into the small bedroom decorated in Sponge Bob Square Pants to find his wife lying on the twin size bed beside Lil Jay, who sat upright the second he noticed him coming through the door.

"Hi Daddy," he mumbled, rubbing his eyes.

Jabarie walked over and took a seat on the bed beside him. "What's up, little man? You don't feel too good?"

Lil Jay shook his head with tears in his eyes.

"Francine says he's been running a low grade fever all day," Brenna informed him as she reached up and brushed the tears from her baby's eyes.

"How about a popsicle?" Jabarie suggested. He'd buy him a pony if that's what it took to bring a smile back to his face.

Lil Jay's hazel eyes grew large and he nodded eagerly.

Rising, Jabarie ruffled his thick curly hair and said, "I'll be right back." As he turned to leave he glanced over at his wife lying on the bed in her robe. Knowing she had nothing underneath, he groaned inward.

The things a man's willing to give up for his family.

Shaking his head, Jabarie went back downstairs. He stepped into the state-of-the art kitchen and found his daughters sitting at the island. Norman was lying on the floor in front of the double oven, tail wagging happily. "What are you ladies doing?"

"We're making chocolate milk," Bree announced.

He watched as she poured enough syrup in a glass to cause a bellyache.

As soon as she was done, Arianna reached for the gallon of milk with both hands and filled a tall glass to the brim. Those two were so independent. It was a constant reminder to him how fast they were growing up.

"Daddy, you want one?" Arianna asked.

He grinned. "Sure, why not?"

Arianna stirred her glass while he reached into the freezer and removed an orange freeze pop.

"Bree ... do me a favor and run this upstairs to your little brother?"

"'Kay," she said, climbing off the barstool, holding her glass in one hand and taking the freeze pop with the other. She hurried out of the room, sloshing milk, with Norman at her heels licking away all the evidence and saving Jabarie from retrieving a sponge mop from the utility closet.

"Arie, how was swimming?" he asked as he lowered onto the stool beside her.

She shrugged. "I did a double somersault. Mommy didn't get to videotape it because she was *too* busy talking on her phone."

"I'm sure she didn't mean to miss it," he reassured her.

She gave a pout that said she disagreed.

"Your mother is a busy woman, but no matter what she's doing she always finds a way to be there for all of you."

Arianna huffed out a long breath. "But why does she have to work at all? Brittany and Julia's mommies don't work." Brittany and Julia were her best friends. She pushed a glass of milk in front of him. While she poured in chocolate syrup, Jabarie tried to explain.

"For some families parents have to work, while in other families they dedicate time to the things they enjoy."

"Does Mommy *have* to work?" she asked, still concentrating on filling his glass with syrup.

"Well ..." he began, unsure exactly how to answer her question except with the truth. "... not exactly. She's a business owner so that's a little different." *Damn,* Jabarie scowled inward as he scrambled his brain for a better way to explain. "Your mother loves that bookstore ... just like you love swimming."

"Yes, but doesn't she love me more?"

"Yes, sweetheart, I love you very much," Brenna said, coming up behind them.

Jabarie swung around as she padded into the kitchen wearing nothing but that robe he was dying to rip away from her body.

"You never have to question the way I feel about you." Leaning over, Brenna kissed her cheek. "I'm sorry I missed your dive tonight, but I promise I'll do whatever I can to make sure I don't miss the next one."

Arianna's eyes narrowed with skepticism. "You mean it?"

Brenna nodded and gave a smile that Jabarie noticed

didn't quite meet her eyes. "Yes, sweetheart, I mean it."

Arianna finally lowered the syrup bottle, then reached over and gave her mother a big hug. "Thanks, Mommy."

Jabarie looked over at his wife, brow bunched, and he realized she was avoiding eye contact.

"Daddy ... are we still going camping next weekend?" Arianna asked.

His eyes were still glued to his wife's face as he spoke. "We'll talk about that later. Why don't you go hang out in the family room with Bree while I talk to your mother?"

Arianna jumped down with her glass and pouted as she left the room, clearly not happy with his reply. They'd talk about camping later. Right now he had something more important to discuss.

He waited until he heard Arianna asking her sister for the remote before he turned to Brenna and blinked with disbelief. "Bren ... baby ... what's going on?"

* * *

Brenna paced around the kitchen, wringing her hands together. This was not at all the way she had hoped to bring up the subject, but she figured now was as good a time as any. "I've been giving it a lot of thought, and I want to hire someone else to manage the bookstore."

Clearly confused, he shook his head. "Why?"

She met her husband's eyes. "Because our kids are getting older and I'm missing out. Running the bookstore requires a lot of hard work and dedication. I can't keep putting my family second."

"But you love that bookstore."

Of course she did. All her life she had wanted nothing more than to manage her own store, but she had wanted a family even more. "I can always run a store. I have only one chance to raise our kids."

Jabarie drew quiet as he sat there drinking his syrupy milk. She could tell he wanted to say more but was keeping it to himself.

Leaning against the kitchen counters, Brenna calmly drew a deep breath and folded her arms underneath her breasts. "I thought you'd be happy to hear I plan to spend more time with the family."

"No, what makes me happy is seeing my wife happy," he protested. "Why didn't you say anything? I had no idea you were feeling so overwhelmed."

She shrugged. "Because I didn't want to worry you. I really thought I could manage, but now that the kids are getting older it just isn't as easy as it was before. I'm spread too thin and something has to go."

"But the store? Bren, I know managing that bookstore means everything to you, and I hate to see you sacrificing everything for us. How about hiring someone part-time to manage the store then you'll have the flexibility to be available for the kids?"

He didn't understand. Why was she surprised? "Arianna has every reason to be upset with me. I've missed her recital … her amazing somersault … All her friends and their mothers went on a trip to King's Dominion and I couldn't go because I had to be at a book conference. She notices that her mother hasn't been there for her, and I made a promise I would always be there for my kids."

Jabarie rose from the stool, then walked over and wrapped an arm around his wife, pulling her close. "Bren, you're not your mother."

She didn't respond.

"You are an amazing mother. A man couldn't ask for a better mother for his children. So don't ever think otherwise."

She hesitated. Her back was rigid, her breathing deep. "Thank you, baby."

He brought her closer to him and kissed the top of her head. "I had no idea you felt so overwhelmed, which means I need to start helping you out more. I guess what we need to do is sit down and work on adjusting our schedules to better accommodate our family," he said tightening his hold. "I think a few days away from work and the kids will be a great way to clear our heads, and an opportunity for the two of us to figure out how to better manage our family together so you don't have to give up working at the bookstore."

Brenna shook her head and pushed away from his grasp. He just didn't get it. "Jabarie, have you been listening to a word I've been saying?" she began as she paced the length of the counter. "I already don't spend enough time with the kids and now you want to plan a vacation away from them."

He ran a hand impatiently through the thickness of his hair. "Bren, a *weekend*, that's all, just you and me. Some time for us to talk. Maybe if we had more time together you wouldn't have held back how you've been feeling. Trust me, I have no problem with you being a stay-at-home mom if that's *really* what you want to do. But I don't believe it is. I really think if we can work out a plan you'll change your mind about finding someone else to run the books store."

She loved her job and found running the Cornerstone Bookstore quite rewarding, but being a wife and a mother was much more fulfilling. She just wished her husband would understand that. "It won't matter. I've made my decision. I'm posting the management job tomorrow," she argued stubbornly.

He studied her in shrewd silence a moment longer, then sighed heavily. "If that's what you want to do, then

I'll have to respect that."

Brenna heard Lil Jay upstairs calling for her. "I better get back up there." She turned and started out of the room, but he stopped her.

"I'll go sit with him. Why don't you go watch a movie with the girls?"

Glancing over her shoulder, she saw his lingering stare, vertical lines appearing between his brows. He was confused and disappointed, and she was tempted to go over, wrap her arms around his neck and reassure him that everything was going to be all right, but all he would do would be to try and convince her otherwise. She was making the right decision. She was certain of that, and in time her husband would understand.

With a nod, she turned on her heels and left the room.

* * *

Jabarie headed up the stairs and watched as Brenna flopped down on the couch between the girls and wrapped her arms around them.

Brenna was tired and overworked, and with the kids home for the summer she had been pulled in every direction, but quitting the job she loved most was not the answer. Maybe it was partly his fault, he thought. He hadn't realized how hard she'd been working, and it was time for him to take up more of the slack. He didn't have a problem with that. One of the beautiful things about being the boss was that he could pick his own hours.

Brenna was not only beautiful, she was independent, and Jabarie knew how much running that bookstore meant to her. It wasn't a job, it was her passion, yet she was willing to sacrifice the store not because she wanted to but because she felt she *had* to and that's what bothered him.

Why do I feel like a failure?

Jabarie dragged a hand across his head, feeling increasingly agitated. What he and his wife needed was some time away from everything so they could talk, *and* so Brenna would have a chance to clear her head and see that they were a team and together they could do anything.

He scowled as he reached the top step because he couldn't remember the last time he had felt so frustrated. His wife was a sexy mama bear with attitude. She was territorial, and when it came to their kids you better look out! Getting her to change her mind would be next to impossible. Jabarie shook his head. How come he hadn't realized she needed his help? Now the situation had become a lot more complicated.

He pondered the problem as he moved down the hall, and by the time he reached Lil Jay's room he decided that he had no other choice. He was going to have to pull out the big guns.

He sat with Lil Jay until the little guy finally drifted back off to sleep. Then Jabarie went down and retrieved his cell phone from the top of his dresser drawer. He scrolled through his address book and dialed. As soon as he heard the raspy voice on the other end he realized he had made the right decision.

"Hey, it's Jabarie. I need your help."

Chapter 6

Jabarie was up to something.

Brenna wasn't sure what, but she had been married to him long enough to know something was going on. It had been a week since she'd announced hiring a manager, and Jabarie's behavior had gotten weirder with each passing day.

For starters, despite her protest he'd hired a cook, and an amazing one at that, who made chocolate chip pancakes and grilled cheese sandwiches without the crust. And then there was Jabarie getting off work early enough to scoop up the kids and drive them to their extracurricular activities. He even had the housekeeping service coming in five days a week now instead of three. It was so overwhelming and wonderful that with each surprise she was left speechless.

And that wasn't all.

She had left the house this morning before Jabarie, and that seldom ever happened. Then as soon as she'd arrived at the bookstore he'd called to let her know he and his sister Bianca were taking the kids school shopping that afternoon. Jabarie shopping? For real? She couldn't get him to shop for groceries, let alone spend the afternoon hanging out at the mall with five hyperactive kids.

With school starting in two weeks Brenna already had scheduled the afternoon off, yet Jabarie told her to spend the afternoon doing something for herself. She decided she'd have to make sure when she got home tonight to pull out a thermometer and take his temperature.

Brenna finished inventory, then moved back out onto the floor. There were several customers in the store and Craig seemed to have it all under control. She was heading back to her office to work on payroll when laughter stopped her in her tracks. She knew that infectious sound anywhere. She hurried toward the coffee shop, and as soon as she turned the corner she found Aunt Nellie sitting on a stool in front of the counter.

"Aunt Nellie, what are you doing here?" she gasped with surprise.

Grinning sheepishly, her aunt replied, "I thought I'd make a surprise visit."

"Oh, my goodness!"

She slid off the seat just as Brenna closed in and planted an affectionate kiss to her upturned cheek, then wrapped her arms around her neck and hugged her tight. This woman was the closest thing she'd ever had to a mother.

Brenna's smile widened. "It's definitely a surprise. I thought you and Tina were planning to spend part of the summer in Jamaica."

Aunt Nellie's chestnut-colored eyes sparkled with excitement. "We spent three weeks there and then Tina was dying to get back here to see if her grandson was running her business right. I tell you … it's all about work with that woman. I don't know how we've managed to be best friends all these years. She doesn't know how to just have fun."

Brenna's lips curled downward slightly at the comment. Was that how Jabarie felt? She had gotten so overwhelmed with work and home that she no longer had time for them to have any fun? She had hoped hiring a manager would change that, but she still had yet to advertise the position. For the last few days Brenna had been asking herself, *what are you waiting for?* Deep down, she was hoping Jabarie was right. That if they worked together as a team, maybe she wouldn't have to hire any help. So far, the assistance Jabarie had been giving all week was proof they were heading in the right direction.

Brenna slid onto one of the wooden stools at the counter. "Chelsea, let me have a latté." While they sipped, they chitchatted about how beautiful Jamaica was this time of the year. Afterwards Brenna gave her aunt a tour.

"I see business is steady as usual. You've done a fabulous job with this place." Aunt Nellie complimented as her eyes traveled around the store.

"Thanks," Brenna said, feeling an overwhelming sense of pride. The compliment meant a lot. Aunt Nellie had owned the bookstore for almost twenty years before giving it to Brenna.

Brenna took a moment to admire her aunt. For a woman in her mid-sixties her walnut complexion was smooth and wrinkle free, and her dark-brown shoulder-length hair claimed very few strands of gray. Packing about ten fewer pounds than she had since the last time Brenna had seen her, she looked amazing. Probably better than she'd looked in years.

When they were done with the grand tour, Aunt Nellie swung around and grinned. "So tell me ... how are the little munchkins doing?"

They moved into her office, and as soon as they were seated Brenna brought Aunt Nellie up to speed on the Fabulous Five. "They are going to be so excited to see you!" she beamed. "How long are you planning on staying?" Since she had moved to Georgia they rarely saw her except for Easter and Thanksgiving.

There was a noticeable pause before their gaze locked. "I'm thinking about coming back home for good."

Brenna's eyes widened. "Are you serious?"

She nodded. "Yes, I've been thinking about it quite a bit. Hanging out with my girlfriends and attending my new church is great, but I miss home."

Excitedly, Brenna started squirming on her seat. "I've been trying not to be selfish, but I was hoping you'd come back home!"

"Well, I've been seriously considering it. My summer tenants are gone so the house is empty right now. I plan on spending the week cleaning up and putting my plan in place."

"This is wonderful! Wait until I tell Jabarie." The Beaumonts were wonderful and made sure Brenna always felt a part of the family, but there was nothing like having her Aunt Nellie back in Sheraton Beach.

They were laughing when she heard a light tap at her door. Brenna's gaze shifted from her aunt as soon as she caught sight of Craig standing in the doorway holding a beautiful summer bouquet.

"Craig ... you shouldn't have," she joked.

"I didn't," he replied and took that as his cue to step into the room. "These were just delivered a few moments ago."

Brenna sprang from her chair and moved around to take the vase from his outstretched hands. "Thank you." He moved back onto the floor while she carried the bouquet over to the small table at the corner of her office and placed it at the center.

"Who are they from?" Aunt Nellie asked, as if she didn't already know.

Brenna giggled. "Who knows? I might have a secret admirer." Leaning forward, she brought her nose to the bouquet and took a deep breath.

"My ... those sure are pretty. What did you do to earn something that romantic?" Aunt Nellie asked her.

"He probably felt I deserved them after giving birth to five Beaumont babies," she said with animated laughter, and Aunt Nellie joined in. Brenna reached for the envelope and removed the card.

Dinner tonight...seven o'clock...and wear something sexy.

Her heart thumped a little harder at the seductive words. "He didn't sign his name, but whoever sent them invited me to dinner tonight and said to wear something sexy."

"Sexy, huh? I can't remember the last time a man asked me to wear something sexy."

Brenna gazed at her aunt with a playful smile. "I haven't done sexy in a while." She'd been too busy dressing in flats and t-shirts, anything wash-and-wear and childproof.

"Then it's about time. In fact," Aunt Nellie began as she rose from the chair. "Why don't you run along and do some shopping while I help Craig watch the store? As a matter of fact, don't come back. I'll close up."

As tempting as the offer sounded, Brenna voiced skepticism. "Aunt Nellie, I couldn't ask you to do that."

"You didn't ask ... I offered. Now go," she commanded with a gentle push.

Brenna hesitated for another few seconds before she danced happily around her desk and reached for her purse. She had already planned for Craig to watch the store a few hours while she took the children shopping. Instead, she could spend the time buying something for herself. And sexy was just what she planned to look this evening. It was time she reminded her husband why he married her.

* * *

"Ladies ... we need to do this more often."

Brenna looked up and nodded at Sheyna, with her

wide eyes and a generous mouth. "I definitely agree." She couldn't remember the last time she'd had a girls' day out.

The moment Brenna went racing out of the bookstore, before Aunt Nellie had had a chance to change her mind, she'd called Sheyna and Danica, who were not only her sisters-in-law but her closest friends, to join her for an afternoon of pampering. Sheyna took the afternoon off while Danica left Jasmine and Joshua with the nanny.

Sheyna, who recently had been promoted to VP of Customer Relations for the Beaumont Corporation, had opted out of the idea of riding around in a minivan, so the three hopped into her CL550 Mercedes and headed up the coast to the outlet mall at Rehoboth Beach. They'd spent the last hour buying clothes for the kids before they had lunch. Afterward, it was time to focus on their reason for being there, finding Brenna something to wear for tonight.

Danica's expression was sheepish. "So what exactly does Jabarie mean when he says sexy?"

Sheyna sucked her teeth. "The same as all men. Something short, tight and easy to take off."

The ladies laughed while Brenna moved over to a rack of after-five gowns. "I want something sexy but classy at the same time."

"It would really help if we knew where he was planning to take you to dinner," Sheyna declared.

Brenna shrugged as she glanced over at the mahogany beauty. "That ruins some of the excitement."

Danica nodded, reddish brown curls bouncing against her shoulder as she agreed. "It also kills the romance. How about this?"

Both ladies turned around to stare at a lime green dress with a plunging neck line.

"Uh-uh. Green doesn't look good on me," Brenna

replied with a frown. "I want something red ... brown ... pink."

The tall leggy honey-brown woman nodded and returned the dress to the hanger.

Not finding anything she liked, Brenna moved to the next rack. She had no idea what she was looking for, but was certain she'd know it the second she saw it.

"How are the plans going for the family reunion?" Danica asked.

Sheyna glanced in their direction and a frown tugged at her full lips. "Puh-leeze! The next time I volunteer to be on the planning committee for the Beaumont Family Reunion, knock me upside my head. Between the Beaumonts here and the ones in Richmond, we've been going back and forth about location!" she exclaimed. "Like I was telling Jace, a reunion in the summer would probably be nice in Richmond, but summers here is where it's at. Sunshine and sandy beaches. And the way the Force MDs love women, you would think they'd be dying to see them walking half-naked on the beach."

"I know that's right," Brenna laughed. "How long is Remy here?"

Sheyna tossed her dark shoulder-length hair away from her face, then scrunched up her lips disapprovingly. "Long enough to have some unsuspecting female fall in love, then break her heart."

Brenna shook her head. Some things never changed.

"Anyway, Uncle Richard wants a catered meal while the chefs in the family want to prepare the meal themselves."

Danica chuckled. "Sounds like you've got your hands full." Whatever they decided, it was going to be a tripped-out weekend.

Sheyna huffed out an exasperated breath. "It's a headache. The rate we're going, there won't be anything lined up before spring."

"If anyone can work it out, you can," Brenna said reassuringly. Her best friend always did have a way with people.

"Ooh, look at this!" Danica squealed as she swung around, holding up a bright red dress that plunged dangerously low in both the front and the back. "It looks perfect!"

"Ooh! I agree. Go try it on," Sheyna insisted.

Brenna took it from her hand and scrambled into the dressing room. She stepped out of her sundress and slipped into the slinky red gown, then raised the zipper that stopped right beneath her generous cleavage. As soon as she glanced in the three-way mirror her heart pitter-pattered. The gown fit as if it had been designed just for her. It had a cinched waist, a short skirt that hugged her lush hips and a front zipper that allowed Jabarie easy access.

Brenna sashayed out of the dressing room to where her sisters-in-laws were waiting and twirled around so they could see the dress at all angles. The second she saw the expression on their faces, she knew the dress was exactly what she had been looking for.

Sexy.

Chapter 7

"Where are we going?" Brenna asked as they stepped out onto the front porch of their house.

"It's a surprise," Jabarie said with a lazy wink, then placed a hand at her waist and escorted her out into the circular driveway where his Jaguar was waiting.

Brenna studied him with a speculative gleam in her eyes. She was sure she could get it out of him if she insisted, but that would spoil the surprise, and she loved surprises.

He helped her into the car, then walked around to the passenger's side. As he moved she was completely aware of how vibrantly attractive her husband looked in a crisp white shirt, blue striped tie and navy slacks. Jabarie slipped inside the car and fastened his seat belt.

As soon Brenna had finished shopping, they'd had manies and pedies and stopped at Annie's for crab bisque that was to die for before driving back to Sheraton Beach. When she got home she found Aunt Nellie in the kitchen baking an apple pie with the girls. To her delight, she'd insisted on watching the children for the evening.

"Did I tell you how beautiful you look tonight?" His gaze swept over her body, taking in her red dress and high-heeled strappy black pumps that accentuated her shapely legs.

She gazed over at him, waiting for his eyes to meet hers. Tingling with pleasure, she spoke. "Yes, but you can tell me again."

"You're beautiful, Mrs. Beaumont." He leaned across the seat and pressed his lips to hers. And she savored the taste of his mouth against hers. She was definitely looking forward to the evening.

Jabarie finally put the car into drive and she reached over and turned on the CD player. The sounds of *Earth, Wind & Fire* filled the air. Brenna sank deeply in the soft leather comfort of his seat and sighed. Tonight she was going to try and put all her worries aside, although there was one thing that was bugging her.

"You think Lil Jay is feeling any better?"

"He's fine," he assured her.

"Maybe I need to have Aunt Nellie take his temperature again." She reached down to retrieve her phone but Jabarie grabbed her hand, stopping her.

"Bren, he's fine. Aunt Nellie raised you. I'm sure she can take care of him."

She curled her bottom lip between her teeth. If anyone could handle a toddler, it was Aunt Nellie. "I guess you're right."

He brought her hand to his mouth and kissed it. "Sweetheart, tonight is about us."

Us. They really did need an evening out together. "Okay," she finally conceded. "Aren't we lucky Aunt Nellie returned when she did?"

He brought her hand over onto his lap, then quickly looked to his left. "Yes, how lucky was that?"

"Aunt Nellie told me she's thinking about moving back to Sheraton Beach. Wouldn't that be wonderful?"

"Oh, yeah, that would be great."

It was better than great, Brenna thought. Having her aunt back in town would be magnificent. She hadn't said anything yet, but once her aunt had had a chance to settle back at home, she planned on asking her aunt to help manage the bookstore. That way she could be at home with the children and Aunt Nellie could go back to doing something she enjoyed. It was a win for everyone.

Brenna was so excited she could barely contain her excitement.

"What are you smiling about?" Jabarie asked, breaking into her thoughts.

She looked over and her smile broadened. "I'm just happy to be out, spending time with my husband," she said by way of an explanation.

Jabarie turned onto the highway and Brenna realized they were headed south toward the bay. "Are we going to Shelby's?"

Quietly, he shook his head.

"You're not going to tell me, are you?"

Jabarie gave her a sidelong glance. "Nope."

"Fine, keep your stupid secret." She faked a pout and tried to resist a smile. Her response was rewarded by a hearty chuckle.

She crossed her legs and settled back on the seat. Resting her hand on her husband's thigh, she closed her eyes and listened to the soulful sounds and allowed the music to relax her as she thought about the last week and had to admit her life was slowly starting to fall into place again.

When the car came to a brief stop, she opened her eyes and gazed out the window to discover they were heading toward the pier. She gasped and turned on the seat. "We're having dinner onboard the *Beaumont Beauty*, aren't we?"

Jabarie gave her a teasing grin. "You think you know me."

With amusement dancing at her lips, she settled back against the seat and said, "You forget, Jabarie, I've known you almost my entire life." And it was a life she wouldn't change for anything in the world. "So ... are we having dinner on the yacht?"

"Yes," he finally confessed. "And plan on staying the

entire night."

Brenna swung around abruptly on the seat again. "The night? But w-we can't be gone that long. Lil Jay is still running a fever."

"Yes, and the pediatrician said he'll be fine," he assured her.

She released a heavy breath, trying not to think about Lil Jay being without her all night.

Jabarie reached out and squeezed her knee comfortingly. "Bren, he'll be fine with your aunt."

He was right. If anyone could take care of the kids it was Aunt Nellie. Brenna leaned back against the soft leather seat and tried to clear her mind. She worried too much. She knew that. It was only for one night. What could go wrong? They were only a phone call away, and besides, she and Jabarie deserved some time alone. Since the kids had been born she could count on her hands the number of times she had left them overnight with someone else. Okay, so she was a mother hen. So what? But tonight she was going to focus on her husband, because he deserved an uninterrupted night alone. Her body began to tingle just thinking about the night ahead. She intended to make sure it was a night that would send them both home smiling.

By the time he pulled the car into a parking spot near the pier, Brenna was grinning and looking forward to sharing a romantic evening. She waited until Jabarie came around and opened the door and offered his hand before climbing out. She rose from the car and met the intensity of his eyes.

"You ready for our date?" He looked down at her quizzically and she realized the meaning behind his words. He wanted to know if she was ready to put all her worries about the kids and the bookstore aside for just one evening. How could she possibly deny her adorable husband anything?

"Yes," she leaned closer and tilted her chin and he kissed her. "But I wish you'd told me you were planning to sail me away for the evening so I could have packed an overnight bag."

"If you'd known what I was planning you'd never have gotten in that car."

She couldn't stop herself from laughing softly as she gave a slight shake of the head. "You think you know me."

"Oh, I know you better than you know yourself." He kissed her once more, then pressed the button on his key and popped the trunk. Brenna stood by with a curious look and watched Jabarie lift the trunk lid and remove a small suitcase before making eye contact.

Her brow arched. "How long have you been planning this?"

"Ever since Aunt Nellie called and asked me to pick her up from the airport yesterday."

"Yesterday?"

Nodding, he moved over beside her. "Yes, dear. She wanted to surprise you."

She shook her head. "You never cease to amaze me."

"Yes, that's the plan. I need to do whatever it takes to keep the relationship interesting. I can't have you trading me in for a younger model."

She smiled up at him. "Really?"

"Really." Leaning forward, he lowered his lips to hers in a kiss that was so gentle and soft she was suddenly looking forward to having him all to herself. Jabarie pulled back, winked, then reached down for her hand. "Now let's get this evening started."

The sun had begun to set in the west. Brenna laced her fingers with his and followed him along the pier until they reached the seventy-foot structure with *Beaumont*

Beauty in beautiful scripted gold lettering on the side. She followed him up the ramp and onboard the yacht.

"How big a crew do we have tonight?"

He winked. "I figured three were more than enough."

She nodded and couldn't resist another smile as she moved down to the stateroom below. She was suddenly anxious to get their evening underway.

* * *

Jabarie couldn't believe they were finally alone.

Grinning, he followed her down to the master stateroom, then lowered the overnight bag onto the floor in the corner.

They stood in the middle of a luxurious room, taking it in, from the dark woodwork and opulent ivory furnishing to the large bed dominating the elegant room. His eyes were immediately drawn to the burgundy comforter covered with plush pillows. To the left was a private balcony overlooking the clear blue water. To the right was the adjoining bathroom with a Jacuzzi complementing the suite.

"I can't believe we're here!" Brenna said excitedly and flopped down on the bed.

He grinned and took a seat beside her. "Believe it. It's just me, you and a small crew until tomorrow afternoon."

"I don't know how to act with all that time on my hands," Brenna declared.

"I'm sure we can think of something." He gave her a knowing grin. They were alone and the very air surrounding them crackled with awareness. He couldn't get enough of staring at his wife, with her flirty laugh, bedroom eyes, and delicious body in that dress. He rolled over onto the bed and pressed her lips to his. The kiss was deep and passionate and nowhere near enough. "Baby, just say the word and we can skip dinner."

Brenna laughed. "Oh no! I didn't buy this dress for nothing. We have all night. No kids, remember?"

"Yes, and the sooner we eat, the better," he grumbled.

* * *

After the chef assured him that everything was going according to plan, Jabarie left the galley and moved up the staircase onto the main deck, staring off into the water while the captain prepared to sail on their romantic cruise.

It felt like déjà vu.

He remembered the first time he had brought Brenna onboard. It had been ten years ago. Brenna had been home running the bookstore while Aunt Nellie nursed a sprained ankle. He had invited her onto the yacht with the hope of sleeping with her and finally getting her out of his system once and for all. However, after two insatiable nights he had to finally admit what he had known all along, that Brenna had still been in his heart and in his soul.

"What are you thinking about?"

Jabarie turned around as Brenna came up the staircase and sashayed over to join him. He drew in a sharp breath. He was physically aware of everything about her. The amazing red dress showcased her slender and curvaceous body. Shoulder-length brown hair flowed free around her shoulders, the way he liked. Her full sensual red-painted lips curled into a tantalizing smile that caused excitement to spiral through his body.

When she finally reached him, she slid her arms around his neck, then arched forward, pressing her breasts to his chest. Their gazes locked for a long moment and she gave him one of those looks that would make a man do just about anything. Dipping forward, Jabarie took her mouth with enough heat to make sure there was no doubt in her mind how sexy she looked tonight.

Brenna kissed him back with a hunger that made his head spin. He traced her lips, coaxing them to part, and as soon as she moaned his tongue slid inside her mouth. She tasted so minty sweet he was ready to take her right then and there. Her lips were soft and hot, and so damned delicious; he explored, teased and tasted, allowing desire to consume him. Brenna sank into the hunger, the taste, meeting his passionate strokes. One hand cupped her head, the other slid to her buttocks and pressed her against him. He wanted to make sure she felt him growing long and hard. And for a moment he allowed himself to think about how good it felt buried inside her wet core. A moan erupted from her throat, glorious and wild.

"You feel that?" he asked, forcing himself to slow down. He dragged his mouth from hers and cruised across her cheek and neck.

Brenna brought her hand to his crotch and squeezed. "You sure don't waste any time now, do you?" she chuckled.

"Sorry, babe. I've been waiting all day for this."

He slid his fingers gently up her arm and along her shoulder until he cupped the back of her neck and pulled her close again. "You're breathtaking," he whispered.

Brenna brought her hands up, then leaned into the solid wall of his chest while her breath caressed his nose, sending shivers raging through his body. Then she slowly planted light kisses from the corner of his mouth, along his cheek and down to his throat before he finally pulled away with a groan.

"If you want dinner, then we better go *now*," he warned. "Otherwise, I'm throwing you over my shoulder and carrying you down below." *Because the sooner they were done, the sooner he could focus on his dessert.*

"I guess I better try and keep my hands off of you at least until we finish eating," she cooed, eyes sparkling mysteriously.

Jabarie gazed up toward the heavens and whispered, "Thank you."

Laughing, he took Brenna's hand and led her down to the dining room. Soft classic jazz music was playing in the background. At the center of the room was a candlelit table covered with a white linen tablecloth. It was perfectly romantic and the exact ambience he was trying to capture. As soon as Brenna stepped into the room, he heard her release a slow breath.

"I take it you like what you see?"

"Absolutely," she replied. "I feel like I did the first time you brought me onboard." She glanced up at him, eyes sparkling with excitement. That was exactly what he was hoping to see.

He pulled the chair out for her and waited until she was seated before pushing her closer to the table. "Thanks, babe," she replied.

As soon as he settled into the chair across the table from her, their server came out to pour their wine.

"Mrs. Beaumont, it's so good to see you again." He tipped his head with a smile, then reached for their flutes and filled them with white wine.

Brenna glanced up at the handsome slender man with berry-black skin and large round eyes, and smiled warmly. "The same here, Toliver. I can't wait to see what you've prepared."

"I hope everything is to your liking," he said with a distinctive Caribbean accent.

"It always is."

Jabarie nodded in agreement. Toliver had been his father's chef for more than fifteen years. Thank goodness his parents were out of the country, because otherwise he would have had a hard time stealing him away for the evening.

It wasn't long before Toliver came back out carrying two bowls of black bean soup. Reaching for her spoon, Brenna brought the family favorite to her lips and moaned. "Oh, my, but that's good."

Jabarie watched her eyes sparkle in the candlelight. "Yes, indeed."

While they ate, Brenna talked to him about a romance conference that was coming to the area. Cornerstone Bookstore had been asked to provide the books for the mega book fair. "They're expecting more than one hundred authors. Imagine all the people who'll be in attendance at the conference."

As he lowered his spoon to the table, Jabarie nodded. "I think Bianca mentioned something about that. They've already reserved a large block of rooms at the Beaumont for the guests."

Dinner salads were served with homemade croutons, jumbo shrimp and balsamic dressing. While eating, Jabarie gazed at Brenna across the linen-covered table. "Have you thought about asking your aunt to help out at the store?"

She speared a cucumber and shook her head. "Yes, but I thought I'd give her a few days to settle back in first."

Jabarie took a sip of his wine, watching her over the rim. "Baby, I'm sure she won't mind helping."

She gazed across the table and met his gaze. He hated to see the uncertainty return. "I sure hope so," she finally said between chews.

"I'm sure she'd be happy to put in a few hours a week and give you a break," he suggested studying her.

"A *few* hours? Hmmm, maybe," she replied but didn't look totally satisfied. "I'm hoping she's willing to at least manage the store part-time."

The candlelight flickered cross her face, illuminating the gold in her beautiful eyes. "Bren, I know that I haven't been doing my share with the kids, but I'm willing to do whatever I have to do to lighten your schedule. I'll hire a full-time staff to run the house if needed. I just wish you'd told me you were feeling overwhelmed," he added with a long breath.

Brenna gazed over at him and appeared almost surprised to hear his confession. "Yes, I should have," she murmured. Brenna would never say it to him, but he knew why she hadn't mentioned feeling overwhelming. She thought she should be able to juggle everything by herself. Well, she was wrong. Last he checked, there was no "I" in team. "If Aunt Nellie and I are both helping, you think you can hold off on trying to find someone else to run the store?"

She smiled and had tears in her eyes. "Yes, baby. I never wanted to give up my job. I was just willing to make the sacrifice for my family."

"Now you don't have to." He rose and leaned across the table and kissed her lips.

Her smile widened as he lowered back into his seat. "I knew there was some reason why I loved you so much."

"Thanks, baby. That means a lot. Especially considering everything I'm dealing with right now at work."

She gave him a puzzled look, then gasped. "Oh, the layoffs! I'm so sorry, I've been so consumed with the store that I forgot all about what you were going through." Brenna reached across the table, gently laying her hand over his. "What have you decided?"

He felt a muscle at his jaw tick as he replied, "Nothing. We've been crunching the numbers and trying to figure out what it's going to take to save these employees' jobs, but everything we've come up with means just temporary fixes. Jace suggested lowering the employee ration per room but none of us are interested in cutting hotel quality or staff."

Brenna hesitated before asking, "Have you spoken to your father?"

He shook his head. Contacting Roger Beaumont was the last thing he wanted to do. For more than forty years his father had invested blood, sweat, and tears into that corporation. And look where they were today. "He and mom are having a wonderful time in Barbados. I didn't want to ruin the rest of their vacation."

Brenna nodded in understanding. "When are you planning to make the announcements?"

"We have a board meeting first thing Monday morning."

"Now it's my turn to make you feel better." She leaned across the table and gently kissed her husband's lips.

"If you want to make me feel better, why don't you just come around here and straddle my lap?" he suggested with a cocky grin.

Brenna rolled her eyes and Jabarie tossed his head back with hearty laughter. She always did know how to make him feel better.

Leaning forward, he said, "Bren, this evening is about us. No more talk about our problems. We left them out at the pier with the car."

She laughed and nodded. "I agree."

Jabarie reached for his wine glass and held it up. "Here's to a wonderful evening together."

"And morning," she added, as she raised her glass as well. "Just think, we can sleep late in the morning."

His eyes widened. "Here's to staying up late and sleeping even later."

"Here, here." Laughing, they clicked their glasses, then brought them to their lips.

The rest of dinner was relaxing. The sun had set and the sky was filled with stars. They sat at the candlelit table talking, laughing and enjoying dinner while listening to the soulful voice of Billie Holliday. The entrée was blackened ribeye, lobster, new potatoes and asparagus. As they dug into dinner, followed by a sinfully rich dessert, they continued talking, totally engrossed in each other. Jabarie realized he was the happiest he had felt in a long time. Once again his wife had managed to ease the tension from his day. As he watched her eat a slice of cheesecake, his hard-on returned and he was ready to rush through dessert and run below with Brenna over his shoulder. But the night was too important for anything to be rushed, he reminded himself. Taking their time and savoring the moment would only heighten the intensity, and when they did finally come together, the night would be explosive.

* * *

The breeze blew across the deck of the ship, stirring Brenna's hair. The night air was relatively warm, and typical for August in Delaware. She stood at the stern and glanced out at the view. They were moving further out to sea and the city sprawled before them as far as the eye could see. Jabarie stood behind her, pressing his chest to her back, his groin against the swell of her ass. "You enjoying yourself?" he murmured against her hair.

Leaning her head against him, she sighed, "Yes, I'm having a wonderful time."

"Come. Dance with me," Jabarie suggested.

Smiling, she took his hand and followed his lead out onto the middle of the deck, where they could hear the music coming from the surround system below. Jabarie wasted no time pulling her into his arms.

"I've been waiting all night for this," he whispered thickly against her cheek.

Brenna tipped her head up and looked him in the eyes, brows raised. "Oh, really? I thought you've been waiting all night for something else."

Jabarie tossed his head back and chuckled. "Okay, yes, that too."

He gathered her close again. Brenna rested her head on his shoulder. Together they swayed to the music, her soft breasts pressed to his chest, her lips against his throat. Tonight nothing else mattered. A half moon was hanging in the sky and the ocean was calm and relaxed. The same way she felt.

"Are you happy?"

"What?" Brenna pulled back. "Why do you ask that?"

"Because it's important to me that my wife is happy," Jabarie replied, expression serious.

She smiled, staring up into eyes that she adored. "Baby, I couldn't be any happier."

The music changed and their hips swayed in the same motion, with his hands resting at her ass. As he drew her closer, she felt the crush of his body and his erection throbbing against her belly, causing her sex to clench with yearning. Tipping her head back, Brenna looked up and made eye contact. Love and desire was evident in his gaze.

One dance turned into one more and she spent the next hour in her husband's arms. Her fingers caressed the length of his back in slow measured strokes as she pulled him closer, absorbing the heat of him through her clothes. Brenna couldn't stop looking at Jabarie, and he couldn't stop looking at her. His gaze was hot and fixed on her lips, causing her heart to throb and setting off a fierce pulsing between her thighs. His tongue slipped out and glided across his lips, and she suddenly wanted those lips and that tongue sliding down between her legs, slipping between her folds, satisfying the erotic ache. Just the thought of him going down on her had her so aroused, she was wet.

"What's on your mind?" Jabarie asked, as if he didn't already know. The cocky grin on his lips told her he was quite aware of what she was thinking.

"You and me," she purred playfully then ground against his erection. "And this."

His eyes darkened dangerously. "Good. That's the only thing that should be on your mind."

Jabarie's lips brushed her forehead and temple, then she tipped her head back and Jabarie claimed the side of her neck with his lips. With every warm caress she couldn't think, only feel. All she knew was she wanted her husband sliding deep inside her body, making love to her until the wee hours. Driven by need, she arched against him.

Her lips were already parted when they met his. She slipped inside eagerly, meeting his glorious strokes. Jabarie groaned and pulled her closer against him, pressing the evidence of his arousal against her belly as he deepened the kiss.

Gently their tongues danced, stroking in a harmonious rhythm that made her think of the two of them lying in bed between the sheets, Jabarie thrusting as he made sweet love to her. Brenna moaned, grinding her body as they continued to sway to the music. The song ended, and her hands that had been resting lightly on his chest began to unfasten the buttons on his crisp white shirt.

"Tired of dancing yet?" she asked.

"Never. But now I'm ready for a different kind of

dance before I lose my damned mind."

Jabarie lifted Brenna into his arms and carried her down to the stateroom and laid her at the center of the bed.

* * *

Jabarie lowered the zipper of her dress, revealing the round caramel swells of her bare breasts. Brenna gazed up at him, then seductively licked her lips.

"You like what you see?" she asked.

"Yes, Daddy likes," he cooed.

Staring down at her, Jabarie didn't think it was possible to be any more turned on than he was right now. Seeing his wife lying there with her hair cascading on the pillow and round breasts only inches from his mouth caused his penis to throb impatiently.

Without wasting another moment, he brought his mouth to her breasts, sweeping his tongue across her soft skin. He took one sensitized peak into his mouth and teased it. Brenna moaned and he felt a trembling deep within her body as he suckled first at one breast, then the other, until desire burst from between her lips in a raspy cry of pleasure.

"Ooooh, yes!"

He continued to tease her swollen nipple with his teeth while she squirmed beneath him. "You like that?" he whispered between sucks.

"You know I do," she said with arousal apparent in her voice.

Jabarie knew she loved the way he nibbled gently with his teeth before closing his lips around the hardened nipple and sucking. At the same time, he held the weight of her other breast in his hand.

Brenna cried out again and clasped his shoulders, digging her nails into his flesh. Her head fell back and her breath caught as she arched closer toward his mouth.

"Oh, baby," she gasped, her fingers grazing his shoulders. "That feels so good."

"I aim to please," he answered, sucking even harder, his warm wet mouth once again causing her back to arch off the bed.

He could have stayed there all night, licking and stroking her round breasts, except parts of his lower region had other ideas. Tonight he wanted to rediscover his wife, every single part of her. The way she tasted. The way it felt to be inside of her. The way she cried out his name.

Gently, he ran his hands down the length of her legs stretched out before him and slowly worked his way up. When he reached the crotch of her lacy red panties, his breathing became shallow. The fabric was soaked with the scent of her arousal. "Awww," she cried out on contact.

Jabarie cupped her soft mound with his hand, rubbing her through the thin fabric. She whimpered and moved against him, rubbing her pussy against the palm of his hand. Gazing down at her, Jabarie found her eyes closed, her head tossed back, her hands grasping the edge of the bed. Propping her feet on the mattress, she spread her legs wide.

Damn, he was going to enjoy this, he thought with a wicked smile. He guaranteed he was going to make every second count before they returned to Sheraton Beach.

* * *

Brenna wasn't sure how much more she could handle. She lay there, breath shallow, body on fire, legs parted and waiting for his touch.

Jabarie's lips traveled to her neck and shoulder, and

at the same time she felt his long fingers sliding across her crotch. When he finally pushed her panties aside and his fingers skated her delicate folds, her breath hitched, parching the back of her throat.

"You like that?" he whispered.

"I like everything you do to me," she said between breaths.

Brenna parted her thighs wider, aching to be filled with him. And when he brushed a thumb across her clit, she cried out with pleasure as heat surged through her body.

"That's exactly what your man likes to hear." Jabarie probed at her opening with his fingers and she rocked against it trying to push it in further.

"You want something?" he asked with a slight chuckle.

"I want … that … I want … you," she moaned with growing frustration. Her body was on fire and yearning for something that was right there stroking her sensitized skin.

"You like that?"

She thought she was going to lose her mind by the time he slid two fingers between her moist folds. And the instant he did her entire body quivered.

"I take that as a yes," Jabarie whispered roughly while he played with her clit. "I can't wait to be inside you."

He slid in a third finger and thrust deeper, and within seconds her feminine walls clutched him tightly and an orgasm seized her body. Jabarie brought his mouth down over hers as she cried out in pleasure. Brenna collapsed on the bed, legs trembling so hard she allowed them to fall limp onto the mattress.

Gently, Jabarie licked her neck, driving her crazy. His breath was warm. His lips so damned soft and barely brushing her skin, but it was enough to tease her senses.

The tension in her body began to build again and Brenna started rocking against his hands. Touching and fondling was okay but she wanted ... she needed something more. Long ... thick ... rough, and so so satisfying.

"Jabarie," she gasped, not knowing how much more she could take. "Please." She reached down for her panties and struggled to get them over her hips. She fumbled several times, then cried out with frustration.

"Let me help you with that," Jabarie hissed. He yanked the panties down her legs and tossed them aside. He then shifted away and she watched as he hastily removed his clothing. Then he was back with her again, skin against skin, kissing her as they cradled in each other's arms. By the time he slipped his tongue inside her mouth the urgency had subsided and in its place a slow fire burned.

Silence throbbed around them. All she could hear was her heavy breathing as he slid down on the bed and positioned his head between her thighs. Before she had a chance to catch her breath, his tongue began its courtship, skimming her outer lips, then slipping between them before rising to lick the little nub of flesh that hid the most sensitized spot on her body.

"Oooh," she cried out, hips rocking.

At first he teased it, sending her higher and higher on the steep path toward ecstasy.

"You taste good," he hissed, using his thumb to stroke her engorging clit. "So damn good."

She started bucking her hips, squirming wildly, meeting the steady rhythm of his tongue. Her body was burning up and soaring toward release.

Jabarie's mouth grew more insistent, driving her toward the edge of sweet madness. Her moans turned into whimpers as she tried to recapture her sanity, because she was certain she was getting ready to beg for mercy. She was bucking and calling his name when he finally pressed his thumb firmly against her clit, causing her to cry out with ecstasy. And just when she was getting ready to come, he moved up on the bed. She cried out her frustration. "Dammit, Jabarie!"

"Baby, I got something even better," he explained as he positioned himself between her legs. "Don't you want me inside of you?"

"Yes," she panted. "*Puh-leeeze* hurry."

Reaching down, he parted her folds and nudged at her opening. Brenna pushed up to meet him, and when he finally drove inside she cried out in shock. Rocking her hips, she drew him even deeper. As she tried to catch her breath, he began thrusting, pounding his length into her. "Jabarie! Yesss ... *yesss*," she cried out and the bed rocked. Or was it the yacht?

"That's it, baby," Jabarie groaned as she clamped tightly around his penis. Within minutes she was hit with an orgasm so powerful it rocked her entire body while Jabarie continued stroking her deeper. She pressed her lips to his neck, loving the taste of his smooth skin, savoring the way their bodies connected. Jabarie continued his strokes, calling out her name close to her ear. There was no mistaking the passion in his voice as he pumped into her welcoming body. Then he began to move faster. "Baby ... I'm about to come," he growled.

As soon as she began to rock her hips he gave a strangled groan and she felt the muscles at his back flex as he came.

* * *

An hour later they were still lying in each other's arms, stroking and kissing.

"How in the world did we go this long without sneaking away for a little quality time?" Brenna asked, her chin resting comfortably on his chest.

He let out an agonizing moan. "I don't know, but let's not do it again."

"I agree." She smiled down into his beautiful eyes and her heart did that silly pitter pat. It was crazy how much she still loved that man after all these years. At one time she thought romance only happened in books, but she and Jabarie were proof that true love clearly existed.

"Do you forgive me for being so difficult to deal with these last few months? I've been trying so hard to juggle everything in our lives and prove that I'm super woman that I forgot I have a strong man standing beside me whom I can lean on."

"Absolutely, and don't you ever forget it. I want to be your anchor. My job is to keep my wife happy, and I can't do that if I have no idea she's not. I love you, Brenna, and I'll do whatever I have to do to provide for my family."

"I know."

"You also know that you have the luxury of not working at all. Wait! Before you bite my head off, I still remember what you told me when you first found out you were pregnant."

She took a moment to think, then released a heavy chuckle. "Tell me, what did I say?"

"Yeah, right. Like you'd forget. You told me, 'don't even think about me being barefoot and pregnant'," he replied in an animated falsetto.

She started laughing harder. "That's because your mother said it was time for me to give up working at the bookstore and focus on raising her grandbabies."

"And you told her running the bookstore was your life and you wouldn't give it up for anyone."

"I guess I did, didn't I?"

"Yes, sweetheart, you did." He leaned forward and pressed a kiss to her forehead. "And that's why I know how much that store means to you."

She grinned. "I'm glad you made me get away."

"I'm just glad I didn't have to toss a pillowcase over your head and stuff you in my trunk." Jabarie laughed, then as soon as he sobered he added, "Seriously ... how about we stay onboard until Sunday?"

"An extra night?"

"Yes, Bren, an extra night. I'll even let you out of bed long enough to call home and check on the kids."

Surprisingly, it didn't take her long to think about it. She didn't realize how much she'd missed their time together. "I'll agree, but only if Lil Jay isn't still running a fever."

"Agreed."

Chapter 8

Jabarie stared down at Brenna snuggled close to him, trying to figure out what it was about this woman that had kept his loins on fire and his heart thumping for more than ten years. Something about her was always on his mind. Her throaty laughter, long and loud, that signified how much she enjoyed life. A delectable body with enough curves to stop rush hour traffic. Her caramel satin beauty that was so smooth he couldn't keep his hands away. And her amazing warmth that he never wanted to wake up without curled beside him.

He watched her lying there, her beautiful breasts bare and voluptuous. Breasts he had kissed and licked only a few hours ago. By the time they had finally fallen asleep from exhaustion, sunlight had already begun to stream through the glass.

"Why are you staring at me?" Brenna asked with her eyes still closed.

"Are you saying I can't look at my wife?"

She grinned slowly. "Quit answering a question with a question."

Jabarie chuckled softly and leaned down to kiss her. "I'm staring because I'm a lucky man to have such a beautiful wife."

"Thank you, sweetie. You don't look half bad yourself."

He kissed once more then leaned back to gaze at her. "Toliver's probably already in the galley. How does fruit, croissants, and coffee sound?"

Her eyes twinkled with mischief. "Heavenly. After

last night I worked up quite an appetite."

"Well, then, you're going to need your strength, because we have a long day ahead of us." Just thinking about having his wife all to himself for another twenty-four hours already had him aroused. He was in no rush for the trip to end, and judging by the naughty looks Brenna was giving him, neither was she. Brenna was nibbling on her lips and had him throbbing with anticipation.

"I feel that," she laughed, making his dick pulse even more.

"It's what you do to me. With one look that boy stands to attention!" he said chuckling. "You gotta problem with that?"

"Not at all," she cooed.

With a ragged groan, Jabarie zoomed in for another kiss, tasting, seeking, stroking. Their tongues began to mate and the kiss became so eager they were touching and caressing as well. Brenna rolled Jabarie onto his back, straddling him, and then slowly rocked her clit along the length of his arousal.

"Hmmm," he moaned. "Whatever happened to needing food?"

"I suddenly feel energized," she purred, then leaned forward and placed light kisses to his lips as she continued rocking her hips.

"You like that?" she asked huskily. "Or would you rather I do this?" Reaching down, Brenna gently massaged the head of his dick. In response his breathing grew ragged.

"Yes," he said hoarsely. "Hell, yes." He moaned again, then reached for her gently swinging breasts.

"Glad to hear it," she managed as he caressed her nipples, "I gotta keep my man happy."

"That's exactly what your man likes to hear. Now I

need to be inside of you."

"I—oh!" Her gasp ended in an incoherent moan as Jabarie lifted her up until the very tip of his erection was just grazing the entrance to her kitty. Then with one swift thrust he pushed deep, lowering Brenna onto his dick, filling her to the core.

"You like that?"

"Dammit, you know I do," she murmured, breathless, then began to move oh so slowly. Raising up to the tip and then back down again and again. Her hips began to rock convulsively as pleasure radiated through her body. She felt Jabarie's hand slip between them and then his thumb grazed her clit that pulsed and swelled in response. It was sweet torture.

"Harder, baby," Jabarie growled. His hands gripped her hips, guiding her down onto his shaft. She screamed at the impact while savoring the feel of his thickness stretching her. Closing her eyes, she allowed her head to fall to the side as she followed his rhythm. She was on the verge of another orgasm. "That's it, baby," he murmured as he rocked his hips forward to meet hers. She felt the pressure of his hands on her buttocks, kneading the flesh, driving her on, faster.

Brenna heard the gasping of her own breath. She knew she was spiraling toward madness as she bucked her hips and tightened her muscles around him.

"Sssshit!" he groaned.

My words exactly. Her head rolled back and she began to move slower this time, the jerking of his body beneath hers. The moans escaping her own lips added to the moment, fueling the movements, and she rode him like she'd never ridden before.

Holding on to her waist, his hips thrust desperately upward to meet hers and their mingled cries filled the room as they exploded together in a shuddering climax.

Brenna collapsed, covering his body, breathing heavily against his shoulder. Jabarie shifted slightly and she buried her face in his neck and inhaled his masculine scent. With his arms wrapped around her, she inhaled and wished they could freeze this moment in time.

Just as her heart began to slow, the phone on the wall rang and Jabarie swore under his breath.

"Who could that be?" she said lazily.

"The only person who knows where we are exactly is Jace." He slid out from underneath her and snatched it off the wall. Rolling onto her back, Brenna watched her husband with curiosity.

"This better be good," he barked into the receiver.

Brenna knew something was wrong before he even said it. Jabarie tried to paint on a smile but she could see it in his eyes. Abruptly, she sat up on the bed.

"We're on our way," he said, then ended the call.

She was shaking so hard she was afraid to ask, "What's wrong?"

Jabarie took a deep breath then locked his gaze with hers as he said the one thing no mother ever wanted to hear, "Arianna is missing."

Chapter 9

By the time they made it back to Sheraton Beach, two patrol cars were in front of the house. From a distance she could see uniformed officers combing the area. "Oh God," Brenna gasped, heart pounding rapidly. "This can't be happening." During the entire ride back from the pier she had been in a daze, hoping that it was just some kind of joke, but it was all too real.

Before Jabarie pulled the car to a halt she was already out the door. Frantically, she ran toward the porch where Aunt Nellie and an officer were standing. As soon as the older woman saw Brenna coming up the sidewalk, she turned and the guilt was all over her face.

"Brenna … I'm so sorry."

She forced a nod when what she wanted to do was scream at the top of her lungs for leaving her children in the first place. *What was she thinking?* That was the problem. She hadn't been thinking about anything or anyone but what she had wanted. And now one of her babies was missing.

Jabarie exchanged a few words with the officer, then looked at the nervous woman standing beside him. "Aunt Nellie, when was the last time you saw Arie?" he asked, taking Brenna's hand.

"Last night. We had movie night. I popped popcorn and we watched *Tangled*. She was laughing and having such a good time during the movie." Aunt Nellie sighed with despair. "That was before I told her you wouldn't be returning until morning. Then she started sulking. After the movie I had a little talk with her and she seemed to be okay when I finally kissed her goodnight. I guess she was more upset that I thought."

Brenna blinked back the tears threatening to fall. Her baby was missing. Tilting her head, she looked up into her husband's eyes, silently pleading for him to find their daughter. She didn't even have to say the words out loud.

"Don't worry. We'll find her," he said with confidence, and the hand holding hers tightened its grip.

Nodding, she wanted so badly to believe him, but she wouldn't be able to relax until she was again holding her daughter in her arms.

One of the police officers stepped forward and started asking a lot of questions. Her head started spinning and she couldn't find the words to speak, so Jabarie took over, stroking her back while he spoke, trying to make her feel better.

"Bren, why don't you go in the house with the kids while I go help look for her?" he suggested lightly.

She was ready to object but the rest of her children were standing in the window and there was no mistaking the fear in their eyes. She nodded.

Jabarie brought her against him and pressed his lips to her forehead. "I'm going to find her. I promise."

Reluctantly, Brenna released her hold, then followed Aunt Nellie inside. The kids immediately dashed over to her, asking a hundred questions she couldn't begin to answer. Brenna was shaking so hard she swayed over to the sofa and flopped down. No longer could she ignore the tears running down her face.

"Mommy, why you crying?" Julian asked.

Realizing what she was doing, Brenna quickly wiped the tears from her eyes. The last thing she wanted was to scare her children. "Mommy's just worried, that's all." She pulled him close to her and gave him a big hug.

Bree stood in front of her, hugging Norman. "When's Arianna coming home?" she asked, lip quivering.

Pushing the lump from her throat, Brenna painted on a smile, "Soon, sweetie. Don't you worry."

Aunt Nellie rose from the chair. "Who wants cookies and milk?"

Brenna found comfort in her aunt being there. As soon as they all moved into the kitchen, Norman trotted happily behind them. Despite everything she was feeling Brenna couldn't resist a small smile. In such a short time the dog had brought so much happiness into their house. Even Arianna had grown attached to him. Two nights ago Brenna had gone in to kiss her good night and had found Norman curled up at the bottom of Arie's bed. As she thought about her daughter, a lump rose to her throat and once more tears began to fall freely. Brenna wiped them away and walked across the Brazilian floor of her sumptuous living room.

Standing in front of the large picture window, she gazed out at all the land before her and closed her eyes against the rush of emotions ripping through her. How could she just stand there when her daughter was out there somewhere, missing?

Hearing footsteps, she swung around just as Aunt Nellie stepped into the room.

"Bren, I am so sorry."

She held up a hand and shook her head. There was no way she was going to allow her aunt to blame herself for something she'd done to herself.

"No need to apologize. It's not your fault."

Aunt Nellie came over and draped an arm over her shoulder. "I feel it in my heart. She's fine. Just wait and see."

"Yes, I want to believe that." She needed to hear that. She needed to have hope.

"I was just trying to help," she began, and her voice cracked before she was able to maintain her composure again. "When Jabarie called last week and asked me about coming back and helping you at the store —"

"Whoa!" Brenna interrupted, and Aunt Nellie's arm slipped away. "Wait a minute ... My husband called you?"

Aunt Nellie's eyes grew wide as she realized her mistake, and she quickly tried to explain. "Yes, but at that point I'd pretty much already made up my mind about coming home. Jabarie said you both were stressed and needed some time together to talk, and I agreed to come down for a few days and give the two of you a break."

And you see what that got me.

Brenna couldn't believe her husband had gone to her aunt for help. She was getting ready to question Aunt Nellie further when she spotted Jabarie walking back up the road alone. Brenna felt the color drain from her face as she rushed out the door and down the steps, halting a few feet from him. As he stared at her, her breathing somehow felt constricted. "W-What did the police say?"

He gave an irritated frown. "They've sent out an Amber Alert while they continue canvassing the area."

She swallowed back the sick feeling that had risen to her throat. The shock was fading and reality settled in. Amber Alert? Police canvassing? "This can't be happening," she whispered, unsure what to do, and brought her hands up to her face. "It's all my fault."

Jabarie rushed over beside her just as she staggered uneasily on her feet. As soon as she found her footing Brenna pulled away abruptly.

"Bren, it's not your fault."

Her mouth tightened. "Yes it is," she bit out fiercely. "I should have been here. I told you I didn't want to go, but you told me it was okay," she said cuttingly.

"What? Baby you can't think like that," he added gently.

"Don't you understand? I'm supposed to protect them. I should have been here last night. Not on the yacht. I should have been here with my baby!" She burst out suddenly with anger, then started crying so hard her entire body shook. Jabarie wrapped an arm around her and pulled her close, and this time she didn't pull away. He tried soothing words as he stroked her hair, but she didn't hear anything except the thumping of her heart.

"Those are *my* babies."

He pulled back slightly and she saw the pained expression as he said, "They're my babies, too. I'd give my life to protect them."

Pushing way from his grasp, she shook her head. He didn't understand. He never would understand. He'd had his mother around all his life. She hadn't.

She looked at Jabarie mockingly, swiping tears away. "Really? What's this about you calling Aunt Nellie and asking her to come back because *I've* been stressed lately?" she snapped, leaning forward, getting into his face. "What you should have done was respected my decision to hire someone else to run the bookstore and focus on my kids. Instead, you whisked me away for a weekend, trying to change my mind," she came back tartly.

A nerve pulsed at his jaw. "Bren," he warned. "Now is not the time to be throwing punches."

She sighed at the awkwardness she could feel growing between them. What in the world was she doing? "Oh God! I'm sorry. I just don't know what to do. I'm so scared," she replied with quiet conviction.

Winding one arm around her waist and placing the other at her back, he drew her to him again. "Right now we need to stay strong. Pointing fingers is not going to bring her back."

Jabarie was right. He was her rock. She needed his strength. "Jabarie, I just—"

He interrupted her. "I told you. I'm going to find our daughter. And I meant that."

She dropped her head to his chest and sobbed while he soothed her.

* * *

After she'd had a chance to get it out, Jabarie convinced Brenna to go inside and start calling all Arianna's friends. As soon as she stepped back through the door a black Range Rover pulled in front of the circle drive. Jaden, Jace and Remy all jumped out.

"Have you found her yet?" Jace asked.

Jabarie tried to hold his emotions in check but was finding it harder to do as he shook his head.

"We're here to help," Remy replied.

The hollow feeling deepened in his stomach as he stared at the three ready to do whatever they could to help. Jabarie had to clear his throat to speak. "I appreciate that."

"I just called and left a message on London's phone. I know he'd want to be here," Jaden explained, referring to Bianca's husband. When times got tough, all of them came together. "Where do you want us to begin?"

The panic climbed higher, clogging his throat. It took several moments before he maintained enough control to speak. "There's a mile between me and Beaumont Manor. She could possibly be anywhere between here and there," he said in a voice filled with emotion.

Jaden nodded, dreadlocks swinging. "No problem."

Jace stepped forward, eyes narrowed, while a dangerous light glittered in their depths that Jabarie knew all too well. *Nobody messes with family.* "Whatever it takes. I've got all the time you need."

"That goes for me, too," Remy said, scrubbing a hand over his square jaw. "If I need to round up the rest of the clan I will."

It meant a lot having them there, especially since the three were supposed to be heading to Philadelphia to hang out with their cousin Diamere for the evening.

"No point in getting the rest of the family upset just yet."

Nodding, Jace replied, "I've already called the house and the ground crew is out checking the area. Robinson says she hasn't come by the house."

Robinson was their parents' live-in butler and an honorary member of the family. While the Beaumonts were in Barbados, he managed the house. "Whatever you do, I don't want Mother and Father to find out." Arianna was their first grandbaby. His father's health hadn't been the best, and he didn't want to do anything to upset him or ruin their vacation.

The men nodded in understanding.

For the next hour they combed the woods, searching for Arianna. There were a couple of officers also out searching, and it was driving Jabarie crazy because he had no idea where she could have gone. He blamed himself, because when she had asked why Brenna was never around he should have taken the question more seriously. He had just been so worried about the layoffs, his mind had been preoccupied. It never occurred to him that maybe Brenna had every reason to be concerned.

By the time he'd reached Beaumont Manor, Jabarie had an uneasy feeling. His cell phone rang at his hip and he grabbed it and glanced down at the screen. It was Brenna. He released a heavy sigh. There was no way he could answer it yet and tell her he still hadn't found their daughter, so he let it go to voicemail. *All I need is a few more minutes,* he tried to tell himself.

There was a patrol car parked in the circular driveway and an officer was standing beside the vehicle talking to Jace. As he grew closer, Jace looked over at Jabarie and met his eyes. The dismay was apparent as he shook his head. They still hadn't found her.

Closing his eyes, Jabarie forced his body to remain calm, and inhaled a breath nice and slow. It didn't help. Instead, he suddenly felt hot and cold at the same time.

He moved inside the house, nodded at Robinson, headed straight for the kitchen and removed a bottle of water from the refrigerator.

Where the hell is my daughter? Jabarie thought as he took a painful swallow. Walking over to the window, he stared out across the yard. Uncertainty made his hands begin to shake. Arianna was out there somewhere and he had to find her. He had given his wife his word and he was not one to go back on a promise.

Once again his cell phone vibrated. This time he removed it, took a deep breath and hit TALK. "Bren."

"Have you found her?"

He swallowed hard. "No, baby ... not yet."

There was a long silence before he heard the sob in her throat, causing his frustration to spike. "This isn't happening."

"We *are* going to find her."

"I believe you."

He took a moment to pull his thoughts together. "Did the kids say anything about what she was doing before she disappeared?"

There was a pause and he could tell she was thinking. "They were watching a movie. Aunt Nellie mentioned she was sulking earlier, saying she didn't believe you weren't taking her camping again."

Camping. Jabarie's heart started pounding heavily. Why hadn't he thought of that before? "Bren, check her closet and see if her sleeping bag is there."

"O-Okay."

Jabarie squeezed the phone while he waited. He heard voices, footsteps, and turned around just as his brothers and Remy stepped into the kitchen. He held up a hand signaling them to be quiet.

"Jabarie?" Brenna came back on the line.

"Yes, baby."

"It's missing."

He released a long breath. "I know where to look. Bren, relax. I'll call you back in a few minutes." He ended the call. Jaden was the first to speak.

"Jabarie, what's going on?"

He started toward the back door. "I know where she was going. To our old camp spot. I took the kids there every spring."

Jace's brow rose. "The log cabin tree house? I already checked that."

Sliding a frustrated hand across his head, Jabarie replied, "Then she's somewhere in the area."

Jaden nodded. "Alright, then, let's check that area again more closely."

"Absolutely," Remy chimed in.

Jabarie swung open the door, then said over his shoulder. "She has her pink sleeping bag with her. Call if you see *anything*. Otherwise, I'll meet you back at my house." He hurried out the door.

With adrenaline surging through his veins, Jabarie climbed into the patrol car and had the officer drive a half a mile down a dirt road. As soon as he saw the old wooden fence he jumped out of the vehicle and raced down the trail into the woods. She was close. He could feel it, and Jabarie said a silent prayer that his daughter

was alright. He had been promising all summer to take
the kids camping again, but had kept putting it off. At
the fork in the trail he headed left toward his house, and
the closer he got the more his heart began to pound in his
ears. At the end of the road, under a tree, he found it.

Arianna's sleeping bag.

"Arie!" he called out and stepped lightly over twigs
and plants while he listened for her to call his name.
From a distance he could hear his brothers also shouting
her name. He walked over to her sleeping bag. It had
been rolled out and a flashlight was right beside it, which
indicated she had left some time during the night. The
thought of his eight-year-old daughter wandering
around in the woods at night caused his stomach to
clench. He didn't even want to think about what could
have happened to her.

But she's probably more afraid she's going to be in trouble.

He took a deep breath, then shouted, "Arie! If you're
out here please say something, honey. I'm not mad at
you. Arie, please, your mother and I are worried." There
was a moment of silence during which he didn't hear
anything but the sound of his own breathing. And then
he heard it. Soft crying.

"Arie, baby, where you at?" he called, almost frantic.
He hurried towards the direction where he heard the
sobs coming from. Behind a bush he found his daughter
curled up in a ball on the ground. "Arie."

"Daddy?" She looked up at him, eyes red and lips
quivering.

Reaching down, he scooped her up into his arms and
cradled her close to his body. She wrapped her arms
around him and rested her head against his chest as she
cried. He was certain she could hear his heart racing.
Closing his eyes, he took a moment to give thanks and
allowed the first tear to fall.

He heard rustling in the bushes and looked over his shoulder as his brother Jaden and the officer came rushing over.

"Jabarie, did ...."

He turned around so they could see Arianna was safely in his arms. They nodded, then backed away, understanding the two of them needed some time alone, and retreated to tell the others the search was over.

Eventually Arianna's sobs began to quiet and she pulled back and looked up at him. "Daddy, I was so scared!"

"It's okay, Arie. You don't need to be scared anymore."

"I couldn't find my way home. I thought I'd never see you again!"

He felt her fear and allowed her to cry some more while he held her tight. She hadn't been the only one who'd been scared.

Eventually the sobs quieted. Jabarie slowly lowered her to her feet and then took a seat on the ground. She flopped down next to him and crossed her legs Indian style.

"Why did you run off like that?"

She hung her head low with shame and avoided eye contact. "When you and Mommy didn't come home, I decided to go camping by myself. I thought I remembered where the tree house was." She looked at him for a fleeting moment. Her hazel eyes were red and swollen.

"Don't you know you scared a lot of people?" he scolded softly.

She nodded her head. "I'm sorry. I just wanted to spend the night at the tree house, but I couldn't find it. So I just slept in my sleeping bag the way you let us do in the backyard. I heard someone calling me but I was afraid you were gonna be mad at me."

"I *am* mad at you, but that doesn't mean I don't love you." He wanted so badly to be angry, but it was hard to do with her looking so small and helpless. "Come here."

Arianna practically leaped into his arms and he held her tight again, stroking her hair as he spoke. "Don't you ever scare me like that again, you hear?"

"I won't."

He tried not to think about her spending the night out in the woods in a sleeping back, but he couldn't shake the image. Jabarie pulled back and stared at her. "Look at me while I'm talking to you." Timidly, she raised her head and met his intense stare. "We're not done with this conversation. I'm sure your mother has plenty to say about you scaring her. Right now I need to get you home so she'll know you're safe."

She pouted her bottom lip. "Okay."

He swatted her playfully across the butt and released her. "Come on, let's go home."

* * *

Brenna was pacing the length of the living room when she saw the patrol car pull up and Jabarie and Arianna step out. Jaden, Jace and Remy had just stopped through long enough to let her know Jabarie had found Arianna. It was Remy's idea to take her other four children down on Main Street for ice cream. She appreciated their giving her and Jabarie a chance to have some private time to talk with Arianna. Aunt Nellie went along as well. As soon as they were gone she had stood in front of the window and waited.

Brenna rushed out of the house and hurried down the stairs as Arianna ran into her arms. "Oh, sweetheart," she sobbed and squeezed her daughter tight. She didn't even want to begin to think how long her daughter would have been missing if they had not returned when they had.

Jabarie came up beside her and wrapped his arm around both of them. And for a long moment they all just stood there, happy to be together again.

"Little Missy here decided she was going camping," he finally said, once the car pulled away.

Brenna stepped back and stared down into her little face. Her bottom lip quivered. "Is that true?"

Arianna nodded her head. "Daddy's been promising to take me, but he didn't, so I went by myself. But I got lost, Mommy, and couldn't find my way home!" she wailed.

Brenna took a deep breath and searched Arianna's face as she stood in front of her and saw the anxiety in her eyes. Aunt Nellie said she had been sad all evening, saying her mother was never at home and neither was her daddy. She reached up and removed a leaf from her daughter's hair and said, "Let's go inside and get you a bath, and then we'll talk." She pressed a kiss to her forehead and led her into the house.

Several hours later the children were back at home and everyone was safely tucked away in bed. Brenna was standing out on their terrace, gazing out along the ocean. Even with her back turned she knew the exact moment Jabarie stepped through the French doors. The tension between them was so thick she could have reached out and touched it.

It was several moments before he finally spoke.

"Bren, you okay?" he asked.

She took a deep breath of the salty air, shoulders finally settling down with relief. "No, I'm not okay," she answered. "I can't stop thinking about my daughter wandering around lost in the woods."

The scent of his cologne drew closer and she knew

Jabarie was standing behind her. "Yeah, it's my fault," he
began and drew in a ragged breath. "I should have taken
her camping weeks ago, like I'd promised. But I'm
certain that as scared as she was, she'll never try that
again."

That was only part of the problem. The other part she
was guilty of. "I should have been there," she said in a
far-off voice, then turned around, arms crossed over her
chest, and gazed up at him. His eyes were clear and
unwavering when he met hers.

"Baby, we can't be everywhere all the time."

"Jabarie, she never would have gone out in the woods
alone if I hadn't gone with you to the yacht."

"Bren ..."

She held up a hand. "No, I should have been there.
I've been having this feeling for weeks that something
was going to happen, and sure enough it did," she
explained as she took a shaky breath. "I can't do this
anymore."

Jabarie reached out, taking both her hands tightly in
his. "Baby, please, let's sit down and talk about this."

She wrenched away from his grasp. She had to
swallow back a sob, then took a deep breath before
saying, "I'm going to ask Aunt Nellie to manage the store
for me until I can find someone full-time to take over."

"Bren, I–"

"Jabarie, please, it's my decision!" she cut in firmly,
eyes narrowed to steely slits. "My children need their
mother. I need to be with my children." Angrily, she
pushed past him, then headed toward the stairs so she
could check on them.

Chapter 10

On Monday, Jabarie moved through the lobby of the hotel, greeted by a chorus of "Good morning, Mr. Beaumont" before he made it to the elevator. He scowled irritably. They were going to have a meeting this morning, and if they couldn't come up with a solution, then tomorrow Jace's staff would start handing out severance packages to fifty unsuspecting employees.

The elevator doors opened and Jabarie stepped inside and released a heavy sigh. Brenna still refused to talk about what had happened over the weekend. Yesterday she'd closed the bookstore, something she seldom did, and spent the entire day with the children, doing everything they wanted to do. He had to admit they'd had a wonderful day together. They had gone down onto the boardwalk and had taken the kids to the amusement park.

By the time all the kids had been bathed and were sound asleep he was ready to talk, but Brenna had kissed him, and one thing had led to another, and soon they were making love and the conversation was long forgotten. She was determined to advertise for a manager for the store and nothing he could say was going to stop her.

Pushing open the double doors, Jabarie stepped into the conference room. Immediately the conversations around the table ceased.

"Bianca, can you have your assistant order takeout?" he asked as he reached for the top button of his black suit jacket. "Folks, you might as well get comfortable because we have a long day ahead of us."

* * *

Brenna pulled in front of her aunt's small ranch-style house and turned off her Mercedes. As she climbed out, she exchanged waves with several of the neighbors, who were already out this morning working in their yards. Most of the families on the block had owned their homes for more than fifty years.

"Brenna!"

She swung around to see Ms. Barker standing on her porch, waving her over. Brenna threw a hand in the air, then shut the door of her car and strolled across the street. "How are you doing, Ms. Barker?"

The sixty-year-old petite mother of six moved over to the edge of her porch, wearing a wide smile and glasses that took up most of her face. "Just fine, chile. Nellie was telling me you found a dog."

Brenna's eyes widened as she walked over and leaned against the white picket fence, resting her elbows on top. "Yes, we did. A big brown dog. Possibly a St. Bernard."

Ms. Barker nodded her head. "Yes, chile. Does he look like that crazy dog from the movie Cujo?"

Laughing, Brenna nodded her head. "Yes, that's him! Does he belong to you?"

She patted her grey afro and shook her head. "Goodness, no! That's my grandson's dog."

Brenna felt relieved to have finally found Norman's home, but at the same time she was disappointed. How in the world was she going to be able to pry that dog away from the kids? "My kids are going to be crushed. Can I have your grandson's number so I can bring him home later?"

Ms. Barker gave a dismissive wave. "Oh, poo! That boy done joined the Navy and left the dog with my sister to find him a home. She wasn't paying that dog no mind and he ran off."

"Does that mean we can keep him?" Brenna asked, and realized she was holding her breath.

"Chile, yes. You'd be doing us a big favor."

"Oh, what a relief!" she exclaimed. Her children were going to be so excited.

They chitchatted a few more minutes, then Brenna waved goodbye. She moved up the sidewalk and onto Aunt Nellie's wide front porch, where she had spent many years sitting on the swing that hung in the corner. The door was open so she stepped inside the house and grinned. It didn't matter that Brenna had a house of her own and no longer lived there. Every time she came to the house she felt like she had returned home.

Almost every knick-knack was handmade, from the afghans draped across the aging furniture to the crocheted tablecloth and homemade drapes. The thing she loved the most about the house was the abundance of windows overlooking the smooth, sandy Atlantic shore.

"Aunt Nellie, where are you?" she called.

"I'm in the kitchen," she heard from the right.

Her sandals clicked across the hardwood floor as she moved into the small kitchen. Aunt Nellie looked up from the countertop with a warm smile.

"Hey, sweetie. How's Arie today?"

Brenna took a seat at the small wooden table and replied, "She's fine. Better than fine, actually. She and I had a long talk, and I know why she's been so unhappy. She wants her mother to be around more."

Smiling, Aunt Nellie came over and took a seat across from her. "You were the same way at that age. You loved being with Shaunda. That's why you hung out at the hotel all the time."

"Yeah, and you see what good it did me," she

retorted with a scowl.

Aunt Nellie gave a sad smile, then reached over and patted her hand. "You and my sister are two different people. Unlike Shaunda, *you're* wonderful with your children."

Brenna appreciated the compliment. "That's kinda what I came over here to talk to you about."

Her brow rose. "What's wrong?"

"I'd like you to take back the bookstore."

Aunt Nellie appeared stunned by her request. "Sweetheart, what's going on? You love that store."

"Yes, but I love my kids more," Brenna replied, certain that if anyone would understand, it would be Aunt Nellie. "My kids need me to be there for them and I can't do that running a bookstore."

"So how about cutting your hours?" she suggested.

"That's what Jabarie said." Brenna shook her head. "I want to be a full-time mom. If I'd been there Arianna never would have run off."

"Dear, so what are you planning to do? Follow those kids around everywhere they go? Because that's the only way you can keep track of them. And even then you can't control everything."

"But I can try," she said with a frustrated breath.

Aunt Nellie shook her head. "And you'll wear yourself out in the process."

Brenna's scowl deepened. "I just want to be a better mother than my mom was."

Tossing a hand in the air, Aunt Nellie replied, "You're already a better mother. Shaunda is my baby sister and I love her, but she's selfish and spoiled and never cared about anyone but herself. Dear, your mother left here *emotionally* long before she left with that sugar-daddy. She never wanted to be a mother. But you do, and it shows. You're loving and giving and those kids couldn't have a better mother."

"Thank you. I guess I'm scared."

"Being scared is okay, but you're driving yourself and your husband crazy. You've gotta stop it. That man loves you and you have to remember that he's just as important as the Fabulous Five. Not only do they need you, but he needs you, too."

Tears brimmed her eyes. "So what do I do?"

Aunt Nellie reached over and squeezed her hand. "Cut your hours to part-time and I'll help you run the store. Even Jabarie promises to help you more at home. Trust me. You need your independence and there's nothing wrong with that. You and I both know you'd go crazy attending PTA meetings and sitting at home watching soap operas."

Brenna couldn't resist a laugh. Goodness, she was right. She couldn't see sitting at home all day, waiting for the kids to come home.

With a smile her aunt leaned in close and whispered, "There *is* a secret to juggling work and family."

"There is?" Her brow rose.

Aunt Nellie nodded. "All you can do is the best that you can. And as long as there are plenty of hugs and kisses, your family will love you for it."

Brenna let the tears fall and smiled, feeling better than she had in days.

"Sweetheart, trust me. You, Jabarie, and the Fabulous Five … you're all in this together."

Chapter 11

Jabarie stepped into the house and Norman came trotting down the hall to greet him. He petted the dog's head affectionately. "What's up, boy? Ready for your walk?"

Woof!

"I'll take that as a yes." Smiling, he strolled down the hall and into the master bedroom, where he found Brenna on the chaise lounge in their sitting room, reading. The second she noticed his presence, she put her book down and met his gaze with a curious look.

"Hey, baby. Where's the kids?"

Her eyes sparkled. "Sheyna and Jace have them."

"All of them?" he asked with disbelief. There was no way he was hearing her right. He'd had a hard enough time getting Jace to take just one.

Giggling, she nodded her head. "Yes. *All* of them. They went to some new pizza joint."

Shaking his head, Jabarie laughed, then removed his jacket and tie, and within seconds his shirt hung loose, sleeves rolled up past his elbows. "Then we'd better enjoy it while we can. Come walk with me and Norman."

She sprung from the chaise and he took a moment to admire her in a white tank top and pink shorts displaying beautiful toned legs. He took her hand and clasped their fingers together and whistled for Norman, then led them through the French doors and down the path toward their private beach. The dog ran off ahead of them and started frolicking in the ocean. Brenna kicked off her sandals and walked alongside her husband, their fingers laced. The wind caught her curls, tossing them hopelessly while they strolled along the shore in silence.

"Bren, I'm sorry about what happened with Arie, but I'm not going to apologize for wanting to spend time with my wife."

Brenna released a deep breath, "I know, and I'm so sorry for getting angry. I was mad and took it out on you."

They grew quiet again. Wet sand ran between her toes and seagulls screeched overhead. When Sheyna and Jace had arrived to pick up the children she hadn't tagged along because Aunt Nellie was right. She couldn't be everywhere all of the time. She would eventually have a nervous breakdown just from trying. Instead, she'd kissed her children good-bye and had decided to curl up with a book she had been dying to read for months. The house was quiet, and in a matter of minutes Brenna had gotten so caught up in the novel she hadn't even heard Jabarie come into the house. It was then that she realized how badly she needed to take more time for herself.

"I really need to start letting go. It's just hard for me." She paused, pressed a hand to her mouth and shook her head. "I want so badly to be a good mother."

"But you *are* a good mother," he contradicted, his voice lowering huskily.

"But I want to be better than better," Brenna reiterated more clearly. "I spent so many years wishing my mother had been around that I've been doing everything in my power to make sure our children never feel that way. In the process, I've been smothering them and neglecting you."

Jabarie stopped walking and turned to face her, and as soon as she met the love in his gaze her heart fluttered.

"Baby, I don't think you could be a better wife or mother. You carried my babies for nine months, then doted on each one for twelve weeks before even returning to work. You've been there for their first step and cried when they each started school. You've managed the store, raised the kids, been my lover and my best friend. You are an amazing woman, and don't you ever for a second think you're not."

She shifted uncomfortably. "You really think so?"

"I *know* so." Reaching down, he took both her hands in his. "It's not about quantity ... it's about quality, and you make sure every second counts."

Tears filled her eyes. "You always know how to make me feel better."

His brow bunched with frustration. "I'm your husband. That's my job. But baby, you have to promise me the next time you're feeling overwhelmed you let me know. Do you know how it makes me feel to be the last to know that my wife is hurting or unhappy? That means I failed as your man."

She nodded apologetically. "I promise to scream the next time I need help."

"Good, and I'm cutting my hours once school starts," he said as his smile returned. "That way I can help you with the kids, getting them to school and to all their activities. I gotta warn you, though ... That means your man will be taking a cut in pay, but, umm, I'm willing to make that sacrifice for my family."

Brenna's brow arched with amusement. Her husband was wealthy enough that he never had to work another day in his life if he didn't want to. "A pay cut, huh? How much are we talking about?"

Jabarie scratched his chin, wearing a smug look on his face. "For the next fiscal year, Bianca, Jace and I have all agreed to be paid one dollar."

"One dollar?" Brenna sputtered with laughter, then smiled as she realized what that would mean for the town of Sheraton Beach. "I knew there was some reason why I loved you so much."

He shrugged one shoulder. "Yeah, I discovered a pay cut would not only save jobs but provide the corporation the revenue it needs to ride out this economic crisis a little bit longer, and hopefully things will start getting better."

Smiling, Brenna wrapped her arms around his waist and gazed up at him. "That sounds like a wonderful idea. Fewer hours, huh?"

"Anything for the family." He pressed his lips against her forehead.

"Anything?"

He inched closer, his gaze on her mouth. "Anything."

"How about a little sex on the beach?" she suggested and a low purr vibrated from her throat.

He flashed her a smile that tugged a dimple at his left cheek. "I think I might be able to squeeze that into my schedule." Jabarie scooped Brenna into his arms and claimed her lips with his in a kiss that told her everything would be alright as long as they had each other.

A Beau for Christmas

~~The Beaumonts~~
Book #7

by Angie Daniels

Caramel Kisses
Publishing

For questions and comments please contact angie@angiedaniels.com or visit www.angiedaniels.com.

Caramel Kisses
Publishing

Caramel Kisses Publishing
PO Box 2313
Chesterfield, VA 23832
www.caramelkissespublishing.com

A Beau for Christmas

~~The Beaumont Series~~
Book #7

Angie Daniels

Caramel Kisses
Publishing

Chapter One

I've got my eyes on you.

Dominique Wellington crossed her legs and leaned back on the seat, holding a watermelon martini in her hand. Laughter and conversations were bouncing around the table, but she was only pretending to be interested in anything being discussed. Instead, her attention was focused on the tall gorgeous man sitting on a stool at the bar.

Reese Beaumont.

She wasn't sure what attracted her most about him. His perfect toasted almond complexion? Hypnotic dark sable eyes? Or that he had a body better than most men half his age?

Even after all this time, his mere presence made her heart skip and caused the private area between her thighs to throb with telltale memories. How she wished she had the strength not to feel that way. Because the last thing she wanted was rekindled emotion for a man who avoided commitment. Yet there they were, front and center. Dominique sighed heavily because she knew there was no denying what those feelings meant. What they signified.

Attraction.

Desire.

Love?

She scowled. Three things she preferred not to feel, especially after so much time had passed. It had been twelve months since that terrible night when he had accused her of the worst betrayal. An entire year since she'd last felt those strong arms wrapped around her waist, and yet she could still remember the power and the strength of that man. And despite everything, her traitorous body yearned for a deeper caress, one she knew firsthand only he could give. When would it end? When would she be over him so she could finally get on with her life? She wondered for the umpteenth time, because after a year-long failed attempt she had begun to discover forgetting was no easy task. Reese was tall, gorgeous and exuded masculinity, but he was also the same man who had accused her of ruining his career, then had walked out of her life without a glance or a single phone call for months. Even then, when they had spoken there had been no real apology. Just lots of unanswered questions and heartfelt regrets.

Well, not tonight.

She had been trying to no avail to apologize. Yet each time they were within several feet of each other, Reese had gone out of his way to avoid her, doing irritating things such as slipping out the side door when she had been silly enough to take her eyes off of him for the slightest second.

But uh-uh, not this time, she reminded herself fiercely. There was no way in hell Reese was getting away from her tonight. That's right. The two of them were going to talk, even if she had to handcuff him to the post of her queen-size bed.

Dominique squirmed on the wooden chair as a similar kinky scene between them flashed across her mind, causing a betraying ache which started to pulse through her lower body. She took a sip from her half-empty glass, then released a weary sigh, irritated at how a single thought about Reese could still affect her so utterly. Sex had never been their issue. It had always been hot, hard, and completely satisfying. What had gone wrong with them had been far worse. Dominique remembered it with feelings of dread. It had been so bad that Reese had blamed her, then cut her completely out of his life, shattering her heart into a million pieces.

Immediately she pushed her disordered thoughts aside. No time for sexual fantasy. No time to feel sorry for herself. Nope. She'd wasted enough months curled up on the couch with a bowl of chocolate mint ice cream, nursing a broken heart. What she needed to do was stay focused on the mission.

Her chocolate eyes quickly scanned the lounge before they landed back on Reese. He was chatting with a sultry-looking brunette in a slinky blue dress who was leaning suggestively against the bar. Immediately Dominique clamped down on the wave of jealousy she had no right to feel. "Why'd he have to be so damn fine?" she muttered under her breath. As much as she hated to admit it, Reese was even more handsome than the last time she'd seen him.

At thirty-two, Dr. Reese Beaumont was panty-dripping gorgeous, with fine, dark wavy hair and a lean, muscular physique. He was wearing a pair of charcoal slacks that didn't begin to hide the defined muscles of his thighs. The sleeves of his black shirt were rolled up, revealing lightly toasted arms laced with golden brown hairs. Even from across the room she could see his perfectly straight white smile and the neatly trimmed goatee that surrounded full succulent lips.

He was truly a Reese's Peanut Butter Cup.

The thought caused Dominique's lips to curve

upward. That had always been a joke between them. There was no denying that man could definitely satisfy any sweet tooth.

While sipping from her glass, Dominique watched him talking and laughing, head bobbing to the beat of the music. She didn't know how long she sat there staring at Reese when she felt someone nudge her arm.

"Why don't you just go over there and talk to him?"

She turned on the seat, trying to shake off the nervousness, and shook her head at her good friend Sheyna Beaumont. "Not yet. Not with all…" she waved a hand in the air. "… all *that* surrounding him," Dominique said and stopped, her lips parted in surprise at just how jealous she sounded. Even though they were no longer together, she didn't want the fact that Reese had dumped her and moved on rubbed in her face, or let it be known how much it bothered her. She couldn't begin to count how many times she'd prayed, hoping that when she saw Reese again he would have no effect on her. That she would have finally gotten him out of her system. *Yeah, right.* The second she had spotted him walking into the nightclub tonight, every nerve in her body clamored for him.

Dominique watched Sheyna as she took a quick glance across to the bar, then spat, "Puh-leeze. Those chicks don't mean a thing. Trust me. *That* there is all about Remy."

Several women were surrounding Reese and his baby brother Remy, also known as Dr. Feel, who loved the ladies as long as the situation made him "feel" good. Dominique tried to convince herself the women were part of Remy's entourage, because skanky women had never been Reese's style, but then again, a lot could have changed in a year.

I hope not, she told herself, biting down on her lip. Her

future depended on it. Self-consciously, she glanced down at her stylish business suit and wondered if maybe she should have changed into something more enticing before arriving at McKinley's for happy hour. She scowled at the ridiculous idea. She worked in the corporate offices located on the seventh and eighth floors of the hotel, so going home just to change clothes would have been silly.

"Go ahead," the dark chocolate beauty urged. "It isn't like Reese doesn't know you want to talk to him."

Dominique groaned inward. *And that's why he's avoiding me.* "I will," she replied with false confidence. "I'm just waiting for the right moment. Then I'll go over there and say hi."

She knew from experience that if she wasn't careful he was sure to bolt out the side door, because talking seemed to be the last thing he was interested in doing. *Too bad.* She had a trick for him tonight. With Reese, she planned to swoop in when he least expected it and demand answers.

"I can't believe he's sitting over there trying to pretend he doesn't see you. Men are such a trip," Sheyna added with a scowl.

"Tell me about it," Dominique murmured, and frustration spiked, making it hard to maintain her composure. What she wanted to do was storm over, grab Reese by the collar and demand he listen to her. Instead, she swallowed and looked away, then simply shrugged, trying to come across as if it were no big deal. "All I plan to do is talk. If he's not interested, then oh, well, but at least I can finally close that chapter of my life." Actually, she'd planned to do a lot more than just talk, but she was embarrassed to mention how far she was willing to take things if needed.

Reaching under the table, Sheyna comfortingly

squeezed her hand. "Good luck. If you need back-up, let me know. Me and the girls know what it takes to handle a Beaumont man," she added with a dramatic sweep of her hand.

With a smile, Dominique's eyes traveled across the table at Danica and Brenna, wives of Jabarie and Jaden Beaumont. Both were deep in conversation. Brenna owned the Cornerstone Bookstore, Danica, a former runway model, owned a cute little bikini shop on the beach, and Sheyna was the VP of Customer Relations for the Beaumont Corporation. Dominique admired all three beautiful women who had managed to snag the brothers and heirs of the Beaumont Corporation, a hotel chain with locations dotting the map from coast to coast. The Beaumont brothers were once confirmed bachelors until they each met their match in a good woman.

Now if only she could say the same about their single cousins, also known as the Force MDs. Rush, Roman, Remy, Reese and Rance. Half African-American, half Samoan, all five sons were tall, educated, and coochie-clenching gorgeous doctors ... each in his own unique ways.

Just thinking about Reese Beaumont and his career as a surgeon filled her heart with another moment of panic. Shrugging those thoughts away, Dominique lifted the glass to her lips and finished the martini with one gulp. Nothing was going to stop her from talking to him and finding out what she desperately needed to know.

Nothing.

* * *

Dr. Reese Beaumont reached for the glass of bourbon sitting on the gleaming bar, then swung around on the stool and allowed his eyes to travel over the thinning happy hour crowd at McKinley's, a popular nightclub located in the lobby of the luxurious Beaumont Hotel of Sheraton Beach. Clubs were no longer his thing, but this was one long weekend he decided to make an exception. However, as he glanced over at the voluptuous bombshell sitting in the far corner of the room, he was starting to think that maybe returning to Sheraton Beach hadn't been such a good idea. Dominique Wellington looked like a feline ready to pounce. And apparently he was her prey.

For the last year, he had done everything within his power to avoid her. And this weekend was no exception.

Reese was reaching for his glass again when a deep voice called out to him.

"Yo, bruh... check this out."

His eyes rolled in the direction of his younger brother Remy, who had flopped onto the stool beside him. By the size of the grin on his face, Reese knew he had to be up to something.

"You see that chick over there?" he asked, then nodded toward the stage where Reese spotted a gorgeous red-bone. "I'm gonna roll back to her place."

Meeting the glint in his eyes, Reese shook his head. "Don't you ever get tired?" he asked, even though he wasn't the least bit surprised. Especially since less than an hour ago Remy had been hell-bent on hooking up with some tall beautiful dentist.

"I never get tired of sexy women. You know what they say, the more the merrier," he commented with a hearty chuckle. Remy loved women, but the second one tried to put on the chains, he was off to the next beautiful honey.

Reese shook his head again. His younger brother, known as Dr. Feel, was the host of the syndicated radio talk show, *He vs. She,* where he and his co-anchor gave relationship advice to people all across the country.

Remy was destined to be the next Steve Harvey with the book his agent was currently shopping. With women falling at his feet, the bona fide playboy had no intentions of settling down any time soon.

"Reese… Bruh, you need to be tryna get hooked up yourself."

He scowled and answered in a husky voice. "Nah. As soon as I finish this drink, I'm heading to the house and chill."

Remy swiveled on the stool, his position relaxed, his eyes alert. "If you say so, but by the look on Dominique's face, I don't think you're going anywhere, anytime soon. It's on and *popping* tonight, Big Papa!" he added with hearty laughter.

Unable to resist, Reese stole another look to the far side of the room where Dominique was sitting at a round table with his cousin Jace's wife, Sheyna Simmons Beaumont. He cussed under his breath. When the two of them were together it meant nothing but trouble. They were definitely up to something. Reluctantly, he allowed his eyes to travel around the table at the other Beaumont wives before they landed on Dominique's smooth coffee-colored face, and froze.

She was looking right at him.

Her stare bored holes through him. Unflinching and steady, even with his eyes locked with hers. Quickly Reese regained his composure and took a moment to admire her beauty. She was curvy and thick, with the prettiest brown skin and short spiky dark hair. Even from across the room he could feel the power of those large chocolate eyes, and there was no denying the determination brewing at their depths. She definitely wanted something, but whatever it was, it wasn't going to happen tonight. He'd avoided her these last twelve months for good reasons, even though his gut still clenched with longing every time she looked his way. And the worst part about it was Dominique knew it. The woman was gorgeous, feisty and had always known exactly what it took to get him aroused. And it pissed him off. Hell, he was downright annoyed at himself that after everything Dominique had done, he still wanted her.

Pushing the thoughts away, Reese cleared his throat and ignored the desire brewing in his chest as he replied, "We don't have anything left to talk about."

Remy's chin-length dark hair was pulled back with a leather tie at the base of his neck. He shook his head, sending his wavy ponytail swinging. "I'm not too sure about that. Yo, bruh…, I'm outta here." He dropped to his feet, held up two fingers, then strolled across the room like a man who knew he had an audience. Several women turned on their chairs and blatantly admired his walk and swag. Reese couldn't resist a laugh. As usual, his little brother was sucking that shit up.

As he brought the glass to his lips again, he felt the heat of Dominique's eyes still on him. He didn't dare look in her direction. The last thing he wanted was for her to get up out of her seat and head his way. Although just being able to see her body in motion was almost worth the risk. The sensual sway of her hips was enough to make any man salivate.

When he had first stepped into the lounge and spotted Dominique sashaying across the floor in that short skirt, Reese instantly knew the weekend in Sheraton Beach wasn't going to be easy. That thought was then followed by him mentally undressing every luscious curve beneath the red designer suit that failed at disguising her voluptuous body. A body he knew all too well. Every curve of flesh had been explored by his hands and lips. Feeling a tightening at his groin, Reese shifted on the stool. There was no ignoring the hum of residual pleasure those memories brought.

And that was the problem.

For as far back as he could remember, Dominique always had that type of effect on him. Whenever he swooped into town and she wanted him heating up her bed, he had been more than willing because the beauty took seduction to a whole new level. In fact, together they had taken a sexual no-strings-attached relationship to new heights. And at one time he wouldn't have had it any other way. But things were different now, or at least they were as far as he was concerned. On the other hand, Dominique seemed fixated on him. And after all these months he couldn't understand why, considering the cruel things he had said to her the last night they had been together.

It was because of *that* night and the months of healing that followed that helped Reese realize the best thing for him to do was to move forward, and that meant leaving Dominique alone.

And it wasn't going to be easy.

He had driven in this evening to spend the weekend with his family, celebrating his cousin Jace's birthday. Born a week before Christmas, the family used to joke that he'd gotten cheated out of gifts every year because his birthday was so close to the holiday. His beautiful wife Sheyna was planning a huge dinner party on Sunday. He probably would have passed on the celebration, but since he had to give a lecture at the University of Delaware on Monday, he decided to drive down to the small beach town for a short visit.

The music changed to Maxwell's "Sumthin, Sumthin," from the movie *Love Jones*. It had been one of Dominique's favorites. It was their song. How many times had he held her in his arms after hours of lovemaking with it playing softly in the background? More times than he cared to count.

Quickly, he tried to shake off the thoughts and steer his mind from of the past.

With a will of their own, his traitorous eyes strayed over to the forbidden table, and when he spotted Dominique rising from the table, his fingers tightened around the glass. Her chocolate gaze was intense as she headed his way.

Bracing himself, Reese released a slow breath as his eyes involuntarily fastened on her generous hips swaying to the beat of the song, with every step in those damn high heels he loved to watch her walk in. He held completely still as his gaze roamed over those curves. Damn, he loved a woman with meat on her bones, and Dominique had plenty. Round succulent breasts, healthy hips and thighs, and a bodacious ass. More to hold, and definitely plenty to love.

As she drew closer, Reese straightened on the stool, shaking off the emotion stirring beneath his chest and forcing a fog of numbness to overcome him. Quickly, he took several deep breaths, so that by the time she had reached him he felt back in control.

"Hey, Reese," she said silkily as she stopped in front of him and struck a pose.

"Whassup, Dom." His heart had already started to thump at the sound of her mesmerizing voice. It was raspy, low and so soothing. Her floral perfume ruffled his nose and he had to fight the urge to lean down and rest his head against her generous cleavage and inhale.

So much for being in control.

At five-four, and even wearing four-inch black pumps, accessorized with a red Christmas bow, she still had to tilt her head back to look into his face. "You look so lonely over here sitting all by yourself." She was standing so close her supple breasts brushed his arm. Instantly thoughts of suckling hungrily at her chocolate nipples flashed in his mind.

Reese shook off the effect, took a swig, then swallowed. "Nah, just finishing up my drink so I can go and lay it down for the night."

She giggled. A sweet, throaty sound that he'd always adored. "You've been nursing that same drink all night."

He lifted his focus to her mesmerize eyes and had to force himself to remain impassive. And that wasn't easy for him to do. "How would you know?"

"I'd know." She shot him an amused look, and when their eyes locked, heat flashed through him so powerful the air disappeared from his lungs.

Dominique was right. She would know. He had never been much of a drinker. Mostly social, and mainly when he was hanging with his brothers or cousins.

He inhaled and chuckled, "Yeah, I guess you would." He brought the glass to his mouth again to show he had every intention of finishing the drink.

"How about I keep you company? While you're finishing your drink we can talk." Without waiting for an invitation, Dominique slid an empty stool over and took a seat, close enough so that their thighs brushed against each other, teasing him, making the blood pump and his breath hitch. She then reached out and swiveled his seat around so they were facing, then put her feet on the bottom of his stool, trapping his legs between hers. How many times had he felt the power of those thick thighs wrapped around his waist?

"Talk?" he managed around the lump in his throat.

"Yes … talk." She grinned and slid her tongue along the seam of her lips, stirring a disturbing response at the pit of his belly.

Reese rolled his tight shoulders and leaned back.

"Maybe tomorrow. It's been a long night. I'd really like to get to the guest house and settle in."

Dominique arched a perfectly plucked eyebrow. "The guest house? You're staying at Jace's when you could have any of the warm... empty... beds right here at the hotel?" she purred and leaned in so close he felt her warm breath on his nose.

"I prefer my privacy."

She nodded knowingly. He'd always preferred peace and quiet and a fully stocked kitchen to the amenities and room services at a five-star hotel.

"I see," she said in a voice that said she was contemplating her next move. Reese had learned his lesson. The last time he had stayed at the hotel Dominique had retrieved a key to his room from the front desk and had been waiting for him inside. Luckily, his cousin Jabarie had warned him. He'd purposely avoided the room and returned home to Baltimore. "There is nothing wrong with wanting a little privacy," she replied, voice laced with wicked humor. "In fact, being alone would give us the perfect chance to catch up and... talk," Dominique added with a wink.

Once again she was determined to talk to him about the night that had changed his entire life. As far as Reese was concerned, there wasn't too much more to be said. He needed to get away from her. Mainly because it was the effect she was having on him physically.

Reese met her eyes, dark and reflecting under the light from the Christmas ornaments flickering around the room. They moved lazily over his face, causing his chest to suddenly flare with a need that sent flames up and down his arms." Maybe tomorrow. It's been a long day and I'd really like to relax."

"The night's young. Why the rush? We haven't had a chance to talk or dance," she commented above the beat of a classic old school song.

"Dance?" Reese repeated, then averted his face as he remembered a different type of dance, where talking wasn't necessary. It had all started the summer before he had turned sixteen, when they had snuck off upstairs into one of the rooms among hundreds in the hotel. He and his cousins were supposed to be working as bellhops for his uncle Roger, the founder of the Beaumont Corporation. Even after all these years, he remembered Dominique had dropped by the hotel for a swim, and had convinced him to *borrow* a key to one of the vacant rooms. That was the summer they had both lost their virginity. After that, talking was no longer a necessity.

"Yes, Reese... dance. Then talk. You... me... alone," she said softly, conjuring up all kinds of lustful images that he immediately blinked away.

Dancing was out of the question. There was no way he could hold her in his arms and not lose his head. And he'd already apologized for that night and his behavior. What more was there to say? He sighed. Dominique never did know when to leave it alone. When she wanted something, nothing stopped her. His shattered hand was proof of that. A year had passed since everything between them had fallen apart. And he no longer blamed her. Not really. Scrubbing a hand over his jaw, Reese dared to ask, "What do we have to talk about?"

"Plenty." Dominique pulled her shoulders back, causing her nipples to brush his arm. Reese shivered, then stared into eyes that darkened whenever Dominique was determined to get her way. Even after all that time he felt caught up under her spell as his heart thudded against his ribs with longing.

"Damn," he muttered under his breath as he watched the way her long lashes practically brushed her cheeks every time she blinked. Reese remembered the hours he had spent staring down at her. He remembered the way her pupils dilated only seconds after he'd positioned himself between her legs and slipped his penis inside her body. Even now he could hear the sounds of her voice, purring his name like a kitten as he plunged in and out of her wet heat, bringing them both pleasure.

Realizing he was staring, Reese jerked his gaze away. "I think we've already said everything that needs to be said about that night." He tried to smile, then glanced down at his watch. "Wow! I didn't realize it was so late. I better get going."

"It's barely eight. Why are you running?" Dominique asked, leaning forward to get in his face.

He swallowed, tightly gripping the glass as he muttered, "I'm not running from anything."

Her luscious mouth curved upward in amusement. "Maybe that was the wrong choice of words." She leaned in closer, licking her glossy lips. "Avoiding. You've been avoiding me since the accident, and tonight is when it stops." She was breathing heavily, her breast rising and falling as her eyes gleamed with determination. "We need to talk about us. We need to talk about what happened."

It took everything Reese had to resist the magnetic pull as he drew back and glared at her. "Now, that's where you're wrong. I accepted your apology and you accepted mine, so as far as I'm concerned there's nothing left to discuss." With that he slammed the empty glass down on the bar, pushed away from the stool, grabbed his wool jacket and walked out of the club.

Chapter Two

Damn that man!

Dominique drew in a long breath, stunned by his response. Had he sensed her determination?

Ever since Sheyna had told her Reese was coming to Sheraton Beach to celebrate Jace's birthday, she had been waiting. And nothing was stopping her from getting what she wanted this time. *Nothing.* He was a stubborn man. Well, guess what? Her stubbornness was just as fierce.

"Dammit, Reese!" she spat as she dropped to her feet. They were going to talk even if she had to strap him to the hood of his truck.

With full determination she stormed out into the well-lit parking lot and cussed under her breath for not having stopped long enough to retrieve her pea coat from the table. Soft white snow had been coming down all day and was still falling steadily from the sky.

"Don't you dare walk away from me, Reese Beaumont!" she shouted as she noticed him sticking the key into the door of his Lincoln Mark LT. She was practically running, determined to stop him from getting inside. "Dammit, you hear me talking to you!"

As she drew closer, she noticed how his shoulders drooped before he slowly swung around and replied, "Dom, what is it you want from me?"

Dominique pursed her lips. Brown eyes narrowed. She wasn't the least bit cowed by his threatening glare. He'd sparked a flame inside her and she couldn't think of any reason not to follow up on a natural conclusion.

Every emotion raging through her body was fully engaged when she charged up to him, ready to wrap her fingers around his neck, but the second she shoved him back against the truck, she reached up, locked her hands behind his head and pulled him down toward her mouth in a kiss.

Oh my goodness!

Reese's lips were explosive, hot and fierce. She half expected him to push her away, and sighed with relief when he wrapped his arms around her waist and drew her even closer. Everything inside her came alive. And she was aware of nothing else except the feel of Reese's lips pressed against hers, the thrusts of his tongue, and her heart surging like a wild fire through her veins. His reaction gave her hope that after months of trying she was finally getting somewhere. She raised herself up on her tiptoe in order to get as close to him as she possibly could, body pressed against body, yet it still wasn't close enough.

While she deepened the kiss the rapid pounding of his heartbeat against her chest was reassuring, telling her that he wanted her, yet she still needed to hear from his mouth where they stood. Her future depended on it.

* * *

As the keys fell from his hand, Reese wasn't sure what shocked him more — the fact that she was kissing him or the yearning that was now pulling at his chest.

Reese wrapped one arm around her waist and the other he rested at the center of her back. He then leaned into the kiss and followed her lead. He had expected a simple innocent peck. But when she opened her mouth and flicked her tongue against his, the flavor damn near brought him to his knees. Hot damn! How could he have forgotten how good she tasted? Not to mention, she kissed with familiarity and expertise, and with skills that any woman would gladly have paid for.

With each second their tongues mated, he grew increasing confused. He had expected Dominique to be angry and demand an apology, slap him across the face maybe, but kissing? Not after the cruel way he had treated her. Now with her soft breasts crushed against this chest and the feel of her mouth coming alive under his, he knew he had to be dreaming. Or could she be after something else?

Before he knew what he was doing, he pulled her tight against his frame and curled his tongue against hers in sensual pleasure. He leaned against the weight of the vehicle with his legs cradling her body and her crotch pressed against his thighs. Damn the clothing between them. He wanted her stripped naked and straddling his lap. He slid his tongue into her mouth the way he wanted to slide his dick inside her sweet essence, and an erection jerked in response. Dominique tasted of heaven, her mouth delicious and downright unforgettable. His body remembered how it felt to be with her, and he definitely didn't want to stop. His body wanted her mouth, hands, tongue, and that sweet something special rubbing against his thigh. How was it with her lips pressed against his that he forgot the reason why he'd ended their relationship? Instead, the only thing on his mind was holding her in his arms and never letting her go. Oblivious to the world around them, Reese felt like he was drowning and couldn't have drawn away from her even if his life had depended on it.

Thank goodness, Dominique did the honors.

She broke the kiss and stepped back, her breathing coming hard and fast. Her eyes wide, lips slightly parted.

"You always did have a way of getting me to listen," he pointed out while catching his breath.

"Only when I wanted something, "she replied, and gave him the faintest smile.

Reese had to shake his head to escape the alluring power of her voice. Looking down at her face, he tried to read her mind, but Dominique made sure to keep her expression neutral. "And what is it that you want?" he finally asked.

Her gaze turned thoughtful. Serious. "We haven't talked. And we need to."

"I already said I'm sorry. I even forgave you," he told her agitatedly.

She waved a dismissive hand. "Yeah and you also said what happened wasn't my fault, but I could tell by your voice on the phone you didn't really mean it." Damn, but she was gorgeous when she was mad.

"What do you mean, *I didn't mean it*?"

Defiantly, Dominique crossed her arms beneath her large breasts. "Just what I said. If you had forgiven me, then why won't you talk to me?" She was shaking mad now. "Why have you completely cut me out of your life as if I'd done something to you if you say I hadn't?"

Self-pity. Anger. Because seeing Dominique and being around her was too hard. All he did was think about the way things used to be and what might have been if that night hadn't happened. And the horrible way he had handled it. And then knowing that she had been seeing someone else....

"I didn't cut you out of my life," he said with a hint of impatience. "I just figured after all this time it was just best for us to leave the past alone." He slid out from between her and his truck and was reaching down for his keys when Dominique grabbed his arm, halting him.

"But why?" she growled. "Because being around me reminded you too much of what happened to your hand? Because it's easier moving on, pretending the past never happened? Or maybe because deep down you know you still want me? Reese, don't even try to deny it. I felt it when I kissed you and I know you did, too."

She was right. He was still attracted to her. And the desire to be with her was pretty obvious or he wouldn't have returned the kiss. "Dom, that's all that's left between us. Sparks."

"Liar! I haven't forgotten about you. I've tried, but I can't. My heart..." she paused, then cleared her throat. "My heart won't let me. There's still unfinished business between us. And I need to know what that is so I can finally move on with my life." She was shaking, close to tears, with a hint of misery in her eyes.

His stomach clenched at her confession. After everything he had said and done, she still cared about him? Or was it because she realized she had made a mistake when she had gotten caught on camera kissing another man? The thought angered him and he felt a wave of jealousy spear through him, viciously sharp. He didn't want any other man with her, even though he had no right to feel like that. He had no claims on her. Not now. Not ever. Dominique was single and free to date whoever she wanted, he told himself grimly. Besides, he'd gotten over her a long time ago. Or at least he'd pretended he had, he thought with a frustrated groan. It was easier when he stayed away from Sheraton Beach and he didn't have to see her around town. And now that he had seen her, and even tasted her, he no longer felt as confident.

"How about we work on being friends again?"

She searched his eyes before finally saying, "Is that all you ever wanted from me?"

At one point during his rehabilitation he'd wanted so badly to believe all could be forgiven and he and Dominique still had a chance, but every time he looked down at his disfigured right hand that had ended his career as a thoracic surgeon, he'd get angry all over again.

While at the hospital he'd said some pretty nasty things when he had blamed her for the distraction that had caused him to miss seeing the deer and lose control of the wheel. There was no reversing that, or going back to what they once were. Not after his hand had been crushed under the weight of his wrecked Cadillac Escalade. Not after seeing the photographs of Dominique kissing another man. Their relationship was in the past, and he preferred it that way.

Besides, it wasn't like they'd had a commitment. Their relationship had been fun and everything a single man could have wanted in a woman who also wasn't seeking a serious relationship. He'd never asked her if she was seeing other people and she had never asked him. He just assumed that she wasn't and that they had an unspoken commitment to each other. But when he saw those photos, Reese felt like someone had reached into his chest and squeezed his heart, and then his mind started spinning all kind of thoughts. It was then he realized how much he really cared about her, and that he was finally ready to define their relationship.

But not anymore. What they had was over. He only believed in moving forward. It was the only way he had learned to cope with his useless hand, his career and the only woman he had ever cared about.

"It doesn't matter what I wanted because what we had… what we were… is over."

* * *

Blinking away snowflakes, Dominique stared up into his face, trying to read his thoughts. Reese had always been such a wonderful liar and she was almost ninety-six percent certain he was lying now. It wasn't over, not until they both said it was over. He had always been stubborn. Hell, all the Beaumont men were. She and Reese had been friends with benefits, which hadn't been easy, considering he had lived in Richmond, Virginia, with his parents and six siblings until college and only came to Sheraton Beach to spend the summers with his cousins at Beaumont Manor. It wasn't until the summer of her sixteenth birthday that they had finally become lovers who joked about getting married and sharing their lives together. It had taken her years to penetrate through that shield surrounding his heart, and dammit, she wanted back in because she had to know. She had a right to know if there was anything left between them, if their jokes had the potential to become a reality that she so desperately wanted, because until she found out, she couldn't move on with her life, and after twelve long months she was tired of waiting and wondering.

Last month Jace had offered her a human resource management position at the Beaumont Waikiki Hotel, and she had yet to make a decision. It was just too hard to decide a future when she still had a past with so many unanswered questions. Was there anything left between her and Reese? That was the big question. She needed an answer and she was determined to have it before he climbed into his vehicle on Monday and headed back to his home in Bowie, Maryland.

She noticed Reese trying again to reach down for his keys and with one kick of her stiletto, Dominique sent the ring under the vehicle and out of his reach.

Rising, his eyes narrowed and swept across her face. "Why'd you do that?"

She tilted her chin defiantly. "Because we're going to talk before you leave town."

He stilled and she could feel his tension. "Dominique,

give it a rest... I'm sorry. I-I was wrong for blaming you, and cutting you out of my life like that, but what more is there to say?" At her silence, he continued. "Listen... I'll beg for your forgiveness if I have to," he added in a deep velvety voice.

She let out a short, abrupt laugh that sent shivers down his spine. "It won't do any good. I'll just stalk you the entire time you're in town until you hear what I have to say. And trust me... I have plenty."

* * *

This was not supposed to be happening.

Reese was standing there staring down at her lips, itching to drag her against his body again and kiss her. He was feeling things he wasn't supposed to be feeling. Anger because she wouldn't leave him alone. Shock at her determination to have her way, and then there was his disbelief at the attraction that was brewing like old times. Not that that should have come as much of a surprise. One thing the two of them always had had was chemistry. Even back when they were still playing kickball in the street it had been there and had only gotten stronger as they grew closer. But that was all in the past.

He blinked, then noticed Dominique was shivering. In her haste to chase after him she had forgotten her coat. Funny how they had both been plenty warm locked in each other's arms.

"Hey, it's cold and snowing. Why don't we jump inside and warm up? The last thing I need is for Jace to go off on me because his *favorite* employee has gotten frost-bitten."

His words caused her to smile. "Is that what he said about me?"

He shrugged. "Yes, I also heard you were offered a

senior level position in Hawaii." Jace had told him over the phone, and for the second time he felt a dull ache at his chest at the thought of her leaving Sheraton Beach and heading to the romantic island. Dominique had always been good at what she had done, so he knew the promotion was well deserved. The beauty had graduated at the top of her class in Business Administration at Morgan State and had later gone on to complete her MBA while he had attended The Robert Wood Johnson Medical School in New Jersey.

Dropping to his knees, Reese fished around under the vehicle until he felt the cold keys beneath his fingers.

"Sorry about that," he heard her say. "I guess kicking your keys wasn't such a smart idea."

He rose and dusted the snow off his knees, then hit the button unlocking the door. "Forget about it. Now get in."

Holding the door open, Dominique wasted no time climbing inside. Reese shut the door, then walked around to the driver's side, climbed in and immediately started the engine. He turned the heat on full blast. "Man, it's cold here."

Nodding, she rubbed her hands together and blew on them. "It always is this time of year. At least we'll have a white Christmas." He had to keep reminding himself the magic holiday was less than a week away.

"Don't remind me. I haven't even started shopping." Reese turned the seat warmers to high and pressed the CD player. Within seconds the soulful sounds of Anthony Hamilton played softly in the background. While they listened, he leaned back comfortable on the seat, waiting for them to heat up.

"Remember when we heard him in concert?"

"Yes, I remember." How could he forget? The first time she had come to New York to visit him was while he was doing a fellowship in cardiovascular disease at the University of Rochester. He remembered surprising her with the tickets and the excitement that lit her face. He would have done anything to see her smile.

Even now.

He ignored the nagging voice. That was so long ago, he reminded himself. Back then he and his best friend were inseparable. Never would he have guessed he would be thinking about them in the past tense.

"We were so happy back then," she said awkwardly as her long slender fingers clutched the hem of her skirt.

Silence ticked on. He flexed his arms with his hands on the wheel. There was no disguising how uncomfortable the conversation made him. "Things change. People change."

Dominique shook her head and gave him a sidelong glance. "Not us. We may be older, but deep down you and I are still the same people. I remember all the years we spent laughing and sharing everything. I miss our long talks at night. And your laughter on the phone."

Reese's face twisted for more than a second. "Dominique. Don't do this. I don't want to hurt you."

Her nostrils flared. "You couldn't possibly do any more than you already have. I'm still hurting about what used to be and what could have been," she said in a soft sad voice. "I might even seem pathetic to you, but I've gotta know. You were my best friend... my lover. Before I can move on with my life and accept the position in Honolulu, I have to close this chapter end our lives together. I need to know if you still blame me and if things are really over between us. I need to know if there ever could have been more going on than either of us realized." There was no disguising the desperation that had crept into her voice.

Reese felt an ache at his chest as her words echoed

between them. Despite all his resistance, he knew she was right. There was so much that they needed to discuss, things that needed to be resolved between them. But he wasn't sure if he wanted to go back there. There had been too much pain and he wasn't sure he wanted to open those wounds again. But part of him still wanted answers. And as much as it hurt, he needed to know why he still felt betrayed by her.

Reaching over, Reese took Dominique's hand and curled his fingers around hers. Despite frequent bouts of tingling and numbness in his fingers, he had no difficulties feeling a shiver of familiarity that rippled through him. Reese knew the last thing he needed to do was touch Dominique. He didn't even want her in his truck, yet there he was sitting beside her, holding hand. It was intimate and felt way too much like old times, and he definitely wasn't trying to go back there. However, there was a vulnerable side to her that he'd never been able to resist. His entire body reacted to her touch. Skin against skin in one of the most intimate ways. At the speed of light, another example flashed across his mind of two bodies, naked between the sheets, doing the one thing they had been so damn good at.

"What are you thinking about?" she asked with softness in her expression, both serious and uncertain.

Her fingers were slender and soft, and the warmth from her hand despite the freezing temperatures outside flooded through his body and made heat pool deep inside of him. Her touch felt good. Too damn good. It had been a long time, and all that softness and beauty drew him in. Not to mention after the kiss they'd shared, he wanted her. Still wanted her, and a surge of physical attraction hardened his body at the thought of holding her in his arms again. "You want to know what I'm thinking about?" he asked. "I'm thinking about you…

me… what we used to have," he answered with a hint of despair, and she knew him well enough not to push.

"What we could still be," she whispered with another hint of despair. "I miss having you in my life."

"So do I," Reese heard himself admit. Turning on the seat, Reese studied her lovely profile, mesmerized by her beauty, and noticed Dominique staring down at the crushed, disfigured hand holding hers.

"Does it still hurt?" she finally asked.

He shrugged. "I have good days and bad days. When the pain is persistent, I take lots of drugs."

She cringing with guilt and closed her eyes briefly. He knew she was having a hard time dealing with the crash that had ended his career as a congenital heart surgeon. Being the person she was, Dominique felt personally responsible. For a long time, he'd agreed. Now he wasn't sure what he thought anymore. Being around her made it too hard to think. His mind was a dizzy circle of scrambled thoughts and feelings.

"Sheyna told me you're still practicing medicine," she said, her voice light.

He nodded and noticed the intimacy of the moment was still wrapped around them. "Despite my limitations I'm still on staff at the Veterans Affairs Medical Center. The only difference is I'm no longer performing surgeries." The thing he'd enjoyed most.

After he received the news that there was a chance he might never perform surgery again, he'd spent six months feeling sorry for himself before his sister, Sedona, a life coach, helped him snap out of his funk and figure out a way to continue to use his gift to help others. Two years ago he'd accepted a position as Director at the Center for Preventive Cardiology for the University of Maryland Medical System, which was one of the top clinical and research facilities on the east coast. They'd performed more than 1000 cardiothoracic procedures in the last six months. Only, to his despair, he hadn't been responsible for a single procedure. It was still hard to accept that he could no longer perform surgery, but it was getting easier. Over time he'd learned to stop blaming anyone but fate. God obviously had another plan for him.

"I'm so sorry!" Dominique blurted out. "It's all my fault. I shouldn't have hit you."

Reese waved his hand dismissively. "There'll be none of that. It's all in the past."

"That doesn't make it any easier," she said in a soft sad voice. "If we hadn't been arguing ..." her voice cracked. "None of this would have happened."

Reese itched to pull her into his arms and assure her that everything was going to be all right, but he didn't trust what he would do once he felt her warm body pressed against his. And when he felt her tugging at his heart he didn't know how to step away.

"Can I ask you a question?" he asked, his fingers still laced with hers.

There was a slight hesitation. "Sure."

"The argument we were having... are you still seeing Gabe?"

"Gabe?" she said with blatant disbelief. "Are you going to start that again?" Dominique looked up, her eyes flashing, then dropped his hand. He instantly missed her touch. "There was nothing going on between us. I told you that. Why can't you believe me?" she asked with frustration firing her words. And why did it feel like déjà vu?

He'd spent months avoiding her, blaming her, angry at her, but now that he was back in Sheraton Beach, now that he'd seen her, he felt the familiar longing he'd experience every time he was around her. He didn't want to feel anything for her at all, yet his heart continued to beat unsteadily as he tried to deny what his body was telling him—it was already too late.

Dominique was right. It was time to talk, if nothing else, so that she could accept the position and move on with her life.

"Okay, if you want to talk, then let's talk, "he finally said.

Dominique swung around on the seat, studying his expression with uncertainty. "Seriously? Okay, great, but not here. I'll meet you out at the guest house in about an hour," she announced in a rush.

Reese was ready to decline, but she had already jumped out the car and dashed back into the nightclub.

Chapter Three

What the hell just happened?

By the time Reese had pulled up onto the long driveway and driven his truck around to the back of the massive farm house that Jace and Sheyna called home, Reese was still trying to find an answer to that question.

One minute he was trying to avoid Dominique and the next thing he knew they were getting busy in a private parking lot. Shaking his head, Reese tried to clear his head of the confusion. But there was nothing confusing about how good the kiss had been. And once he had sampled those lips there was no stopping him. They were everything he'd remembered them to be and so much more. Soft, supple, and sinfully delicious. Nothing could compare to those lips, and for those few seconds it had felt like old times.

As he pulled into the carport and came to a complete stop, Reese wondered if he'd really intended to keep his distance from Dominique all weekend. Even if he had, the thought was abandoned and hope leaped into fresh life the second she had kissed him. All it took was one touch and he melted. He wanted her. After everything that happened, he still wanted her. He wanted her sweetness and touch, the taste of her inside his mouth. He wanted her surrender. To bury himself inside the warmth of her body. Being around her made him feel vulnerable and exposed, to the point that he could barely remember why the relationship had ended in the first place. And that had him more confused than ever.

Right after their split-up, Reese had been too busy feeling sorry for himself to think about a woman. But once he'd started physical therapy and started seeing a therapist to help him cope with his limitations, he'd met Simone, a beautiful news anchor. She'd spent most of her time staring at his hand, and when he touched her arm, she jerked away. It came as no surprise to Reese when she'd sent him an email ending their relationship, admitting that his disfigurement gave her the creeps. Reese had dated a few more women after that, but realized he wasn't being fair to any one of them since all he had done was compare them to Dominique.

Reese cut off the engine, then grew still as he allowed his mind to go over the events of the evening. The encounter with Dominique wasn't at all what he envisioned it to be. What he had expected was anger and resentment, but instead there was passion. Plenty of it. Within seconds he'd felt the anger slip from both of their bodies, replaced with rekindled desire. Even now heat flowed through his veins at the mere thought of the kiss they had shared. The second her tongue slipped inside his mouth and he heard the soft purrs that gurgled at the back of her throat, Reese knew nothing was stopping him from tasting her warm, sweet mouth, or from savoring the heat of her body pressed close against his. His body knew what he wanted, and that something had always been Dominique. What was it about that woman? he wondered for the umpteenth time. Even after all this time, and everything that had happened, she still had that same effect on him.

Despite his reluctance, he couldn't keep himself from wanting to spend a little more time with her, even if it was just for a few days. They were going to talk about that night, the photographs, and Gabe. Just thinking about the man caused the nerve at his temple to tick.

While they were teenagers the two had played football together, and the lanky kid didn't know the meaning of playing fair. Reese had never liked him then, and he definitely didn't like him now.

Not after seeing him kissing Dominique.

He was man enough to admit that it was time to face the past. Dominique was right. They had some unfinished business. He needed to ask some questions that he should have gotten answers to almost a year ago. The only reason he hadn't asked those questions was because of his stubborn pride.

Glancing through the windshield he spotted his cousin Jace coming down the brick path toward the guest house. Reese climbed out just as he reached his vehicle.

"Whassup, cuz!"

Jace grinned. "What's going on, Reese? Glad you finally decided to come out of hibernation."

"Hey, I can't hide this ugly face forever," he joked as Jace came around the car and the two hugged.

"I tried to wait around at the hotel for you to arrive," his cousin explained as he released him and buried his bare hands in the pockets of his bomber jacket. "But I had a six o'clock conference call." Jace was president of Human Resources.

"No problem," Reese replied with a nod. "Sheyna told me. Then I ran into Remy in the lobby and we decided to put down a few at McKinley's."

Glancing inside the car, Jace asked, "Where's he at?"

Reese tossed him a knowing look. "Where you think? Went home with some chick he met."

Tossing his head back with laughter, Jace said, "That boy's never going to change."

"True that," Reese said with a chuckle.

Jace turned and signaled for Reese to follow him. "Come on... let's get inside."

Reese retrieved a duffle bag from the back seat of the truck and followed Jace through the gap in the trees that led them toward a small stone cottage. It was hidden behind tall hedges so it was completely separated from the main house. The garden was now dead, with snow covering the ground, but the paved walkway had been recently cleared by the groundskeeper.

Reaching the carved door, Jace removed a key from underneath the matt, stuck it in the lock and pushed it open.

Reese stepped inside the house. He expected it to smell musty and unused, but was pleased to find a woodsy scent similar to pine cones. His eyes quickly surveyed the large open living area with sofas and chairs. Fresh logs were inside the fireplace, ready to be lit. To the left was a gaming area with a large pool table, a seventy-two inch LCD television mounted on the wall, and a bar stocked with premium top-shelf liquors. He and his brothers had spent many weekends hanging out at the cottage during football season.

"Sheyna told me she saw you and Dominique talking."

Inwardly, Reese groaned. That was one reason he hated coming to this place. Small town folks talked too much.

"If you wanna call it that," he said in a cool tone, hoping it would stop his cousin from asking more questions. For the last year, whenever the family brought her up, he had found a way to avoid the conversation. However, as soon as he saw Jace take a seat on the couch, he knew he wasn't going to be able to avoid discussing her any longer.

"Don't you think it's time the two of you talked?"

Reese dropped his bag to the floor, then looked at Jace for a long moment, contemplating how much he should share, before finally taking a seat and replying, "What's there to talk about? I thought we were both happy with our relationship the way it was and I discovered she wanted more when she started dating Gabe Wolfe."

Jace's brow rose. "Gabe?" he repeated with an amused look. "Yeah, right! Who told you that lie?"

"Katharine," Reese replied.

With a frown, Jace shook his head. "Well, she lied. And knowing the way Kathy feels about you, I can't believe you were stupid enough to fall for it."

His eyes widened with disbelief. "But I saw the photos of the two of them kissing."

"You're not talking about the pictures taken of them under the mistletoe?" The moment he nodded, Jace erupted with hearty laughter. "What you didn't see was Dom slapping the crap outta him for kissing her on the lips."

Reese's went still and lapsed into silence. The night of the accident Dominique had tried to explain, but he was so angry he'd refused to listen. Even tonight she had reaffirmed that nothing had ever gone on between her and Gabe. Why had it been so hard for him to believe her? Had he really been that stupid all this time?

"Damn. The night of the accident...that's why we were arguing. She tried to tell me, but I wasn't hearing it. All those months I blamed her for the accident... my injury, and totally cut her out of my life." Leaning forward, he rested his elbows on his knees and shared details that he had refused to discuss before. And the more he talked, the more Reese realized how foolish he had been.

What have I done?

Jace blew out an exasperated breath. "Cuz, how come you didn't just ask me or Jabarie?"

Yeah, how come?

He shrugged. "Dammit, I don't know. I was so mad when I saw those photos I immediately drove down to confront her, and... well you know what happened next."

He watched as his oldest cousin shook his head. The disbelief was apparent in his eyes. Growing up, he had always admired Jace, wanting to be just like him when he grew up. When Reese had decided to apply to medical school, Jace supported his decision and was standing right there in the crowd the day he graduated. Disappointing him was the last thing he'd ever wanted to do.

"What's done is done. No point in dwelling on the past. Now what are you going to do to fix it?" Jace asked.

Reese's heart slammed against his chest. "I don't know."

"Well you need to figure it out. As much as I want Dominique to take the job at Waikiki Beach, I'd rather see the two of you together."

"Thanks, cuz." Reaching out he gave him a fist pound, then Jace stood in one fluid motion.

"Well, if you need anything, let me know, although I doubt it. Sheyna's anal when it comes to keeping the guest house stocked." There was no denying the love in Jace's eyes as he spoke of his wife.

"I'm sure I got everything I need. Where's JJ?" Reese asked, referring to Jace's four-year-old son.

"He's with Sheyna's brother Scott and his wife Zanaa. They're watching him while we get out in the morning and do our Christmas shopping. But if you really want to see him, I'll be more than happy to have you take him off our hands tomorrow," he offered with a laugh.

Reese released a chuckle. The kid was a true Beaumont, full of energy, rough and tough, with a natural love for sports. For a brief moment Reese stood there and wondered if he'd ever have what his cousin had. At one point he'd had his entire life planned out. All the way to the two-point-five kids, but after the accident all that had changed. "I think I'll pass. It looks like I already got my work cut out for me this weekend."

Jace tipped his head knowingly. He knew firsthand what it took to pursue a woman. "Spoken like a true Beaumont."

After Jace returned to the main house, Reese grabbed his bag and moved down the hall to the master bedroom. He needed to shower and change into something comfortable. He set the bag on a large chair in the corner, then stepped into the bathroom and turned on the water. As he unbuttoned his shirt a smile curled his lips. Dominique would be here soon. One thing he could never argue was that she was different. Dominique had always been feisty, funny and determined. And a woman whom he had considered to be his best friend, his better half, and he'd allowed selfishness and anger to ruin everything they'd had.

Now it was time to bring that to an end.

*   *   *

Dominique stopped in the living room long enough to turn on the CD player that sent Destiny Child's Christmas music flowing through speakers throughout her entire townhouse. With a grin on her face, she crossed the foyer and climbed the curving staircase to the second floor. Her tall heels clicked softly as she walked down the long, narrow hallway. As Dominique entered her bedroom she went straight to her walk-in closet and a smiled curved her lush lips.

"Now let's see what we have in here," she murmured, determined to make sure Reese remembered how good they were together. She planned to entice him. Seduce him. Their encounter would be pleasurable... and possibly meaningless, she thought with a frown. After a few minutes together it was apparent that he wasn't interested in rekindling their relationship or discussing the accident.

"We'll see about that." Her brown eyes scanned the clothes hanging in her closet until she finally located what she was looking for. The outfit was guaranteed to be something he wouldn't be able to resist.

Quickly, she removed the hanger from her closet and tossed it onto her queen-size bed.

Oh yeah. It's on.

Dominique danced over to the right of the room humming, "Spread a little love on Christmas Day," as she rummaged through the lingerie drawers. It may not be Christmas yet, but she had every intention of spreading some love. Her eyes scanned the contents. Pink...red...polka dots...hmmm, she wasn't sure what type of mood she was in. What she required, needed to be bold, daring and downright sexy. Reese was no match for a female hell bent on seducing her man.

She paused and took a second to calm her racing heart. She didn't want to get ahead of herself, but she was definitely on a mission. When she said she needed to know if there was still anything between them, well... the truth was... she already knew. She had loved him since she was sixteen, and despite the car accident and the accusations, nothing regarding her feelings had changed. He still had her heart. Whether he wanted it or not, it was still his. All the same, there was no way she could move on with her life before she—correction, before *they*—had had a chance to see if their relationship could be saved. If they could again have what they once had. And the only way to do that was by throwing caution to the wind and throwing everything she had at him. She had never been one to back down from a fight, so what was the difference? She was fighting for love and her man.

And tonight he was definitely her man. It was her job tonight to make sure he didn't forget who his heart belonged to. If she no longer had his heart, she'd know. And even as painful as if might be, after tonight, if Reese told her it was over, then she would be ready to walk away and start a new life.

Nothing ventured, nothing gained, had been her motto since high school, and because of it she had graduated at the top of her class and had gone on to make her mother proud when she went off to college. After graduation, Roger Beaumont had hired her at the Beaumont hotel, not because she was a friend of his daughter, Bianca, or of her brothers Jace, Jabarie and Jaden, but because she was a woman with a proven record. Once Dominique had landed a position in the employee relations department, she was more determined than ever to succeed and make her mother proud.

An ache of sadness filled her as she thought of her mother, Priscilla, who had passed away due to complications from diabetes. She had spent years being depressed over a man who had abandoned his wife and two little girls. From day one her entire life revolved around them, making sure they made something of their lives. She had worked two jobs to put her daughter through college, and Dominique had never forgotten her mother's sacrifice. Her last promise to Priscilla was that she'd follow her dreams and never let a man hold her back from having everything she desired. Dominique had been holding her hand when her mother had passed away three summers ago.

Quickly Dominique brushed a tear from her eye.

There will be none of that, she scolded. Her mother wouldn't have wanted it that way. Instead, she slid into her slippers and padded into the bathroom. "Mama, I'm about to go claim my man," she murmured, and felt giddy all over.

Twenty minutes later Dominique was stepping out of the shower when she heard the loud shrill of her cell phone. Hoping it wasn't Reese trying to cancel their date, she quickly wrapped a towel around her waist and padded out the adjoining bathroom as quickly as she could without slipping on the wet floor. She grabbed her purse off the chaise lounge in the corner and retrieved her phone before it went to voicemail.

"Hello?"

"Dominique… where you at?"

She groaned at the sound of her younger sister's whiny voice. "I'm at home, why?" she said with an impatient sigh.

"Are you alone?"

"Why would you ask that?" Dominique said as she stepped back into the bathroom and reached for the bottle of cocoa butter.

"I heard that Reese is back in town."

She dragged the phone away from her mouth, covered the mouthpiece, and let out a loud scream. Of course her sister had heard. Even though she was attending college all the way in Atlanta, she still knew everything that went on in the small beach town. There was no telling which busybody was watching the two of them. Dominique groaned inwardly. By morning everyone would know that she and Reese had been getting it on hot and heavy in the parking lot. She brought the phone back to her ear.

"So because he's back in town you just assumed he was over here." It wasn't a question because she already knew the answer.

"Well... I mean... of course. He *was* at McKinley's, and I know that's where you go every Friday evening after work."

Dominique glared at her reflection in the mirror, then rolled her eyes. Reese had always been quite fond of Brittany, and she of him. He considered her like one of his little sisters. Even though he and Dominique were no longer together, he had even come home for Brittany's high school graduation. Reese had laughed and talked with her and had even bought her an iPad 2 for her freshman year at Spellman. Dominique had planned to talk to Reese immediately after the graduation dinner, but while she was in the ladies room he had slipped out the side door.

"Yes, Reese is *here,* but he isn't over here."

Brittany sighed heavily in her ear. "Why not? I thought you were going to talk to him."

Dominique screwed the lid back onto the bottle and hurried into her bedroom to get dressed. For the life of her, she didn't know why she had confided in her sister that she couldn't accept the position in Hawaii until she'd had a chance to speak with Reese and see what was left of their relationship.

"I'm going to talk to him, Brit. Just not tonight," she lied, moving over and slipping on the barely-there red panties with *Naughty* screen-printed in white letters right smack at the center of her ass.

"Why the hell not?" she exclaimed.

"Brittany Ann! Watch your mouth," Dominique scolded, fighting back a smile.

"Sorry," she said, sounding like a small child. "I just want the two of you to make up. This is been going on long enough."

"I see," Dominique mumbled while sliding into the

matching satin corset.

"I'm serious!" Brittany huffed. "The two of you should be married by now. Do you know how long I've been waiting to be a bridesmaid and walk down the aisle with a bouquet of orchids and baby's breath?"

Oh, brother. Her sister could be such a drama queen.

"Promise me you'll talk to him." Dominique didn't miss the desperation in her sister's voice. It saddened her how much her family loved that man.

If only he still felt the same way about me.

"I promise, Brittany. Jace's party's not until Sunday afternoon, so he isn't going anywhere. By then the two of us will have talked."

Brittany released a heavy sigh. "Then I guess I'll call you on Sunday."

"Okay, but I expect you to spend the weekend studying for finals," Dominique replied, then decided to change the subject. "When does your flight leave?" she asked as she took a seat on the end of the bed and reached for her stilettos. Brittany was coming home for Christmas break.

"I land at six on Friday. I hope you're coming to the airport to pick me up. I'll just die if I have to ride with Uncle Clee. All he wants to talk about is football."

Dominique giggled. Cleveland Wellington was a diehard Pittsburg Steelers fan. After he'd ensured his niece had had a safe flight, her uncle would spend the rest of the ninety-minute drive discussing the highlights of the season. Dominique knew, because he used to do the same thing to her.

"I'll come and pick you up."

"Thank you so much!" Brittany cried. "Well, I better get going. My roommates and I are going to the coffee shop to study. I'll call you on Sunday night, so make sure you answer your phone."

"Sure... talk to you then."

Dominique ended the call, then rose from the bed and slipped into her outfit. She then sashayed over to the floor-length mirror and turned from side to side, taking in all her curves. Brittany was tall and slender, while she had taken after her mother and all the Decker women — wide hips, large breasts and plenty of junk in her trunk. In junior high Dominique used to consider her weight an issue, but as she had gone through puberty and entered high school she had learned to appreciate all her voluptuous curves, and loved what she now considered her *ass*ets. There was nothing insecure about her.

Now it was time to play for keeps.

Chapter Four

Shortly after ten, Dominique knocked softly on the guesthouse door and waited patiently for all of five seconds, then knocked again, a little harder. She was nervous, but with her short time schedule she hadn't much time to convince Reese they were meant to be together. Jace's party was Sunday, and according to Sheyna, Reese was speaking at the University of Delaware on Monday before heading back to Bowie, Maryland. Time was of the essence, and she needed every second to count.

She shook her head and sighed as she thought of the games women were forced to play. I guess I'm one of them. She was about to take a gamble, but hopefully she'd come out a winner.

Raising her hand, she was prepared to press a French nail to the doorbell when she heard movement on the other side. Then the lock turned. The second the door swung open, she suddenly forgot to breathe.

Standing in the door was Reese. The man she still believed to be her soul mate. Even thought it had barely been two hours since she had last seen him, it did nothing to calm her heart. He stood in the door with his hands in the pockets of his jeans. Even casually dressed he looked amazing. Dominique drank him in, her gaze lingering on the way his clothes clung to his powerful frame. All that smooth golden flesh pulled taut over rippling muscles that strained against his hard chest and arms. The smooth fit of his relaxed jeans emphasized his trim waist and powerful thighs, sending her heart racing at warp speed. While she stared at him, his eyes traveled over every trace of her in a long winter-white coat. She spied a flash of male curiosity in his eyes.

"I thought maybe you had changed your mind."

Dominique clucked her tongue. "Not on your life." She stepped into the foyer, listening to the sound of her stilettos clicking against the Brazilian cherry wood floor as she passed a plush sofa and chairs and headed toward the entertainment area. A large flat-screen TV and pool table were situated at the far end, beside a fully stocked bar. A warm fire and soft music created an inviting atmosphere. Dominique followed him over to the bar and took a seat on one of the swiveled stools.

"Name your poison."

She rested her elbow on the polished bar and replied, "Vodka, straight up. Are you going to join me?"

"I think I've had enough for one night," he said with a playful wink.

She giggled. "Oh, yeah. I forgot. After *one* drink you're sure to have a hangover in the morning."

He laughed. "I see you've got jokes." Smiling, he walked around the bar and reached for the bottle of vodka. "Glad to see you haven't lost your sense of humor."

"Never that. I might have lost a lot of things in my life, but laughter isn't one of them."

If Reese heard the bitterness in her response he gave no indication as he poured the clear liquid into a crystal glass and set it in front of her. Dominique brought it to her lips and tossed it back, emptying the glass in one gulp. She had a feeling she was going to need another to settle her nerves.

As she lowered the glass she noticed Reese was staring at her oddly, as if he was trying to figure out something. His eyes lingered at her painted red lips a moment, then followed the path down her throat.

"You look like a nicely wrapped Christmas present. Can I take your coat?" he asked, eyes dancing with mischief as he poured her another.

She winked playfully at him while her pulse quickened with uncontained excitement. "I thought you'd never ask." Taking a deep breath, she pushed away from the bar and stepped back just enough so Reese could see all of her. As soon as she was certain she had his undivided attention, Dominique unfastened the last button and allowed the long wool coat to fall to the floor.

"Damn!" he whistled under his breath. "Mrs. Claus ain't got nothin' on you."

She grinned, pleased by his response, and watched as his eyes perused the red corset, white miniskirt, candy-striped leggings, and the emerald green come-fuck-me shoes. The second she had spotted the outfit in the adult store she knew she had to have it, and screamed with joy when she discovered it was also available in plus sizes.

"Oh, wait!" she gasped as she suddenly reached down into the pocket of the coat and removed the Santa hat and placed it on her head. Grinning, Dominique perched a hand at her waist. "Now my costume is complete."

"Yes, it is," Reese cooed as his eyes traveled to the swell of her breasts above the top of her corset.

Dominique chuckled inwardly. There was no mistaking the lust burning in his eyes. And if she could see around the bar she was certain there would be evidence of how aroused he was throbbing at his crotch. Their attraction had always been instant, and the sex that usually followed had always been explosive.

"So is this what you meant by *talking*?"

"Talking is only the beginning," Dominique said with a nervous laugh. "This weekend is really about unanswered questions, renewing friendships, or finally finding closure."

"Closure, huh?" Reese said, as if he didn't believe her. "What if we decide we don't want things to end? It was good between us once, which means it can be good between us again."

Dominique swallowed and forced herself to stay in control. "Anything is possible. Although, I'm the first to admit that with ending the way it did, our friendship wasn't as strong as we both thought it was."

"Really?" he said with a hint of amusement. "I guess, we'll have to see about that." Before she had a chance to respond, Reese rounded the length of the bar and was heading in her direction. Dominique's nipples tingled with anticipation, but she snapped out of it before he could reach her.

"Not so fast, sexy," she said, holding out a hand that landing right smack at the center of Reese's amazing chest. Tonight they were doing things her way, and at her pace. She had to reel him in slowly in order for her plan to work.

His brow quirked. "I thought you wanted to talk?"

"I was thinking that before we… talk…How about a game of pool?" she asked innocently. "In fact, I'd like to place a wager."

His appreciative eyes traveled the length of her before he asked, "What kind of wager?"

With newfound determination, she replied, "If I win… I want you to remove all of your apprehensions… forget about the past, and spend the night with me." It wasn't the weekend, but one night might be all she needed to get in his bed and his heart.

There was a long pregnant pause, then something

flickered in Reese's eyes and his mouth twitched. "And what do I get if I win?" he asked, and Dominique realized her heart was beating just a little too hard.

"If you win… I will bid you farewell and never bother you again." Without waiting for an answer she turned away and walked over to the far corner, adding a little extra wiggle to her hips. She could feel his smothering gaze following her every move.

Dominique selected a stick from those mounted on the wall, then racked the balls while Reese stepped around her and selected his own pool cue. As he passed, his hand brushed her shoulder, causing her to grit her teeth to control the shudder that gripped her. No way was she surrendering this early in the game.

She arched her back and lifted her bottom in the air a bit more. Clearing her throat, she drew the stick back, then jerked forward, executing a perfect break that dropped three stripes. She eyed her options on the table, doing some quick mental calculations. Reese had taught her to play years ago. He'd taught her a lot of things. More things than she cared to think about with the silk panties stroking her kitty with every move. Keeping her mind on the task at hand was hard enough as it was. Yet there was no mistaking that Reese had been her best friend. Her first lover.

Not just the first. The best. Sure, in the last six months, she had tried dating other men, hoping it would help her get over him, but no one came even remotely close to what she'd had with Reese Beaumont. No one made her heart pound or her mouth go dry with a single touch.

Dominique mused over the erotic thoughts for a few more lingering moment as she lined up her next shot. She then leaned forward, knowing she was giving Reese a perfect view of her perky twins as they rose above the scandalous neckline of her cinching corset. Slowly, Dominique lifted her gaze to see if Reese had noticed.

Oh, yeah, he'd noticed.

His dark sable eyes were fastened on the swell of her breasts and blazed with so much heat it made her skin sizzle, her kitty clench, and her breath quiver.

Remember the wager!

Forcing her gaze to the table, Dominique centered her attention on the shot. Ordinarily, she was a beast at pool, but as the game continued she realized that tonight... tonight she couldn't focus. Instead, her brain was a scattered mess and her aim was off. As a result, on her next shot she hit one of his balls and dropped it into the corner pocket. Reese laughed while she cussed under her breath.

"'Preciate the help, sexy," he murmured, then slid past her, his body gently caressing her arm, igniting another slow burn.

Within seconds, he'd studied the table, aimed, then fired, sinking three more balls.

Her heart sank. Unless her luck changed she was minutes away from losing the game and possibly her last chance to win Reese back.

Reese lined up his next shot, but before taking it he paused and looked over his left shoulder. "Babe, what do you think about raising the stakes?"

Her breath caught. There was no mistaking the challenge in his voice. The lustful look that flashed in his dark eyes sparked something carnal deep inside her and had her whole body on full alert. "Raising it how?" she dared to ask.

"How about... if I win, before you bid farewell... you spend the entire weekend in my bed?"

Dominique drew in a slow nervous breath. Had he just offered to give her what she wanted? An insatiable weekend satisfying each other's needs? The penetrating look burning from his beautiful eyes spoke volumes and confirmed any of her uncertainties. She had no idea what had caused him to change his mind since her departure at the club, but whatever it was his intentions were now clear.

He wanted her and planned on having her.

The mere thought sent her pulse into warp speed. Reese took another shot, sank a ball, then look at her as if he'd been waiting for a response. Did he really think they could have a conversation when she was this sexually worked up?

She nodded, then tried to focus. Tried to think of something other than Reese lifting her up onto the edge of the bar, dragging her panties down to her ankle and taking her. Hard and fast. The way he used to when they were both so aroused nothing else would satisfy them.

Dominique took a seat because Reese was on a roll and it seemed a lost cause for her. Besides, her body was shuddering at the thought of him lying between her legs again.

She looked over at the table and her eyes locked with Reese over the tip of the cue stick. His probing expression became dark, intense, and smothering with lust.

And Dominique nearly fell off the chair.

Reese returned his focus to his shot. For a moment, Dominique was sidetracked by him. He was so damn sexy, with shoulders like a linebacker and a chest that could put any body builder to shame. Reese was gorgeous, with powerful hips and thighs, and even now she could feel his magnificent body pumping inside her. Goodness! She suddenly felt hot and shifted uncomfortably on the stool. In a matter of hours he would be exactly where she had been dreaming about for more than twelve months. Where he belonged.

She stared down at the table. Reese aimed and sent the last ball flying into the corner, followed by the eight ball.

The second he straightened and tossed the cue stick onto the pool table, she knew the moment had finally come.

Reese moved behind her, wrapped his arms around her waist, then eased close to her ear. "Dom..."

"Reese," she breathed and leaned back, offering herself to him. "Yes?" His lips brushed her cheek, ear, and neck.

The heat from his warm mouth seeped inside her, heating her. "I take it we're done playing pool?" she whispered.

"Yep," he managed between kisses as he lifted her off the stool and into his arms. "All done."

And not a moment too soon. At the feel of his warm tongue, she felt herself sagging against him, weakening by his mere touch. It had always been that way between them. Wild and deliciously explosive. Where Reese was involved, her body had a mind of its own.

Dominique sighed as her eyelids fluttered shut, "Now what?" she asked as if she didn't already know. She hadn't worn that costume for nothing, and Reese knew her too well to be fooled.

"Now it's time for some real fun." His hand skimmed lightly along her spine, along the satin laces of her corset. Her lips parted and her breath came quickly, lifting her breasts in small unsteady movements.

"What could be more fun than pool?" she purred. Dominique felt his fingers slip underneath the spaghetti straps, then slide them down her shoulders. "Huh? Tell me."

His voice vibrated with arousal as he replied, "I think

I can come up with something."

* * *

Reese massaged her bare shoulders and slid his hands down her arms, and Dominique jerked in response. "Still ticklish?" he said, and chuckled when she shrugged a single shoulder.

"I guess not much has changed," she purred.

He licked his lips. "That's actually a good thing, because you don't need to change a thing." He stepped forward and closed the gap, pressing his erection against her belly.

"Really?" she said, searching his eyes as if she didn't believe him.

"Absolutely." As far as he was concerned, she was perfect the way she was. He allowed his hands to move over the lace at the center of her back, down to her narrow waist, then skimmed across the luscious swell of her ass.

Thoughts of carrying her to the bedroom invaded his mind, making his dick pulse painfully with need. But he forced himself to be patient and savor the moment.

"Sweetheart, I'm dying to take this corset off you." He already knew the swell and softness of her breasts and the shade of chocolate that colored her nipples, but that didn't stop him from wanting to see them again.

Her eyes sparkled. "What's stopping you?"

"That's all I needed to hear," he murmured as his fingers looked for a knot to release the top. After several failed attempts he said in a low growl, "How the hell do I get this thing off?"

Her eyes sparkled with amusement. "It fastens in the front." She reached up at her cleavage and folded back the material, and he saw the long line of hook-and-eye fastenings that held the corset together. "See?"

Nodding, Reese reached up and attempted to work at the tiny hooks for several seconds before he finally growled with frustration. "Fuck it." He grasped the lace and gave a hard yank, ripping the material from top to bottom.

"Reese!" Dominique shrieked with disbelief as he tossed the corset across the room.

"Baby, I'll buy you another one," he murmured while his eyes feasted at her generous cleavage.. Desire coursed through him, landing right smack at his erection, which strained against the front of his jeans. Her breasts were large, firm, and her nipples were like morsels of semi-sweet chocolate.

"You see something you like?" Dominique teased as she shifted, spreading her thighs apart. It was a provocative stance, made all the more arousing by the sexy get-up she was wearing—the tiny red skirt, thigh-high stockings and sexy heels.

And those damn *Naughty* panties.

He had caught a glimpse when she bent over the table to shoot. Oh, he knew what was beneath that little skirt, a luscious chocolate ass, and he couldn't wait to peel it away from her skin. Reese bit back a growl as he felt an overwhelming need to have her right then and there.

"That corset was brand new," she proclaimed with a playful pout.

He smiled. "I'll buy you two more. Hell, I'll order them directly from Paris if you'd like."

Dominique giggled. "I'm going to hold you to it."

Reese stepped forward and allowed his hand to graze the flesh at her midsection and dipped into the curve of her waist. "You didn't want me to waste time unwrapping my Christmas present, did you?"

"I guess you do have a point," she whispered.

Reaching up, his fingers slid along her collarbone and

then down to hold the weight of her large, firm breasts. While he stared into her eyes, his fingers stimulated her breasts and circled her nipples. "No apprehensions, remember? Just you and me sharing my bed all weekend, right?"

"Yes... y-you're right," she shivered.

"Damn, right," he growled as he took a nipple between his fingers and squeezed. "No point in pretending. You wouldn't have come looking for me tonight if you didn't want the same thing I want."

"I came to talk," she rebutted, her breath coming quick and urgent.

"We'll talk later. Right now I need to make love to you," he muttered, fanning her lips with his breath.

Dominique gave him a saucy grin, then curled her hand behind his head and brought his mouth down to her own. His tongue danced with hers as the kiss deepened. Her teeth caught her lower lip while Reese pinched her nipple between his fingers.

"You're not playing fair!" she cried out. "Reese..., you know that's my spot."

"Haven't you heard? All's fair in love and war." He fondled her breasts and grew increasingly aroused by each helpless cry that rose from her throat. Leaning against her, Reese pressed her weight against the pool table. "You started this, and I have every intention of finishing. Now, turn around."

She was eagerly obedient. In record time Dominique turned around, sticking her ass in the air, and braced her weight against the table, using her hand. Her thighs were parted and her legs looked incredible in those sexy-ass shoes. Reese lifted the skirt up over her hips, and at the sight of her he cussed under his breath.

"Damn, look at all that ass." It was round, tight and delicious enough that he had a sudden craving to sink his teeth into it.

His hands left her hips and kneaded her ass. Dominique moaned and rocked against the table. "See what you've been missing?" she teased.

"Yes, Lawd!" he laughed, then sank to his knees before her parted legs.

"Remember that time we snuck into my uncle Roger's office and made love on his desk?" he asked as his lips grazed her smooth skin. His fingers skimmed lower still and slid slightly forward until he grazed the satin fabric covering her mound.

Shakily, she replied, "How could I forget? You had me bent over his desk just like this."

"Tell me you didn't like it?" Reese asked with his warm breath caressing her naked skin.

"Oh, no," she moaned. "I loved it."

The memory elicited a low groan from him. "Do you remember how many times I made you come that night?" he asked as he continued to tease her. The contact made her shiver breathless.

"God, yessss, I remember."

It was the night he had discovered her g-spot. Reese was beyond aroused. He closed his eyes and tried to summon his control. He wanted to touch and taste before sliding his penis inside. He intended to make her feel as turned on as he did.

Reaching up, he grabbed the satin fabric, and with one yank ripped the panties impatiently from her body.

"I hope you plan to replace that as well," she cooed.

"Sweetheart, we can spend the entire weekend at Victoria's Secret if you want, but right now I need to touch you."

Reaching up, he stroked all the way down to her feminine folds. His thumbs slid along her seam and he threaded his fingers through the soft curls with a gentle touch. When he reached her clit he heard Dominique's breath hitch.

"You're so wet," he whispered as he touched her butt cheeks, spreading them slightly apart so he could get a better look at the moist pink flesh right smack in front of him. Her body trembled under his touch and he noticed how she teetered a bit on her heels.

"You okay?" he asked as his fingers traveled down along her moistened folds and slipped inside just enough to make her squirm against his finger.

"Yes," she moaned and rocked her hips, drawing him deeper.

"Yes, what?" he coaxed, and he dipped his finger in and out of her wet heat.

"Yes, that feels good... so good."

When he added a second finger, a long moan escaped her lips. "This is what you've been wanting, isn't it?"

She wiggled and moved with the rhythm of his thrusts. "Yes... Oooh, yes."

He had a steady grip on her thigh, holding her in place. She was so wet his finger made squishy sounds as he delved in and out. Heat pulled and throbbed at his crotch and he had to grit his teeth because what he wanted to do was drag down his zipper and ease his dick inside.

Her soft whimpers aroused him. Her sweet scent ignited him, and he doubted how much longer he could hold out. He rubbed her clit with his thumb, slowly at first, then with purpose, and slid another finger inside her.

"Open your legs," he commanded gently.

She spread her thighs wider, granting him complete access.

"Good girl," he whispered, then leaned forward and pressed his mouth to her most intimate place. Dominique sucked in air at the first touch of Reese's lips. And when he started licking her with his tongue, she moaned aloud.

"Yes!" Dominique cried with appreciation as he licked again and again. "That feels won-der-ful."

He couldn't resist a smile as he swiped his tongue along the hood of her clit, loving the way she shivered with pleasure. She tasted delicious and smelled heavenly. Dominique withered in frustration while his fingers explored.

Soft whimpers continued to slip from her lips as he indulged, taking his sweet time. While he savored the taste of her essence on his tongue he remembered all the years he'd spent satisfying their needs, making sure Dominique had been completely spent and thoroughly made love to before he took care of his own needs.

He had twelve months of pent-up frustration, so he was more than ready.

Although Reese was aroused and eager to fuck her, he was determined to hold out until the thought of not being inside her was unbearable. He'd been with Dominique enough years to know just how much pressure to apply to her clit and when it was time to ease back.

"Please, Reese. Make love to me," she begged.

"Hold tight, baby. I'm not finished with you yet." Confidently, he teased and demanded her undivided attention as he slowly drew her closer to an orgasm that he knew was only seconds away. The thought made his groin tighten to an almost painful degree.

"Feel good?" he asked, his breath warming her tender flesh.

"Do you have to ask?" she whimpered with a hint of frustration. "Oh! Please just don't stop."

"I don't intend to."

Reese's tongue traveled along her folds, then he

reached up and slid two fingers deeper and deeper, to point of insanity. And when he finally applied pressure to her g-spot, he felt her body begin to shudder.

"Come for me, Dominique." With each thrust her body rocked slightly, causing her nipples to rub against the red felt covering the pool table. He felt her quiver inside and contract around him. "Reese!" she cried on a sharp breath as an orgasm rocked her body, but Reese didn't stop his pleasurable assault until he had drawn out every last moan from her.

While Dominique struggled to find her breath, Reese gave her one final kiss, then rose to his feet, waiting patiently. Dominique looked over her shoulder and swallowed deeply at what she saw. Reese stroked his hand along the dip in her back as he watched her, eyes flooded with pleasure, the heavy throbbing between his thighs pounded viciously.

Reese's need to be buried deep inside her was so intense his legs shook. "You ready for me?" he asked as he pulled his shirt over his head and reached for the fly on his jeans.

She simply nodded.

Grinning, he removed protection from his pocket, then lowered the zipper. His jeans fell to the floor in a rush, followed by his boxers. With his eyes focused on her sweet brown ass, he slowly rolled on the condom and hissed against the torturous ache that wouldn't be satisfied until he slid inside. Using one hand he spread her thighs and lifted her ass up, granting him better access. With a loud groan he sank into her warm depth while he placed his other hand to the small of her back to help steady her.

"Awww," he moaned between his teeth.

"Yes... yes..." she moaned.

Dominique held on to the edge of the table for

leverage as she pushed back against him, and Reese thought he was going to die from the pleasure. The pace he set was hard and fast. He pulled out of her and then thrust back inside. As wet as she was, he wasn't sure how long he could hold out.

"Harder, Reese," she moaned.

Gripping her hips, Reese increased the tempo.

"Yes… just like that, Reese. Just like that," she panted. As he pumped at a frantic rhythm, she moaned and begged for more. It was all he could do to keep from coming. She was so hot and wet he was on the verge of exploding.

"Come with me," she said in a strained voice.

"Let me know when," he managed.

"Now. Oh God. Reese… now!'"

She shuddered, then contracted, gripping his erection like a tight fist, shaking him to the core. Reese pumped wildly, no longer able to control his reaction. He pounded hard against her ass, causing his sac to slap against her swollen lips. Dominique screamed his name in a combination of pleasure and pain. She milked him, drawing out every last bit of pleasure until his body went limp on top of hers.

"Damn," he hissed as he fought to catch his breath, his heart pounding steadily against her back.

"My words exactly," Dominique replied, with laughter flavoring her voice.

Reese slowly eased from inside her and stared down, noting how beautiful she looked lying across the pool table, breathing heavily.

"Come on." His hands circled her waist as he eased her off the table and lifted her into his arms. He could feel her heart pounding beneath her breasts.

Her brow quirked. "Where are you taking me?"

"To bed. I meant what I said. This weekend is mine,"

he said possessively as he moved purposefully down the hall.

Chapter Five

Why did things always feel so right when we were together?

Still half sleep, Reese opened his eyes lazily and stared at the beauty lying peacefully beneath the white cotton sheets. He tried not to think about anything beyond the next few days, but his mind was already thinking about so much more.

When he had agreed to talk to Dominique, he'd really thought she'd meant spending the rest of the evening reliving the events that had led up to that night, and the bitterness that that had colored the last twelve months that followed. He'd had no idea Dominique had meant body language. Not that he was complaining, he thought with a grin. She had always had a way of wiggling past any kind of resistance with a kiss, tongue, and those delightful costumes she loved enticing him with. What they didn't say with word their bodies said in a rhythm all their own. The fire still burning between them was scorching hot.

Reese rolled onto his back and gazed up at the ceiling in disbelief. All this time they'd lost filled with resentment and anger, yet now he vaguely remembered why he'd ended the relationship.

Stupid! Stupid!

How could he have ended a relationship based on an assumption? He hadn't even given Dominique a chance to explain, because as far as he was concerned the proof was in the photograph. But it was what it *didn't* show that proved how wrong he had been. All because of his anger and pride. What was even more disturbing was that if it hadn't been for Dominique's determination to fix things between them they would not have a second chance.

And what an opportunity it had been.

The second he'd opened the door and found her standing there in that long wool coat he knew there was no way he was leaving town without making love to her again. And now that he had, he wanted more.

Rolling back onto his side, he gazed down at her. His body went hard while his heart turned over in his chest.

How could he have forgotten how perfect they fit together? Staring down at her now, soft and naked in his bed, was everything he'd remembered it to be. In fact, making love to her again had surpassed his wildest dreams.

Reaching out, he lightly stroked her arm. Dominique moaned and shifted onto her back, exposing her large breasts. The sight caused a shudder of desire to course through him. He stared down at her dark nipples, remembering how they had tasted in his mouth. How often had he rolled a nipple around on his tongue while he pushed her thighs apart and then thrust inside her body? Just remembering how many times they'd made love last night was overwhelming. Once, twice, three times... hell he'd lost count. All that mattered was that he couldn't seem to get enough of being inside her, hearing her cry out his name and gasping as he brought them both to completion.

His rigid penis throbbed against her thigh. It had barely been three hours and already he wanted her again. How was it he had gone twelve months without and now had an insatiable appetite he couldn't seem to satisfy?

"I can't get enough of you," he groaned as he lowered his lips to a nipple and drew it between his lips.

He had once believed God had created her perfectly just for him. Now... now he wasn't sure what he believed since his mind was a big jumbled mess. But one thing was sure. They had unfinished business, and he owed it to both of them to spend the rest of the weekend figuring out what it was.

Starting now.

Dominique moaned as he sucked hungrily at her nipple. With his other hand he reached out and rolled the other between his fingertips until it was pebble hard.

"Reese," she murmured, still half asleep.

"Sorry, baby," he began. "But I need to be inside of you again." With that he grabbed a condom from the nightstand and quickly rolled it on. Opening her eyes, Dominique lay there waiting as he spread her legs apart and he pushed in with one hard thrust. He pounded inside her and she rocked her hips and met his thrusts. As far as he was concerned, no matter how hard he pumped it still wasn't deep enough. One thing was for sure. He wasn't going to be satisfied until she was back in his life as well as in his bed.

* * *

Dominique lifted her heavily lidded eyes, then rolled her head to the side and smiled. *Reese.* "I guess I wasn't dreaming."

He gave her that heart-throbbing smile. "Dreaming about what?"

"You... me... here... together." As soon as the last word came out of her mouth she regretted it. The last thing she wanted was for him to think she was making more of last night than it really was... even if she was. They weren't a couple, at least not yet. They had just agreed to spend the weekend together. Nothing more. But if the comment bothered him, Reese barely blinked as he reached out a hand and pushed the hair away from her forehead.

"No, babe. I'm really here."

Yes, he was for now, and she was glad she had a little more time to convince him they were meant to be together.

"What would you like to do today?" Reese asked,, kissing her cheek. She savored the feel and a shiver moved through her chest. She hated to ruin the mood, but some things couldn't be prevented.

She leaned back against her pillow and said, "We still need to talk about that night."

Dominique noticed the exact moment the defensive wall returned. With a groan he rolled over to his side of the bed. "I thought we already talked."

She flipped onto her side. "No... We made love. The one thing we've never had a problem with. Communication has always been a problem," she admitted.

He frowned. "Communication? Why you say that? We used to talk all the time."

"Yes, but not about the things that really mattered, and what happened that night mattered. It's practically destroyed us."

The annoying muscles at his jaw ticked, and ticked some more.

"We need to talk about what happened," she repeated, knowing she needed to be firm.

There was a long pause, and she could see the wheels turning in that stubborn head of his.

"I agree," he said, and she realized she had been holding her breath. "But not until after we have breakfast."

She searched his face, making sure it wasn't just another stall tactic, before she finally nodded. "Okay, but

I get the shower first!" She jumped out from under the covers and screamed as she slipped away from his grasp and onto the floor. Laughing playfully, he made a mad dash after her, and before she could secure the door he'd swooped an arm around her. She screamed with pleasure as he pulled her against him and lowered his mouth to hers.

"I'd rather we showered together," he murmured against her mouth, then pressed his lips against hers in an explosive kiss.

* * *

After their shower Reese went down to the kitchen to get breakfast and she moved into the bedroom to find something to put on. There was no way she could put on the outfit she had worn yesterday. She'd always gone out of her way to find something different and enticing. But it was all a game, and she usually went home afterward. Which is why she hadn't bothered bring a change of clothes. Something about looking at what she'd worn the night before in daylight always made her feel like a slut, even though Reese never seemed to mind.

She walked over to the bed and looked at the mess they had made and smiled. Last night was one for the record books. But it had always been like that between them. He'd swoop into town. They'd get together, and it would be hot and so damn arousing. Then he'd be gone again for another couple of weeks. She dug in his bag and spotted a UVA sweatshirt and slipped it over her head. It was like a warm dress, which would have to do. They'd been doing that for years, and even though deep down she had wanted more, she'd been content with what they had. Because she loved him. But now that she was older she wanted so much more, and it scared her.

The difference was that this time she refused to settle

for less than what she deserved. Her heart thudded against her ribs, making her dizzy with emotion. In the last twelve months nothing had changed. She still yearned for a committed relationship. She wanted a ring, babies, and a man lying in bed beside her. And there was only one man she wanted those things with. Reese.

The problem was that before the car accident Reese had been adamant that he didn't want those things, which was part of the reason they had been arguing in the first place. And unless he was willing to offer her more than just friends with benefits status this time around, then they would just have to go their separate ways after the party on Sunday.

* * *

Reese was taking bread from the toaster when he heard movement. He looked to his right to find her standing there. Dominique in the kitchen, hair damp, feet bare.

"I was about to come in and get you."

"Sorry, but it's not my fault. I didn't plan on taking a shower and then getting all dirty again," she said, and felt herself blushing at the things he had done to her in the master bathroom.

"Nothing wrong with a little loving in the morning," he said with a smile as he moved toward her.

"You're right. Nothing at all."

She tilted her head and met his mouth in a sweet kiss before he pulled back and said, "I see you found something to wear."

She struck a pose in his sweatshirt. "Sexy, huh?"

He laughed. "Absolutely. Now have a seat."

Smiling, she moved over to the small table and took a seat in front of a plate of scrambled eggs and bacon. Both were a little overcooked, but it was the thought that counted, he tried to convince himself. He placed a plate of toast at the center of the table, then carried over two mugs of coffee.

"Thanks."

"No problem. We worked up quite an appetite," he added with a boyish grin as he took the seat across from her.

"Sounds like someone is fishing for compliments."

"Not at all. You know I'm confident in my ability to please a woman."

"Well, this woman is quite pleased."

His grin widened. "How about going to see the James Patterson movie this afternoon?"

Dominique nodded. "Oooh! I'd like that," she managed between chews. While they both ate there was a long silence that grew increasingly uncomfortable with every passing second. Reese finally lowered his fork and spoke.

"I want to apologize for accusing you of trying to kill me."

*   *   *

Dominique searched his eyes and saw they were filled with remorse.

She shrugged like it was no big deal, but the apology meant a great deal. She had spent weeks feeling guilty for making such a stupid move.

"Thank you, but I was wrong for hitting you."

Briefly she closed her eyes as the night came flooding back. It had been the subject of her dreams for the last several months.

When Reese had appeared at her job that December evening, she had thought he had driven in to surprise her. It wasn't until he had whisked her away in his car that she discovered the real reason for his visit...

One year ago....

"So what's been going on?" Reese asked as he pulled his Escalade away from the hotel.

Dominique glanced over at him from the passenger seat, shrugged, then replied, "Nothing new. Same old, same old."

"The same old, same old? *Something* must be going on," he said with dangerous softness.

She swung around on the seat and regarded him curiously. "Something like what?"

Dominique swore she heard him mumble, "Never mind" before he asked, "How was the party?"

She studied Reese's profile, his expression blank. "What party?"

"What party?" he parroted. "The Christmas party."

Dominique bit her lip. There was something going on. Yet she wasn't sure what that something was. "It was cool, like every year. Why?" Her words were careful and controlled.

"Cool, huh? This year must have really been special," he persisted.

Okay, he was starting to get on her nerves. "Reese, what are you talking about?"

"I saw the photographs of you and Gabe at the party. Care to explain?"

"Explain what?" she asked, staring at him with bewilderment.

He gave a bitter laugh. "Wow! Really? You gotta ask?"

"I'm asking because I have no idea what you're getting at!" she snapped.

He glanced at her, his eyes dark and blank, yet she could hear the accusation. "I'm talking about the pictures of you and Gabe kissing at the party."

Her head whipped around. "Kissing? What

pictures?" she asked in confusion.

Reese tore his eyes from the road long enough to narrow his gaze at her. "The photos I saw on Facebook."

"Photographs?" she frowned. "I have no idea what you're talking about. And unless you're going to just tell me and quit playing this ridiculous game, you can take me home." The nerve of him picking her up for dinner, only to give her the third degree.

"Well, let me refresh your memory... you're at the hotel Christmas party...wearing that red dress... kissing that fool in the corner," he replied.

"You're crazy."

Sure, she had attended the party, and yes, Gabe Clements had been there as well. He was the head of security for the Beaumont Hotel. She started to shake her head and protest further, but then stopped when it suddenly hit her.

She *had* been kissing Gabe..., or rather, he had kissed her.

But only because he had caught her under the mistletoe, and in the spirit of the holiday season she had offered him her cheek. Only she hadn't turned her head before Gabe managed to plant one right smack on the lips. Somebody had taken a picture of the two of them. Dominique blinked as anger sank in, because if the photographer had stuck around a second longer they would have also caught her slapping Gabe across the face.

"*Are you serious*?" she said, voice filled with ridicule. "We were under the mistletoe."

Reese laughed. "Is that what we call it these days?" he asked sarcastically. "I didn't see a damn mistletoe. All I saw were the two of you locking lips." There was no disguising the jealousy in his voice, and she might have felt flattered if it hadn't been for the accusing tone.

Or the fact that she and Reese were nothing more than friends with benefits.

Fury raced through her veins and burst at her heart. "Is that why you drove down here to see?" she snapped. "Because someone told you they saw me kissing Gabe?" There was no point in him denying it. The answer was written all over his face. "And let me guess who posted the photo on Facebook? Was it Katherine?"

Oh, his silence was all she needed to confirm it. Katherine was the hotel's accounting manager, the same stuck-up bitch who'd been wanting Reese since forever. For some unknown reason she still hadn't gotten over him dumping her their sophomore year in high school and choosing Dominique instead. They were now in their thirties, and yet Katherine still looked for any chance to wiggle her skinny ass in front of Reese's face.

"Thanksgiving you mentioned you were ready for a serious relationship. So is that why you were with him?" he asked stiffly.

"Is *what* why I was with him?"

She noticed how Reese tensed and his body stilled as he replied, "You want a serious relationship with Gabe."

"That's not it, and you know it!"

"I don't know anything anymore," he said, voice laced with impatience as he dragged a hand along the length of his handsome face. "I told you, I care about you and I don't want any other woman but you, and you said you were okay with our relationship the way it was. Now I see photos of you kissing that asshole, Gabe."

Her mouth dropped in outrage as she realized what he was implying. "Do you know how ridiculous you sound? I never said I was okay with our relationship. I told you I wasn't going to sit around waiting for you to decide what it was you wanted. I am thirty years old. Most of my friends already have families. I want the same. And if it isn't with you, then I'll find a man who is ready for the same."

Reese lifted one shoulder and shrugged. "What's wrong with our relationship the way it is? We laugh and have fun... it works for us."

She folded her arms. "No... it works for you. Reese, you want your cake and eat it, too. Unfortunately, I want more."

"I didn't say I never wanted to settle down and have a family, I just said I loved the way things are between us right now. Who's to say I might not eventually change my mind and want more?" he replied, not bothering to look her way as he maneuvered his Escalade along the winding back road.

Dominique paused, heart beating with sudden desperation. "What make you think I'm going to sit around and wait for you to decide you want to marry me?"

"I never said I didn't want to marry you. Hell, if I ever decided to get married, that woman would be you. You're the only one I've ever cared about... Who I enjoy spending time with." He stopped and drew a long breath. "I'm just not sure if I want more than that right now."

They drove for several second in silence. Leaning her head back against the headrest, Dominique closed her eyes to calm her nerves. She was tired of this endless conversation. What was wrong with wanting love? "I'm sorry, but that's no longer acceptable," she said in a sad voice. There was no way she was going to continue settling for less.

"So what are you saying? You want to end our relationship?"

Dominique rolled her eyes and turned away. She stared out her window and decided to focus on the road instead of Reese and his self-centered behavior. They were heading down a narrow wooded road that was a shortcut to Rehoboth Beach where they were planning to have dinner at her favorite restaurant. Any other time she would have been excited about eating at Garbera's, but tonight she suddenly had no appetite.

"Dominique, I asked you a question. Is that what you want to do? End our relationship?"

Men could be such idiots. "You are ridiculous!" she cried as she swung her small handbag at him. "You are the only man I have ever loved, and yet you don't have a clue about women!" she added with another swing, this time hitting him square in the forehead.

"Ouch... watch it!" he yelled as he ducked out of her reach.

"I want to spend my life with you... only you, you idiot," she punctuated with each swing. "Just take me ... Reese, watch out for that deer!" she cried.

She watched in horror as he swerved, trying to avoid the doe, lost control and ran the car into a cluster of trees. The Escalade began to tumble down the hill toward the river. Dominique screamed and then she felt something slam against her forehead and everything went black.

Chapter Six

"You had every right to be mad at me for hitting you with my purse."

Dominique's comment brought Reese back to reality. There was no way he was letting her take the blame. "No, not like that. You didn't deserve that. What I said was cruel and uncalled for."

"Dom... it's over. Now stay the hell out of my life!"

The echo of his voice rang hollowly in his ears. He'd never forget the look of surprise followed by hurt on her lovely face before she started sobbing and hurried out of the hospital room. Even then he knew what he had said was hurtful, but he was too busy feeling sorry for himself to care. Had he really been that selfish?

"True. You were mean, but I knew you were hurting and scared. I walked away with a mild concussion while you were thrown and..." she paused to swallow. "...and your hand pinned under the vehicle. I should have understood what you were going through and stood by you. Instead, I did exactly as you said and stayed out of your life." Tears momentarily blurred her vision as her feelings got the better of her.

"Listen, Dominique. Who's to say I wouldn't have hit that deer, anyway?"

Immediately she shook her head. "You're just saying that to make me feel better."

"No, what I'm saying is it wasn't your fault."

"I don't believe that. Do you have any idea how long I blamed myself for what happened? I wanted so badly to talk you."

"No, it's my fault. I had no right, rushing down there, hassling you about a kiss." He dragged a hand down his face. "I don't know what it was, but when I saw that picture I went crazy."

Hearing himself saying those words warmed his heart, and Reese suddenly realized he missed Dominique more than he'd realized.

"Yeah, you were acting like a jealous boyfriend," she commented with an infectious grin.

"Exactly, and we both know I'm not your boyfriend. You and I are best friends with an unspoken understanding," he said by way of explanation, and punctuated it with a wink.

* * *

Dominique's heart sank. That was not at all what she'd wanted to hear. Part of her was hoping he would have realized how much she meant to him and how badly he wanted her in his life—exclusively.

"Yes, I guess you're right." She reached for her mug and took a sip to swallow the lump in her throat.

"So where do we go from here?" she heard him ask.

"I don't know," she replied, since it appeared that nothing about their relationship had changed.

Reese reached across the table and covered her hand with his. "I missed you, Dom. I didn't realize how much until last night. I was stupid and made a mistake, but with that said, I know I won't be happy until you are back in my life."

She looked up from her mug and said, "In what way...? Available whenever you decide to drop in town?" She didn't bother to hide the sarcasm from her voice.

He gave a tender grin. "I like what we had. We

traveled, laughed, talked, and enjoyed life. Dominique, you are my closest friend. I don't want to lose that."

She gave him a trembling smile. "You know that I want more than just a casual relationship with a man. Why is that so hard for you to understand?"

He stared at her. "I understand, and after seeing you with another man I have to admit I don't want you with anyone else but me."

"So let me get this straight… you don't want me, but you don't want me with anyone but you. I'm going home!" Abruptly she rose from the table and was prepared to leave the room. Leaping, from his seat, Reese caught her wrist, halting her departure.

"Dom," he began and swung her around so she was facing him. "What would ever make you think I don't want you? I've cared about you for along as I remember, and you know that there isn't anything I wouldn't do for you." He pressed his lips against her forehead and then her cheek. There was no denying that before the accident Reese had always been there for her. "I don't want to lose what we have."

As pathetic as it sounded, neither did she. She loved that man enough that she was willing to accept their relationship for what is was for the duration of the weekend, and then she would decide if she was ready to finally close that chapter in her life, accept the promotion, and move on.

"Then we'll just enjoy the time that we have together." She took a deep breath and then added quickly, "We'll make the most of this weekend."

He scowled and pulled back so she saw his eyes as he spoke. "I want more than just a weekend. I want you in my life. It's always been you, Dominique. I don't want any woman but you." With his lips pressed against her temple, she allowed her eyes to flutter shut.

That wasn't at all what she wanted. She'd rather Reese confessed his love and admitted that he was tired of playing games and was ready to settle down and spend his life with her. She could only hope he would realize how much they were meant to be together before she had to make a decision about her future.

There was no denying Reese wanted her. He just wasn't ready for marriage or children. Would he ever be? she thought with a sigh.

Men can't change who they are, her mother used to say. And in her heart she knew her mother had been right. Why was she trying to change someone who was obviously happy the way he was? She could only hope, but at least one thing could be said about Reese. He was honest.

* * *

"I think the movie was wonderful," she argued.

Reese held up his hands in surrender. "I didn't say the movie wasn't good. I just have a hard time seeing Tyler Perry as a detective when I'm used to seeing him in that dress."

Dominique responded with a peal of laughter.

Reese grinned. "I'm just saying…"

"I can see your point," she agreed with a laugh. "But it was still a good movie, and you have to admit he's an excellent actor."

They discussed the details of the movie as they moved out the theater. Reese reached for Dominique's hand and she felt the warmth radiating up her arm. This felt like old times, so she didn't want to make more of it than it was. Although this was the way it could always be if she decided to turn down the promotion and stay in Sheraton Beach.

Or if Reese would just realize what a prize she truly

was and commit to a serious relationship.

They were stepping out of the theatre when Dominique spotted one of the human resource assistants coming her way.

"Hey, did you just see the new Alex Cross movie?" she asked, blue eyes sparkling with anticipation.

Dominique nodded. "Oh, yeah, it was fabulous!"

Miley smiled, but Dominique noticed the way she kept looking from her to Reese.

"Hello, Miley," Reese said with a nod.

She gave a shy wave, then walked toward the ticket box. Even before they had made it into the parking lot Dominique looked over her shoulder and spotted Miley pulling out her cell phone.

"You know we're going to be the talk of the weekend," Reese said as he pulled into a vacant parking space along the curb. On the drive down Main Street with its mom-and-pop stores and cobblestone streets, Dominique saw several people she knew. They waved and looked at her curiously, or they just simply pointed in their direction.

She groaned. "What else is new around here?"

"True, that." Smiling down at her, Reese softly stroked her cheek and met the sparkle in her eyes, then turned off the car and stepped outside. Dominique watched him walk around the car, feeling her body heating up. She was almost afraid to blink because she might discover she had been dreaming. And she just wasn't ready for the afternoon to end.

Holding hands, they walked onto the recently shoveled sidewalk. Main Street had been transformed into a winter wonderland with Christmas lighting, wreaths hanging from the front doors of all the stores and lampposts that had been covered in red and white garlands.

They stepped into Clarence's Chicken &Fish where the décor was red-and-white check and R&B memorabilia. The hostess escorted them to a booth near the window. Reese waited until she left to greet more customers coming through the door before he asked, "Does it bother you?"

Dominique glanced up from the menu. "Does what bother me?" she asked chocolate eyes sparkling with curiosity.

"That folks are talking about us?" he asked and leaned back on the bench, legs spread wide.

She gave him a long thoughtful look before she finally shrugged. "Why should it bother me? We are two friends spending the weekend together. What's the big deal about that?"

She was right, so why did her answer bother him? Truth be told, there wasn't supposed to be anything more going on than the two of them spending an insatiable weekend together. Nothing more. So why did he feel a rumble at the pit of his stomach that hinted at something else? Reconciliation, maybe? He wasn't sure what it was, or if he was even ready to try and define it. All he knew was that he was enjoying having her back in his life, even if it was temporary. He tried to convince himself that if nothing more came of the weekend than their parting as friends, he would return home feeling at least somewhat satisfied.

Liar!

He sat up on the bench and forced a smile. "Absolutely, and I must say I am enjoying every moment of it."

She grinned, showing off her beautiful smile. "So am I."

They stopped talking long enough to order the catfish special. The restaurant had been around for generations and was a popular spot. Once it had been featured in Delaware Magazine, and weekends lines were seen wrapped around the building.

"Have you seen Bianca since you got here?" she asked, referring to his first cousin who was married to London Brown, the owner of the famous franchise with several locations from here to Philadelphia.

He shook his head. "No. I'll see her at the party tomorrow. I'd much rather spend my time with you."

She stared over at him and their eyes locked. Something in their depth made his heart pound against his chest. He missed her more than he even knew. And he didn't want to lose her again.

"What do you have planned for Christmas?" he asked.

"I'm picking Brittany up from the airport on Monday. We're having dinner with my uncle, like always." She looked up at him. "What about you?"

"The usual. Mama is having her annual Christmas party and Dad's out looking for the perfect Christmas tree. All of us will be home. Sage is back from Germany."

"So tell me, honestly... How have you been managing?" she heard herself say, and when his smile vanished she wished she could take it back.

Reese held his hand out in front of him and gazed down at the long scars on his fingers where his knuckles had been crushed.

"I can still use my hand, with limitations." He raised the fork to demonstrate and she noticed that even though he could hold the instrument, his index finger had almost no mobility.

Dominique reached out and caressed his hand, wanting to let him know it was okay. His deformed hand didn't bother her at all.

"Can you feel that?" she asked.

His gaze locked with hers. "Not there, but I definitely feel it somewhere else."

She jerked her hand away. "You're nasty," she laughed, and he joined in. She loved the way his face lit up and the sadness disappeared. This was the Reese Beaumont she knew and loved. Funny, and with sex always on his mind. Just thinking about sex had her body heating up of thoughts of this morning in the shower.

"Sheyna told me you're speaking at a conference at the University of Delaware on Monday?"

He nodded, and she loved the way his eyes lit up at the mention of his chosen profession. "I'm conducting a lecture on coronary risk factors and clinical trials to reduce atherosclerosis."

Playfully, she rolled her eyes. "What is atherosclerosis? And before you start, speak in a language that regular folks can understand," she teased, because Reese had a terrible habit of talking way over her head.

He smiled. "Atherosclerosis is hardening of a blood vessel from a build-up of fatty deposits and cholesterol that can slow and even stop blood flow. It can cause coronary heart diseases and strokes."

She gave him a thoughtful look. "So in other words it's caused by eating fried greasy food like we're about to eat?"

Reese tossed his head back with laughter. "Exactly." While they waited for their food, he talked in detail about his recent research and the clinical trials they were conducting at the University of Maryland. Dominique always loved hearing him talk about his work, even though half the time she didn't understand a word of it.

The waitress returned with their food. Dominique held out her hands. Reese placed his in hers and they bowed their heads while she said grace.

Reese took a bit of his fish before asking, "When are you supposed to give Jace an answer about the promotion?"

His questioned pulled her away from her thoughts. "By Friday."

He nodded and she could see the wheels in his head turning.

"What?"

"I'm just curious. Why the hesitation when this is something that you've always wanted?"

No. What I have always wanted was you.

"I always dreamed I would get promoted right here in Delaware, not hundreds of miles of way from my friends and family."

"You know they'd never want to stand in your way," he said tenderly.

"True. But I need to make sure it's a good move because I can't just come home whenever I want."

I can't see you when I want.

She searched his eyes, hoping to see something that said he didn't want her to move so far away, but his expression was blank and his thoughts too hard to read.

Dominique stabbed a fry with her fork. "I have to admit this is the opportunity of a lifetime. I'm finally going to have my own department."

"How many people?" he asked between chews.

"Fifteen in my department, and more than three hundred employees total at the hotel, including part-time staff."

His brow rose. "Nice."

Dominique nodded. "I know, right? Jace and I flew down two months ago after the manager quit, and I fell in love with Waikiki," she said gleefully.

"I can understand. I heard the beach is beautiful," he said, resting his elbows on the table. "That's one place I haven't had a chance to visit."

"Maybe you'll come visit me when I move there. That's if I decide to take the job," she added in a rush of words.

His expression became serious. "I get the feeling you already have."

She stalled. Was it really that obvious how badly she wanted the position? Deep down maybe she was only fooling herself.

"I'd be lying if I didn't say I don't want to see you go."

She looked down at his hand them gave a sad smile. "If I take the job I won't be leaving until after the holidays."

He stared at her. "It won't be the same here without you."

Dominique completely understood. Being without him for twelve months had been unbearable. She could only imagine how she would feel being miles away. All he had to do was ask her to stay and be his wife and she wouldn't hesitate to pass up the promotion.

She forced a smile. "Why don't we just enjoy this weekend while it lasts? I haven't made any decisions, so there's no point in spoiling the mood."

He scowled and said, "Yes, you're right."

Reaching over the table, she entwined her fingers with his. "I promise, when I make a decision you'll be the first person to know."

* * *

Finished with their food, they each ordered the sweet potato cheesecake. Reese settled back on the bench and was unable to keep his eyes off of Dominique as she dug into her pie.

Clarence's was extremely busy for a Saturday

evening, with dozens of shoppers who had been patronizing the shops up and down Main Street, stopping in for a delicious meal before returning home. Their dinner conversation was filled with laughter and reminiscing over the years while Christmas Carolers sang merry songs right outside the picture window.

It was nice. Really nice. But nothing made Reese happier than sitting across the table from Dominique, staring at her in skinny jeans and a pink V-neck sweater that not only complemented her complexion but showcased her tantalizing curves.

"Oh, my goodness! I'm sitting here stuffing my face," she said when she caught him staring. "This pie is one of my biggest addictions this time of year."

"Just think, you won't be able to get this in Honolulu," Reese made it his business to point out. He knew he was itching to convince her to stay, and he had no right. But Dominique needed to make a decision about the position by Friday so he couldn't afford to avoid the possibility of her moving over a thousand miles away. If he wanted any shot of being a regular fixture in her life, he needed to act fast. "Christmas won't be the same."

"You're right. It won't," she confessed between chews.

"There won't even be any snow."

She sat forward on her chair. "You know… I hadn't thought about that. Oh, my goodness! Warm sunshine in the winter. That would definitely take getting used to."

"And nothing beats shopping on Main Street." The small beach town was popular for its unique gifts.

Dominique stopped chewing and pointed her fork at him. "I know what you're up to."

He gave her an innocent look. "I'm not up to anything."

"Yes, you are. You're trying to convince me not to take the job."

"No I ... "

She cut him off. "Yes, you are. I supported your decision to leave Richmond and accept a position in Baltimore."

"Yeah, but my moving to Bowie meant I was closer to you."

She reached for her coffee and peered at him over the rim, regarding him curiously. "So this is about me moving far away."

"Hell, yeah," Reese responded with slight laughter. "Now that I have you back in my life, I don't want you to go."

Dominique shook her head. "That sounds kind of selfish to me."

He shrugged. "I'm selfish when it comes to you. I'll admit that."

Laughing, she shook her head again. "You are too much. When the time comes, I'll make my decision. If I need advice, I'll ask for it."

"So let me ask you this... if I hadn't come down this weekend, would you have taken the job and moved before we'd even had a chance to talk?"

Dominique took a moment to chew and consider his question before saying, "We wouldn't have had any reason to talk, now, would we? As far as you were concerned, our relationship was over, and as much as it hurt I would have had to just find a way to close that chapter of my life on my own."

Seeing her again, he was glad he had come down. Maybe it was meant to happen this way. In some ways they both seemed older and wiser.

"But since you're here, we were able to put all our cards on the table. Now we'll both know where we stand.

I've got my friend back and that means more to me than anything else," she said.

"Same here," he heard himself say, and met her smile.

"Now it's on to new beginnings and getting everything we want in life," she said, waving her fork in the air.

It was becoming pretty clear that Dominique knew what she wanted and nothing was going to influence her decision to have all or nothing. She was planning to start a new life somewhere else, far away from him.

"What's Brittany think about all this?" He was depending on the teenager to be on his side.

"She's excited about inheriting my Honda Accord when I leave. As part of my offer, I'll get a new car," she explained.

He'd have to make sure he thanked good old cousin Jace for sweetening the pot.

As she talked about the package that she had been offered Reese realized more and more that there was a tremendous possibility this was going to happen.

All the years they had talked about their hopes and dreams, and here she had been managing her own department. Now the promotion was becoming a reality. Right before his eyes she had grown into a beautiful, mature woman. She had changed, and starting fresh somewhere new meant her new life would have absolutely nothing to do with him.

Reese shifted on his seat and their eyes met, and this time it wasn't solely about physical attraction. It was about the years they had spent sharing their lives together.

How could he live without her?

"Would you like anything else?" a cute waitress asked as she cleared their empty plates.

He glanced over at Dominique, who shook her head.

"You can pay me when you're ready." She lowered the bill to the table and Reese scooped it up a second before Dominique could reach for it.

"You know better than that," he scolded. "Jolene would have my behind," he said, referring to his mother. She believed all men should treat women like queens, and that meant never letting them pay for a thing.

"So what do you want to do now?" he asked, wanting to make every second together count.

Her eyes twinkled and he knew that look anywhere. "Since we're already on Main Street..." she purposely allowed her musical voice to trail off. "How about doing a little Christmas shopping?"

Reese laughed. "Sure. Why not?" he was willing to do just about anything except let her go.

Chapter Seven

He didn't want to stand in her way. And yet he couldn't bear the thought of Dominique leaving him.

Not yet, Reese thought as he stared out the window. He had already lost twelve months with her, and he wasn't ready to lose any more time.

He shook his head angrily, at what he wasn't quite sure, but it wasn't fair. He had made a mistake and now he was paying for it. Dominique was getting everything she deserved. She was beautiful and intelligent and her passion for her work was so strong it shone from her eyes and could be heard in her voice. And he wanted nothing more than to be happy for her, but that meant he would lose her again, and he wasn't ready to deal with that. If he had his choice, he wouldn't have to deal with it at all.

For the first time he wanted more than stolen moments together and weekend rendezvous. He wanted a relationship with her. And yet it still wasn't enough for her. Seeing her again made him want her again, and the twelve months they had been apart caused him to hunger for so much more. It was easy to say he didn't want her in his life when there was distance between them. But with her right here, he couldn't imagine her anywhere but standing right before him.

All you have to do is offer her a future with you.

He didn't want to hurt her by promising something he could not promise. As desperate as he was, he could have lied, but he had always prided himself on his honesty. But now she might be moving and he would lose her. He didn't like it. He didn't like it at all. But she wanted all or nothing, and he felt he couldn't give her that.

Couldn't she at least be happy that he was ready for a commitment? Why couldn't that be enough for now? Who was to say that eventually he wouldn't be ready for more? Only Dominique wasn't willing to take that risk. Why, dammit? He had never felt this way before. Didn't that count for something?

He turned away from the meeting and paced the length of the living room. He stared at the fire crackling in the oversized hearth in the middle of the wide open space. It was cold outside and the fire added just the right amount of warmth to the room. Although he could think of another way to heat up the room.

A sizzling jolt rushed through his veins. He would enjoy the rest of the weekend, and on Monday he would be on his way home and back to his simple life. No shackles, just the way he and his brothers liked it.

Right?

He and Dominique had two nights left, and he planned to make every second count.

* * *

Dominique stepped out of the bathroom, feeling clean and completely refreshed, wrapped in a thick terry towel. When she moved into the bedroom and found Reese missing, she padded down the hall into the living room, where she found him staring out the window.

"What are you looking at?" she asked, walking slowly toward him. The soles of her feet were cold against the wood floor.

Reese glanced over his shoulder and smiled. "How beautiful the snow looks coming down."

Dominique wrapped her arms around his waist and

glanced out the window. Outside was a blanket of white show. Christmas lights coming from the main house could be seen blinking through the gaps in the hedges.

"It's pretty," she whispered.

"And so are you."

She looked to her left and caught him staring at her. She gave him a goofy smile. "Thank you."

Leaning forward, Reese pressed his lips to her hair. "You smell good, too." He kissed her again. "Damn good."

She turned in his arms and allowed the towel to fall. "Oops! Did I do that?" she said with false modesty.

Reese stepped back, his eyes focused on her mouth. "Let me take a look at you." His eyes lowered and fastened on her breasts. "All of you."

Under his intense gaze her breathing was shaky. "I hope you like what I see?"

"I love everything about you." He stepped forward. "Do you forgive me, Dominique?"

She stepped backwards until she felt the cool wall at her naked back. "Yes, I forgive you." And she did. After the way he had dumped her, she swore there was no way she would ever take him back, but now she knew she had only been lying to herself. She loved him, and love made you do crazy things.

"Tonight I want you to forget about the last twelve months, the promotion and Hawaii, and focus on just you and me. Can you handle that?" Reese asked as he traced her lips with the tip of his index finger.

Dominique could handle his request and she could certainly enjoy another night of pleasure. All she had to do was keep her mind and her heart out of it, which wasn't going to be too hard to do, considering he hadn't made any promises to her beyond the weekend. "I think I can handle that."

"Good. How about a little game of Reese Says?"

She giggled. "We haven't played that in a while."

"I'll take that as a yes," he teased before his expression grew serious. "Let's begin. Reese says take off his pants."

Grinning, Dominique reached for the black leather belt, unfastened it, then popped the snap of his jeans and slowly lowered the zipper, allowing her fingers to graze the length of his delicious penis beneath the cotton briefs. She purposely stroked the head, loving the way he swelled into a rigid state in a matter of seconds.

"Reese didn't say touch him."

"No, but Dominique did," she purred, and she squeezed the head of his dick.

On a swift intake of air, he stilled. "Shit! Dom, don't," he warned.

A smile tugged the corner of her mouth. "Sorry, Dr. Reese." Parting the opening of his jeans, she slid her hands along his hips and around to his ass, where she slipped her hands underneath the band of his boxers and slid her fingers inside. "My hands seem to have a mind of their own." She squeezed his tight sculpted ass, a result of years of bicycling. She drew him close and arched her back so his erection throbbed against her belly. "Someone is happy to see me," she murmured.

"Damn, right," he murmured.

Dominique didn't even bother to stifle a moan when his pants fell to his ankles with a whoosh. Leaning forward, she pressed her kitty against his muscular thighs and wiggled her hips, enjoying the friction that made her clit twitch.

"I see you planning on teasing a brotha tonight."

"Who? Me?" With a wicked grin she lowered to her knees in a squat position, running her fingers along the front of his thighs, and feeling the muscles underneath his tight flesh flex beneath her touch. "I'm just following instructions. Now... lift your leg," she commanded.

"Yes, ma'am," he said with amusement.

Dominique helped him step out his pants while brushing her hands up the length of his calves. "Very good." She purred, then pressed her lips to his thighs. Oh, she had always loved the way he smelled and tasted. Her hand crept slowly up his leg, drawing closer to the beautiful erection that was putting a tent in his boxers. She reached inside the material to draw him out, and Reese groaned as her fingers closed over him. "What do we have here?" she teased.

Reese grabbed her hand, dragged her to her feet and pushed her hard against him. "Reese didn't say," he reminded.

"I—"

Reese lowered his mouth over hers in a fierce, hungry kiss that made her body heat with need. Wildly, he dragged his fingers through her hair, fisting and releasing the spiky strands. She held on, rocking on her heels, breathing heavily as she savored the kiss, until her entire body was on fire. And when he abruptly ended the kiss she cried out in disappointment.

"Enough of the games," he growled. "Now it's time to get down to business."

Reese pushed her gently against the wall, then raised her arms and pinned them to the solid surface. She stared up at him, eyes locked. His were filled with desire and something else. She wasn't sure what, but she wasn't about to make assumptions.

"Open your legs," he commanded, and she complied without hesitation. "Wider." He nudged her thighs further apart until she felt stretched, naked, and completely exposed.

"That's it. Damn, you are so beautiful," he

complimented while running a hand down her arm, across her hips and around to skim her ass. "So very beautiful. I don't think I could ever get tired of looking at you." His fingers traveled up her side and caressed the side of her breasts. "You like when I look at you, don't you?"

"Yes," she said barely above a whisper as his hands slid across her belly, working their way to the inside of her parted thighs.

"You also like it when I touch you," he told her with a soft confident laugh.

She shuddered when his fingers brushed the mound of soft curls, then delved slightly inside. Gasping, she tilted her pelvis and felt herself rocking, eager to feel the pleasure his fingers were sure to bring.

"You especially like it when I touch you here." Reese slid a long finger inside her warm sex. "No one knows your body like I do. And as far as I'm concerned, no one else ever will." Possessively, he slipped in a second finger. Dominique cried out and bucked against him. Reese drove deeper.

"Yesss," she moaned.

"Yes, what?" he coaxed.

"My body belongs to you. It's always been you. Only you," she managed between moans.

"Show me," he demanded. Reese drove his fingers deeper, stroking and caressing while his thumb pressed against her clit. "Show me by coming for me." As his fingers slid in and out, she rocked against him, moaning, panting, her large breasts bouncing with the rhythm of his moves.

"That's it, baby," he whispered, then lifted her left leg off the floor and wrapped it around his waist, granting him deeper penetration. Dominique leaned back against the wall as she wriggled along his fingers. "You like the way my fingers feel stroking that pussy?"

Lord, yes, she loved everything she was feeling, and yet it still wasn't enough. Dominique's moans grew louder as the moment of climax grew closer. Reese's fingers teased and tortured until she thought she would lose her mind. Then he took her clit between his thumb and forefinger and applied pressure.

"Answer me, Dominique."

She nodded, resting her head in the crook of his arm.

"I'm waiting."

"Yes," she panted. "I can't get enough of the way you make me feel."

Reese removed his fingers from inside of her and lowered her leg, ending her pleasure. She opened her eyes and studied his face with confusion. Taking her hand, Reese led her away from the wall and over to the recliner.

"Have a seat," he ordered.

Not sure where this was going, she took a seat and waited anxiously to see what happened next.

"Now spread your legs over the arms of the chair," he instructed, eyes twinkling with mischief.

Obediently, she lifted first one leg and then the other over the arms spreading her kitty wide and leaving it completely open for Reese to explore. Looking up, she watched the intense look in his eyes as he stared down at her pussy that throbbed with anticipation. His intent was obvious.

"Damn," he hissed under his breath, and she noticed the way he was licking his juicy lips while he lowered his boxers and kicked them away. His erection jutted with desire to be buried inside her. He walked over and reached down for his pants to retrieve a condom. He slipped it on and moved toward the chair.

Dominique's breath quickened as she watched. Reese

knelt and gripped the back of the chair on either side of her head. "Ready for me?"

Her eyes traveled down to his beautifully defined dick and back up to his face. "Yes, I'm ready."

Reese pushed his generous penis inside her, feeling her in entirety, then stalled and gazed at her. "You like that?"

"Dammit, you know I do," she whispered. Reese eased out to the head, then thrust back hard inside of her. "You know I do," she whimpered as she arched her pelvis forward, wanting more of him, desperate to feel all of him.

"No, I don't think you do." He withdrew to the tip again then plunged forward, again and again, pounding, driving her crazy with every passing second until he finally withdrew completely and she opened her eyes to find him staring down at her.

"In fact, I think you want me to stop." Reese wrapped his hands around the base of his erection, then rubbed the head along the sensitize folds of her kitty.

Overwhelming heat raged through her and she couldn't find the words to speak. "Please..."

"Please, what?" he encouraged as he continued to tease her with the tip. "What is it that you want?"

How in the world did Reese expect her to respond with the way he was arousing her kitty-cat? Each caress set her body on fire. She wanted — correction, needed — more. So much more. "Please, I ..." Her words caught in her throat as he leaned forward and captured a nipple, drawing it into his mouth. "I ... "

"You what? How will I know what you want if you don't tell me?" He asked, then suckled at her breast, tugging at the pearl with his teeth. "Tell me how you feel."

Dominique fisted her hands. He was demanding

more than just sex. He was trying to drag out everything she was thinking and feeling. Every emotion. Every want and need. Reese wanted to know if her body and heart still belonged to him, but she was holding back until she had a better understanding of what was happening between them. Because as far as she could tell, it was still nothing more than another weekend rendezvous.

Telling him how she felt required her surrender. To give her body, mind, and heart without fear of what pain may come when he left. To give and admit how she felt, when she knew he didn't feel the same way, would make her become like her mother. And as much as she loved Reese, that wasn't even an option. With Reese it had to be all or nothing. Two nights. That was all they had left, and she planned to make the best of it.

"Make love to me, Reese."

He brought his mouth to hers and she locked her arms loosely around his neck, then wrapped her legs around his hips. "Make love to me," she repeated as he stood and carried her to the bedroom.

* * *

"Lie down," she ordered as soon as Reese lowered her to the floor. "Now it's my turn to be in charge."

"Yes, ma'am." He obeyed her instructions and lay down on the bed, his head on the pillow, and closed his eyes.

"Good boy," she approved.

"Good boy? What am I now, a puppy?" His eyelids fluttered open with laughter.

She joined in. "Silly, now close your eyes and don't move."

Standing on the side of the bed, she stared down at him. She had every intention of climbing on and straddling his lap and immediately satisfying her craving for something sweet, but as she watched him lying there she had other ideas. He was on his back, chest rising and falling with each breath and his gorgeous penis thrusting in anticipation underneath her gaze. Damn, he was sexy, she thought as she licked her lips.

She moved over to the bed and fell onto her knees in front of him. His breathing sped up as she wrapped her hand around him. "*Shit,* Dom..."

Such a gorgeous dick, she thought as she stared down it. Smooth..., silky soft..., and delicious. Slowly she stroked the entire shaft to the sensitive tip and he nearly came up off the mattress. Dominique was truly enjoying being in control. "Now it's your turn to tell me what you want."

He looked up at her. "You know what I want."

"Yes, sweetheart, I believe I do," she purred and took his shaft into her mouth.

"*Awww,*" he groaned, then lifted his hips off the bed, forcing his dick deeper down her throat. Dominique moaned, loving the way his penis tickled the roof of her mouth. She had always enjoyed giving him head. She knew exactly which vein to run the tip of her tongue across, how to apply just the right amount of pressure when she sucked.

"You still haven't told me what you want," she said, slipping him out from between her lips and licking the head. Then she sucked the tip of it into her mouth again.

"I don't have to tell you because you already know." His hips jerked upward and he gritted his teeth. "You've always known."

Dominique gave a satisfied smile. *Yes, I guess I do. And I have.* The problem was that Reese had yet to realize she was the woman for him.

By the time she ran her tongue up his thick shaft and sucked, Reese was gasping for air, hands clenched into tight fists at his sides.

"Dom, ride me, dammit!" he begged. "I need to be

inside of you."

"If you insist," she cooed, and gave the tip of his erection a final kiss. It jerked, responding eagerly to her caress. She climbed onto him and straddled his lap, then reached down to guide his erection to the entrance to her kitty.

"Damn!" Reese gasped as she settled there, and rubbed the tip of him along her feminine folds, allowing him to feel how wet she was, how very much she wanted him.

"Dom, quit teasing!"

He didn't have to tell her twice. Dominique pushed down hard, feeling herself stretching to accommodate every masculine inch of him. And being the gentleman that he was, he arched and met her halfway.

"Ohhh," she moaned once he was buried to the hilt, and then she began to rock. Oh, was it good. She felt his entire length stroking her as she rolled her hips.

"Damn," he groaned and brought his hands to her waist, guiding her strokes. Whimpers slipped through her lips and her eyes rolled closed. It was heavenly with Reese lifting her up and bringing her down hard onto his dick.

"That's it baby, ride that dick," he chanted. "Keep riding…"

Dominique knew she wouldn't last long and was hoping he wouldn't either, a hope that was rewarded when he began to buck and pant and match her rhythm.

"Now, Dom," he gasped. "Come with me *now!"*

Reese pumped wildly inside her, guiding her up and down hard over his erection to the breaking point.

"Reese!" she cried as she came hard, gripping his erection, and seconds later she heard a fierce growl and his body contracted and jerked inside her.

She sagged against his chest and he had his arms around her, stroking her back as their breathing slowed and their heart rates returned to normal.

Reese planted light kisses to her face and neck, then whispered, "Rest up, because you're in for a long night."

Chapter Eight

The next morning Reese was in the kitchen making coffee when he heard knocking at the door. A frown marred his face as he padded in bare feet across the wooden floor to the front door and swung it open.

"Coffee... just what I needed."

He frowned as the mahogany beauty took the mug from his hand and sauntered into the house. "Actually, Sheyna... that coffee wasn't for you."

Her nose wrinkled. "Too bad. Now where are you hiding Dominique?" she asked, glancing down the hall.

Groaning, he shut the door. *I knew I should have stayed at the hotel.* "She's still sleeping," he informed her as he swung around and forced a grin.

Her chocolate eyes were trained on him as she took a cautious sip almost as if she had half expected the Colombian blend to be spiked. "It needs more sugar." She turned on the heels of her brown ankle-length boots with pom-poms swinging and headed into the kitchen.

Reese debated ignoring her and returning to the bedroom with Dominique to forewarn her, but Sheyna was just too smart for her own good.

"Can I speak to you a moment?" she called from the other room.

He grumbled under his breath but tucked his hands in his pockets and walked into the kitchen. He found Sheyna sitting on a stool in front of the island, jean-clad legs crossed and the right one swinging. He gave the room a quick once-over. She had already found the cream and sugar in the cabinet, but then he wasn't surprised. Sheyna had decorated every inch of the guest house. The apple décor of the room couldn't be anything but a woman's touch.

He leaned against the door frame. "How's the family reunion planning coming along?" Just as he thought she would, she immediately rolled her eyes.

"I'm so sick of your family changing the date! Do any of you have any idea how much work it takes to plan an event?" She didn't bother to wait for an answer. "Hell, no, none of you do. If this wasn't important to my father-in-law I would cancel the whole thing." She continued her tirade while he stood chuckling inwardly. Sheyna had been trying for the last year to coordinate a reunion with brothers Richard and Roger Beaumont and their families. Uncle Roger thought the festivities should be held in Sheraton Beach, while Reese's father wanted the event in Richmond.

Where's Jace?" he asked, changing the subject in hopes getting her out the house, fast.

"In the kitchen making breakfast. I told him I was coming over to invite the two of you to join us."

"Sounds good. I'll tell Dominique when she wakes," he replied, and pushed away from the counter in hopes she would leave.

"Uh-uh, not so fast Romeo." She gave him a penetrating stare. "So what's the deal, Reese?"

"What do you mean, what's the deal?" Like he didn't already know.

"I mean... what are your intentions? Dominique is one of our best employees. She's been given a wonderful opportunity to run the office in Hawaii, but because of *you* she won't commit. She deserves a chance to have a life... even if it isn't with you." He didn't miss the hint of discontent.

Reese rolled his eyes heavenward. *That's what you get for opening the door.*

"Sheyna, you know I would never do anything to intentionally hurt her."

She took another sip of coffee, then nodded. "True, but sometimes we hurt people unintentionally. Look what happened this past year, all because you *assumed* she was sleeping with someone she wasn't sleeping with."

He would have to remember never to tell his cousin anything again.

"Look, Reese... I know it isn't any of my business."

"Really? Well I'm glad to hear you at least figured that much out."

Her eyes narrowed. "Very funny." Reese laughed and her face relaxed, and Sheyna couldn't resist a giggle of her own. "You know I love you, Reese, just like the rest of the clan, but I also love Dominique like she's my sister. So I gotta look out for her."

Reese nodded. He had a lot of admiration for Sheyna. "I know you do."

"Then you understand why I have to say this. Stop it! You've been stringing her along for years."

His brow rose. "No, I haven't. We always had a mutual understanding."

"You don't believe that any more than I do. That girl has been playing along, when what she has always wanted was a commitment from you. And she is about to give up a promising opportunity for the chance to be with you."

Was that true? Had he been holding onto her all this time?

"You need to do the right thing. Either commit to that girl or leave her alone."

Sheyna was truly a fighter and the perfect

complement to his stubborn cousin Jace. Often he had watched the love between the two of them and often felt envious, and once he had wanted the same thing. Now he wasn't so sure. But even as that thought crossed his mind, he couldn't help but think about the insatiable night he and Dominique had just shared, and he couldn't help wondering if maybe he was being unfair to her.

"Don't worry. I'll definitely plan to do the right thing," He said with confidence.

A smirk curled her lips. "I'm glad to hear that."

While he made Dominique another cup of coffee, the two discussed the details of Jace's party. And then he heard another knock at the door.

"What is this, Grand Central Station?" he mumbled as he moved back toward the front of the house. Reese yanked open the door and watched with increasing frustration as four tall men stepped inside.

"Well, well, well, if it isn't the rest of the Force MDs." Sheyna was standing in the doorway with a hand propped at her hip.

"Good to see you too, Shay-Shay!" Rance scooped her up into his arms and spun her around until she screamed at him to put her down. The NBA player was almost two feet taller than she was.

Reese frowned. "I thought you weren't coming in until late this afternoon."

"Traffic was better than we thought," said Rush, the second youngest and most obnoxious of his brothers. He flopped down on the couch and reached for the remote.

"Don't y'all have rooms at the hotel?"

"Sure, but we wanted to come and see what you and Remy was up to."

Reese folded his arms across his chest. "I haven't seen him since he went home with some female the other night."

Sheyna gave a rude snort. "What else is new?"

"How come no one told me we had company?"

Reese whipped his head over his shoulder and found Dominique walking into the great room looking beautiful in his sweat shirt and clean boxers. She had been digging in his duffel bag again for something to wear. His appreciative gaze roamed over curves. The site of her caused a stirring in his jeans. She looked like a woman who had rested well after a night of passionate lovemaking. Her hair was messy and wild and her eyes were large with excitement.

Reese wasn't sure when he had ever seen her look more beautiful.

His heart turned over in his chest and he realized he was in trouble.

* * *

Dominique felt like she had just stepped onto the set of a calendar shoot. What had seemed like a large living space was now crowded with none other than the Force MDs. They had the kind of looks that were made for women to appreciate.

Rance, Reese, Rush and Ryce. The only ones missing were Remy and their sisters Sedona and Sage, also known as the car doctor, whom she heard had just opened her own auto body shop. As she eyed the men a soft smile curved her lips. They had always been like brothers to her.

Dominique couldn't help marveling at the striking resemblance between the brothers. All of them except Rush had dark sable eyes (his were hazel) and beautiful peanut butter brown skin and tall, handsome features.

"Whassup, Dom!" Ryce called out cheerfully, dropping a kiss to her cheek.

"Dominique... is that you?"

She noticed how Rush and Ryce exchanged glances and a smile.

Her smile deepened. "Yep... it's me. How have you been, Rance?"

Dominique noticed his smile didn't quite meet his dark, heavily hooded eyes. "I've been better," he replied as he walked over and gave her a warm embrace. Standing at seven-one, he lifted her slightly off the floor.

"You'll be back in the game before you know it," she whispered against his chest before he released her.

He merely grinned. "I sure hope so."

A knee injury had kept him out of the first half of the basketball season. He was hoping to be back out on the court before the playoff season.

"I can't believe you're over here with this dude," Rush said with laughter as he dragged her close.

For the first time, Dominique noticed Sheyna, who punched Rush lightly in the arm and signaled for him to behave. The R&B star known as Dr. Heart, whose latest single was currently climbing on the chart, had never been good at listening.

"Yo, Dominique, when you're done wasting time with this chump, I gotta good man for you," he joked.

She chuckled at the gorgeous man. She had just read in the tabloids that he was dating a beautiful soap opera actress.

"Rush, worry about finding your own woman," Reese said between gritted teeth. "That's if you can keep one."

His eyes glinted wickedly as he replied, "Dude, ain't you heard? I gotta female for every day of the week."

"Shame on both of you. It's too early in the morning for this nonsense," Sheyna said with a shake of her head. "Jace is at the house making waffles."

"Waffles." Rush and Rance chorused.

She nodded. "Yep. So I advise you to head over

there." She turned to Dominique. "I'm going shopping at two, you wanna come me? I could use your help."

Dominique grinned. "Of course." She never passed up an opportunity to shop.

"I'll see you then." She headed toward the door. "Boys... follow me."

"Bruh, we'll be back," Rance tossed over his shoulder.

"Yeah, we'll holla in a few." Rush followed his brothers out the door.

Smiling, Dominique watched as Reese shut the door behind them and turned the lock. He then swung around and sagged against the cold steel and groaned.

Dominique chuckled. "I see much hasn't changed."

He gave her an apologetic look. "Sorry about that."

With a dismissive snort, she replied, "You know I adore your brothers."

"And they adore you."

As he moved toward her, her thoughts flashed to the night before and she felt her nipples pucker as Reese dragged her into his arms.

"I was hoping to join you back in bed," he murmured, leaning down to brush a kiss across her mouth. His lips were soft and he tasted like hazelnut coffee.

"Then you should have put everyone out," she retorted.

"Guess what? They're out," Reese whispered against her neck.

She giggled and stroked his stubbled jaw. "Now I'm hungry. Sounds like Jace is making breakfast."

"I think breakfast can wait a few more minutes."

Dominique drew back to meet the hunger for something other than food that was burning in his eyes. "Is that so?"

"Absolutely. I think what you need is some more of this doctor's good loving."

She brought her arms up and wrapped them around his waist. "What makes you say that?"

"Because every time I'm near you your breathing becomes quick and shallow, causing your breasts to rise and fall, tempting me, making me want to hold them succulent babies in my hands."

"Don't flatter yourself," she said with laughter.

"Liar," he growled, then reached out and ran his index finger along the column of her throat. "You know you want me. I can see the anticipation in your eyes at the thought of me kissing every inch of your soft flesh, especially one area in particular."

Dominique trembled hard. "Whatever."

"Deny it if you want, but you can't wait for me to taste you, starting here," he said pressing his fingers to her lips. "And here, and here," he murmured as his fingers grazed her nipples and her breath hitched. "And especially here." He brought his hand down and cupped her mound.

He was trying to weave a sensual spell around her, using words that would leave her feeling helpless and aroused with need, and with no desire to resist. Then he could throw her over the edge, which was okay as long as he was willing to take the plunge with her. Dominique sighed, wishing that he was ready to surrender his heart as well.

Placing his hands on either side of her waist, Reese leaned in close, wanting her to feel everything he had to offer and then some. Halfheartedly she pressed a hand to his chest, intending to keep him from getting too close because she was way too weak to resist him, but instead of pushing him away she discovered her hands had a mind of their own as they slid eagerly across his sculptured pecs and down along his tight abs. She heard him hiss and then gazed up into his eyes. The hunger burning there almost stole her breath away. She wanted him inside of her. Pounding, stroking, pushing her over the edge, as long as he was buried deep enough to satisfy her need. Although she had a sinking feeling that she could never get enough of him.

"Sheyna wants me to help her run errands— *Oh!*" she cried out when he stroked his tongue along the length of her neck.

Reese laughed softly, then said, "Let her wait. Right now I have some unfinished business to take care of."

Dominique giggled and raced him back to the bedroom.

Chapter Nine

"So what's going on between the two of you?"

Dominique glanced up from the display of designer watches to meet Sheyna's intense stare. "What do you *think* has been going on?" she retorted with a wicked smile.

Sheyna cocked a perfect brow at her. "TMI. I don't want to hear about what the two of you are doing in the bedroom. I want to know if the two of you have talked about getting back together."

Dominique dropped her gaze back to a slender leather watch that had sparked her interest and heaved a heavy sigh before saying. "Nope. Nothing. We're just taking it one day at a time."

The sales clerk returned with a long box and removed the lid. Inside was a beautiful gold Movado watch with the inscription, *from Precious, with all my heart* engraved on the back.

"Oh, Sheyna. That's beautiful."

"Hopefully Jace will think so. I caught him staring at it the last time we were here."

"That's a wonderful gift."

"Thanks." After inspecting the quality of the work and giving her approval, Sheyna handed the box back to the clerk for gift wrapping. As soon as she moved to the other end, Sheyna leaned her elbow against the long glass countertop and said, "So... let's get back to you and Reese. Taking things one day at a time. Is that his idea or yours?"

Dominique shook her head with a laugh. Her friend had never been short of persistent. "Neither. He wants things the way they used to be and I told him I wanted more and wasn't settling for less."

"Good for you. A man loves a challenge."

"It isn't about that. I want some stability in my life. Like I told him, I'm not getting any younger." She stopped, then shrugged. "I want what you and Jace have."

Darting a wary glance, at her, Sheyna asked, "Have you told him you loved him?"

"Hell, no, and I'm not putting myself out there. I'm the one who initiated this union. I was the one who said I wanted to see if there was anything left between us."

"And is there?"

"Hell, yeah! Things are hotter than ever. I just don't understand why he can't see how good we are together. If he wants to continue to see me, then he needs to tell me how he feels about me."

"And then what?"

That was a good question. And she knew the answer. If he loved her and asked her for a commitment, she would decline the promotion to be with him. The promotion meant nothing if she didn't have him in her life. She wouldn't be happy without him. "The only thing missing from my life is him. Nothing else will make me happy, not even the promotion."

"Dammit! You know how long it took us to recruit for that position?" she reminded with false disappointment. They had conducted a nationwide search. Dominique had beat out more than ninety other qualified candidates.

"I know, but look at the bright side. I'll be there to help."

"You better be," Sheyna scolded playfully, then smiled. "I just want the best for you. You deserve it."

She was such a good friend. "Thanks, Sheyna." They were walking away from the counter when Dominique continued. "Reese is so resistant to marriage. I know how loves me, even though he has yet to say it, but I don't know if he's ever going to realize that we are meant to spend our lives together."

Sheyna halted mid-step, then turned to her friend. "You heard the expression, you don't realize what you have until it's gone? Well that's probably what it's going to take for Reese to realize what life's going to be like."

"But we had an entire year apart and yet I had to make the first move."

"Oh puh-leeze. That's different. That was stubborn Beaumont pride. This is different," she said confidently as she swung her designer purse onto her shoulder and headed toward the car. "Hopefully he's nothing like Jace. It took him forever to realize he couldn't live without me."

Dominique fell into step beside her and mumbled, "He's a Beaumont. I don't expect any less."

* * *

"So what's up with you and Dominique?"

His cousin Jabarie looked down curiously from the ladder at Reese who was running lights around the ten-foot Christmas tree. "We're spending the weekend together."

His brow rose. "Is that all? Because rumors are floating around town that the two of you are getting back together."

He drew a deep breath. In a small town like Sheraton Beach it didn't take much to get the gossips started. All it took was one person seeing you together, and then like a forest fire the word had spread throughout the city. What started out as "I saw the two of them together" translated into "they had been spotted at the jewelry store picking out an engagement ring."

"So is it true? Are the two of you getting back together?"

"No. I mean, I don't know. The plan was to talk and try finding closure." But even as Reese said it he felt a tug at his heart that said things were far from over between them. "But after a couple of days I realize I wanted her back in my life. Permanently."

"Are we talking marriage here?"

Not ready to answer, Reece reached for the cord and plugged it in. The entire tree lit up in a brilliant burst of white and red lights.

"Finally. It's amazing how one bad bulb can screw up an entire string of lights," Jabarie said as he started down the ladder. "By the way... you still haven't answered my question. Are you finally ready to make Dominique an honest woman?"

Reese frowned at his persistence. Jabarie was getting as bad as Sheyna. "No, not that. I just want things back to the way they used to be before the accident."

"If you say so." Jabarie, CEO of the Beaumont

Corporation, started laughing.

"What's so funny?"

His sable eyes sparkled with mischief. "You. Come on, Reese. I was leaving the office and saw the way the two of you were getting at it hot and heavy in the parking lot. Nothing about that look said *closure* or *the way things used to be.*"

Reese faltered, unnerved at being caught. He wasn't sure what he was feeling, but his cousin was right. There was more going on between the two of them than two friends spending a weekend together.

"We're not kids anymore. Things change. People change. So what in the world makes you think that you and Dom can keep doing what you've been doing for years? Women are only going to put up with that for so long before they chalk us up as a loss and move on."

Reese gazed at his cousin for a long moment and thought about what he had said. Dominique said she was tired of things the way they were. She wanted more. The big question was, did he want the same? Sure, he cared about her more than he'd cared about any woman, and she meant the world to him but was he ready for a lifelong commitment? What Sheyna had said earlier had him thinking, too. Had he been holding on to her, keeping here right where he wanted her, and that by doing so he had kept her from moving on with her life? He wasn't ready for a commitment, yet he expected Dominique to always be available to him. Realization begun to sink in. He wasn't being fair to her or their friendship. Everything about what he was asking had been completely selfish. If he really cared about her he'd either commit or let her go.

Why was it so hard to make a decision?

"What are the two of you talking about?" Jabarie's wife, Brenna, came around the corner sipping hot cocoa.

"We're wondering why you didn't make us any hot cocoa," Reese said with a playful grin to the caramel beauty..

"Actually, Bree is in the kitchen making a cup for both of you," she said and stuck out her tongue. "Where's Dominique? I hear the two of you are finally moving in together."

Jabarie tossed his head back with laughter. "See what I mean?"

Chapter Ten

Dominique returned to her townhouse carrying bags from several stores, including her favorite, Ashley Stewart, where she'd spotted a beautiful wrap dress in the display. Once she and Sheyna finished picking up items for Jace's party, they decided to do a little shopping for themselves. Not that they really needed any excuse to go shopping.

She dropped the bags on the couch and moved into the kitchen and retrieved a bottle of water from the large stainless steel refrigerator. She loved her condo and had a real estate management company already lined up to list her property for rent if she decided to take the job in Honolulu.

She twisted the cap and thought about how much was riding on the word "if." *If* she decided to accept the position she had a grocery list of things that needed to be done before she would be ready to relocate to the romantic island.

That's *if* she decided to take the job, and a lot was still riding on that decision. After tomorrow, she had a lot of thinking to do.

"Damn you, Reese," she muttered.

Why did he have to make things so difficult? If he hadn't returned for Jace's birthday, she would have taken her broken heart and moved to Hawaii. But now that she had seen, tasted, touched, and felt his power pounding inside her body, there was no way she could make such a huge decision until she was one hundred percent certain that their relationship would never be any more than it was.

The problem was that she was enjoying being with him too much. Living here, she could see Reese as often as she liked, but if she took the position in Hawaii it would mean a long distance relationship.

She needed to stay focused, and she hated that her entire future was riding on hearing those three little words from him.

"I love you."

That's all it would take, and then she would know where she stood with him, and would finally know if the two of them had a future together.

As she took a long swig, she frowned, hating that she felt so uncertain. She had always been confident in everything she did and with all the decisions she made in her life, but with Reese she felt like an insecure fool, and she hated that feeling. Her entire future had been put on hold for one man who had yet to express his love, or the possibility of the two of them having a future together.

What is wrong with me? she scowled. Her mother would be so disappointed if she knew a man had such an emotional hold on her.

Feeling slightly foolish, Dominique turned on her heels and moved into the living room, grabbing her bag and hurrying up the stairs.

While she slipped off her clothes her mind went over the last few days. No, her mind wasn't playing tricks on her. The signs were there. There was no denying that Reese cared about her. If they hadn't spent the last two days together then maybe she could say she'd been trying too hard or making more of their relationship than it really was. But at the same time, she had an overwhelming feeling that maybe she was setting herself up for failure.

Nothing ventured, nothing gained, her grandma used

to say.

Quickly, she shrugged off the doubt. No point in turning back now. One more night and then she would know which direction to take. She decided to wear a gold dress with wide sleeves that dropped mid-thigh and black tights, with gold and black accent pumps. She wanted to look extra special tonight. She raced into the bathroom to take her shower. Reese would be there to pick her up at seven and she wanted to be ready for what the night was bound to bring.

* * *

"Have I told you how beautiful you look tonight?" Reese said close to her ears as they stepped off the dance floor.

Smiling, Dominique gazed up into his dark eyes. "Yes, you have, but please tell me again."

Reese chuckled and took her hand and escorted her back to the table.

At least two hundred invited guests filled the elegant Princess ballroom at the Beaumont Hotel. Friends and family were dressed to impress in suits and beautiful dresses with complementary accessories. The wait staff made their way around the room, serving coffee and an assortment of desserts. Dinner had been a delicious feast, starting with lobster, prime rib or salmon. The R&B band continued to entertain the guests with hits from the seventies and eighties. Sheyna had truly outdone herself. The room looked fabulous, decorated in black and gold. Jace was a big Pittsburg Steelers fan, so Sheyna felt it an appropriate color scheme for an evening event. Throughout the evening speeches had been given and there had been several champagne toasts.

Dominique reached the table where they were seated, and where three of his obnoxious brothers were seated.

"Bruh, you looked good out there. I guess those dance lessons are finally starting to pay off," Rance joked from across the table. Remy and Rush joined in on the humor.

"Very funny," Reese mumbled as he helped Dominique into her chair and lowered onto the seat to her left. The wait staff was moving around the table, refilling coffee cups and delivering dessert choices.

"Dom, I hear you got a helluva job offer," he heard Rush say as a slice of chocolate cake was placed in front of him.

Reese tried to focus on his dessert and not the sparkle in her eye at the mention of her pending promotion.

"Yes, I feel truly blessed by the offer."

"You're gonna love Hawaii. I try to get down there and surf every chance I can," Remy said, and Reese noticed his brother smiling at him over the brim of his glass. He knew what Dominique's leaving would mean to him.

Rance sat up on his chair. "You got a job in Hawaii?" he whistled. "Damn, you're gonna be living it up! I'll be heading that way for the Pro Bowl in February. Maybe we can hook up while I'm there."

It took everything he had to keep from commenting. Leave it to his brothers to rub salt in his wound.

"Well, I haven't decided yet if I'm going to take the job," she said.

Remy looked from her to Reese with a silly look on his face that made Reese want to ring his neck. "Why haven't you made a decision?" he asked, as if he didn't already know the answer.

Dominique's eyes met his. "There are a few important things I need to sort out first.

"Important? Like what?" Rush asked, who seemed to know what was going on as well.

Remy nodded as he struggled to keep a straight face.

Angie Daniels

"Yeah, like what?"

Reese dropped his eyes. He'd been thinking a lot since he'd left Jabarie's house and come to a painful conclusion. The last thing he wanted to do was influence her decision. As much as he wanted her to stay, it wouldn't be fair to ask her to stay in Sheraton Beach when he lived in Bowie. She had always dreamed of leaving the small town and getting out into the world and tackling her next challenge, and this opportunity would give her just that.

"I hope your decision doesn't have anything to do with my big-headed brother over here. You know what Beyoncé said, 'He shoulda put a ring on it.'" He chuckled, and even Rush and Rance joined in.

Dominique gave a nervous grin. She hesitated slightly before she replied, "There are... several things I need to consider. My little sister is one of them."

"Well, don't take too long. I might have to ask Jace for the job myself," Remy teased. "I can just see living down there with all those beautiful women."

"I'd have to agree," Rush said between chews.

"Bruh... what you think about all that?" Remy asked with amusement.

Reese looked up from his pie to see all eyes were on him. He searched Dominique's eyes and saw the uncertainty.

"I would love for her to stay, but Dom has to do what's best for her."

He cringed at the way her shoulder dropped with disappointment. What he'd said was true. He wanted her to do what was best for her, but he just hoped the best was him.

Remy looked to Rush, shook his head, then reached for his fork.

"He's right. I need to do what's best for me, and that's

exactly what I plan to do." She stabbed her pie and there was no denying the anger in her voice.

During the rest of dessert the boys joked around about the last football game, and Dominique, a diehard football fan, joined in on the fun. Reese noticed that she only spoke to him when required.

The music stopped and he heard someone tapping a fork against a glass.

"Can I have everyone's attention?"

Reese blew out a frustrated breath, then swung around on the chair and faced the head table where Jace was standing.

"I want to thank you all for coming. This probably has been one of the best days of my life, and it's because of all of you. God has truly blessed me with an amazing life, and especially with a beautiful woman who made this all possible. Sheyna, baby, I want to thank you for my beautiful son, and for being my rock, especially this last year while we've been working on restructuring the corporation. I couldn't have asked for a better wife."

Reaching out, he took her hand in his and lifted her to her feet, then leaned forward and captured her mouth in a searing kiss.

At that exact moment Reese felt an unfamiliar stirring at the pit of his stomach. Damn it. No matter how much he denied it, deep down he wanted the same.

* * *

Dominique watched Sheyna and Jace and felt the familiar wave of envy. She wanted what they had. The couple was the epitome of true love. And she wanted the same. She would give anything for Reese to look at her that way, with total love and devotion. She had hoped that tonight would have been a turning point, but after the comment he'd made at dessert it was starting to become obvious that he still wasn't ready to offer her any more than he ever had in the past.

And their time together was almost over.

She had taken the risk of accepting three days of happiness at the expense of finding out if Reese was going to be part of her life. Not what they had had in the past, but what she desperately wanted for her future. A husband. A family. She knew in the beginning what she had been up against, yet despite the odds she had to know. No matter how painful the outcome might be in the morning, she knew she was doing the right thing. They had only one night left. Tomorrow he would be heading back home after his conference and she would be going in to the office, hopefully with a response to the job offer.

Her heart ached. How was it only two weeks ago she had been so excited about a promotion for which she had waited her entire life? And now she couldn't bear the thought of not being within driving distance of Reese.

But she wasn't willing to compromise.

She glanced over at Reese as he stood near the head table, speaking to his Uncle Roger and his Aunt Jessica, who looked amazing as always. The couple would soon be celebrating their fiftieth anniversary. At the office, she had heard that their youngest, Bianca Beaumont Brown, was planning something special for the occasion.

Fifty years. Fifty amazing years. What she would do for that many years with Reese!

Dominique watched him, her eyes clinging to the broad span of his shoulders. His shirt somehow delineated the male shape of his body. What was it about him that he could wear a pair of slacks in a way that focused a woman's attention to the muscles of his thighs? Reese was handsome beyond words.

Forcing her eyes away, she focused her attention on the conversations at the table, and was laughing at one of Remy's corny jokes when she glanced up to find Reese heading her way. Her eyes traveled downward from his handsome face and dark, chiseled jawline with the neatly trimmed goatee and back up to meet his gaze. Their eyes locked and the sexual attraction sparked all around them. There was no doubt she was going to have to make one of the hardest decisions of her life.

"Wanna dance?" he asked.

She grinned up at him, eyes crinkling with delight. "I'd love to." Taking Reese's hand, she allowed him to lead her out onto the center of the crowded ballroom floor. Reese tugged her into his arms and they immediately fell into step.

"Enjoying yourself?" he asked.

"Yes, I am," she replied, stroking his upper arms." The weekend had been most amazing. One thing would make it perfect.

His love.

She stared into his eyes, wishing she could make his lips move to declare the one thing she had dreamed of hearing from him. All it took was for Reese to confess that he wanted a future with her and she would decline the Hawaii offer and stay put in Sheraton Beach while they planned the rest of their lives.

"I've been dying to hold you again."

"We just danced," she said within his arms as her senses burst into life.

"That was way too long ago," he insisted and he drew her closer. The way Reese moved when he danced filled her mind with mental images of hard muscles and the power they contained.

Beneath her dress her nipples peaked, and charged on the surge of desire that rushed through her, Dominique rested her head on his chest and closed her eyes, allowing the slow sensual beat to vibrate through her.

"You smell good." He spoke softly, his breath warm and moist.

"Thank you. It's Nicki Minaj's new scent."

"I never liked her music, but I'm definitely a fan of her fragrance," he said with his breath tickling her as he nuzzled her neck and caused her to giggle.

"You know I'm ticklish."

"Sorry, sweetheart. I couldn't help myself."

They swayed in silence for several seconds as she listened to the words of the love song and allowed her body to relax against his. She breathed in his masculine scent and enjoyed the pleasure and comfort of his warm embrace.

Only one night left.

"I hate to see this weekend end. I'm really going to miss you," Reese confessed as if he had just read her mind.

Swallowing, she replied, "So am I."

Pulling back slightly, he looked into her eyes. "How about coming up on Friday and spending the weekend with me?"

She searched his eyes, trying to read what he was thinking. He definitely wanted to see her again, and that was music to her ears. She would love to stay in his arms forever, but in what capacity? Was he ready for a serious commitment? Until she knew, she wasn't ready to make plans. Because regardless of how much it hurt, the last thing she was going to do was be readily available to him.

Trying to hide the emotion from her face, she answered indecisively, "We'll see. I've got a lot of things to get done before the holidays, so I might be working." Curving an arm around his neck, she rested her head on his chest again and felt firm muscles shift with every move.

"Then if I have to I'll come to you," he insisted. "Now that I've got you back in my life, I don't plan on losing you again." He held her with a possessiveness that excited her, the warmth of his body penetrating the material of her dress.

She closed her eyes and tried to still the runaway beat of her heart. She wanted what Jace and Sheyna had. Love and total devotion to each other. Why was that so hard? They were going to talk, and she was going to let him know that it was all or nothing with her. But right now she was going to enjoy the evening.

Tilting her head back, she stared up into his eyes and saw desire burning in their depths. "What's on your mind?"

"You." He dropped a kiss to her nose. "I'm going home with you tonight."

"Really? Are you assuming you have an invitation?"

"Hell, yeah, otherwise I'll just have to camp out at your door." He pulled her close again. "I want to hold you in my arms and wake up with you in my arms."

She sighed. "What time is your conference tomorrow?"

"Six-thirty," he replied with a delectable grin.

"Goodness, why so early?'

"We have a breakfast and several other guest

speakers before the lecture begins. I'm supposed to speak at UCLA next month, you wanna go?"

She hesitated. There was no way she could say yes. Not until she knew for sure where they stood. Dammit, why couldn't he just tell her they would never be more than they were so that she could pick her heart up off the floor and move on?

The song drew to an end and Dominique wasn't sure how long they stood there staring at each other before she felt someone tap her on the shoulder. It was Rush.

"My turn to dance with the pretty lady."

Reese rolled his eyes and planted a kiss to her cheek. "Baby, I'll see you back at the table."

She smiled up at Rush's handsome face with his thick brows and long lashes. "I hear you're dating one of my favorite actresses."

"You know how I do." Laughing, he drew her into his arms.

Yep. That's the problem. All five brothers were too afraid to commit, especially Dr. Reese. Dominique looked over his shoulder in time to watch him slowly walk away. The same way he would tomorrow.

Chapter Eleven

They were relatively quiet on the ride from the hotel to her condo. Soft music was playing and Reese was holding Dominique's hand.

It was their last night together and they were both aware of it.

"You need to stop and pick up anything before we head to your house?" Reese asked, breaking into her thoughts.

She turned, gazed at his handsome profile, and replied, "No, but thanks for asking."

He squeezed her hand and awkward silence filled the car again for the rest of the ride home.

Once at her condo, Reese took her keys from her hands and she was grateful. As nervous as she was, she wasn't sure if her hands would have stopped shaking long enough to insert the key into the lock.

He pushed the door open and she stepped into the foyer where a seven-foot Christmas tree took up most of the walk space.

"Come on in and make yourself comfortable." She set her purse on the table in the hall and slipped out of her heels. "Would you like something to drink?" she asked, then turned and noticed that Reese was still standing in front of the door. "Is something wrong?" she asked.

"Yes... there is," he replied. "Come here."

Heart beating heavily, she walked slowly toward him, and as soon as she was close enough he pulled her into his arms and nuzzled her cheek. "I haven't left yet and I'm already missing you," he whispered with his breath fanning her ear.

"And I miss you. More than you know."

Cupping her face in his hands, he kissed her with so much emotion, Dominique struggled to make sense of it and figure out what it meant.

"I don't want to lose you. I won't lose you."

His tantalizing words played havoc with her mind. "What are you saying?" she asked, and pulled back slightly so she could look up into his eyes.

"I'm saying I don't want you to leave. Forgive me. Damn! I know it sounds selfish, and the last thing I want to do is stand in your way."

Didn't he realize how much he meant to her? "Nothing means more to me than being with you. Haven't you figured that out? All I want is you."

Reese slanted his mouth over hers. The kiss was deep and so possessive it promised her he was everything she needed and erased any uncertainties or thoughts about their future. There would be plenty of time for that tomorrow. Tonight the only thing she wanted to think about was Reese.

Dominique exhaled and arched toward him, crushing her breasts to his solid chest. Reese wrapped his strong arms around her and with every confident stroke of his tongue, she felt the strength of his hands running along her arms, back and hips.

Goodness, she was drowning in his taste and his touch.

Reese moved forward, walking her backwards until she felt the cool wall against her back.

"You feel that?" Reese asked, grinding against her so that she felt his hard length wedged between her thighs.

"Yes," she breathed. How could she not? Reese forced her legs apart with his knees while putting his hands at her ass, drawing her close enough that she didn't miss a thing.

"My dick gets hard every time I think about you," he murmured against her lips.

"Is that so?" Dominique asked as she slipped her arms around his neck and rode his erection.

"Absolutely. It has always been about you," he confessed. All she knew was that she wanted Reese sliding deep inside her body.

He kissed her softly, gently devouring her. Dominique followed his lead while she skimmed fingers through his thick wavy hair. It was crazy. Even insane, the way her body was driven by a need to be possessed by him.

Reese held her close, kissing her deeply, his tongue moving with skillful strokes. His erection continued to pulse and a moan slipped from her throat. She wanted her panties off, her legs wrapped around his waist, and Reese buried to the hilt.

"Reese," she called out as a pool of hot desire coursed through her that made it impossible not to whimper.

"I'm right here, Dom, and tonight I plan to take my time making love to you." His words were warm against his lips.

She giggled inwardly. *Like she would have refused.*

Reese lifted his head, not enough to break the kiss entirely but enough to meet her gaze.

"What's wrong?" she asked.

He shook his head. "Nothing. Nothing at all." Then his tongue outlined her lips with soft, light kisses before traveling to her cheek, her jaw. "Except I need to get these clothes off *fast.*" In a sudden move he scooped her effortlessly into his arms and up the stairs, and straight to the bedroom.

Reese laid her gently on the bed, then stood over her, watching with dark eyes that promised a night to remember. His smoldering gaze built the excitement, the anticipation, the promise of the pleasure to come.

"Take your clothes off," he commanded.

Dominique smiled up at him, rolling the dress enticingly up her hips and then up over her head, with Reese watching her every move.

"Beautiful," he murmured.

"I'm glad you like what you see," she cooed, then took a seat on the end of the bed while Reese knelt on the floor before her. Suddenly they were nearly face to face. His appreciative gaze trailed down her body.

"I never get tired of looking at you." Although Reese had seen her nude countless times before, he'd never watched her like this before. He'd never looked at her as intensely as he did now, causing her entire body to tingle.

She swallowed hard and was reaching up for the clasp on her bra when his hands covered hers.

"Let me help you with that," he said, and released the clasp. As he slid the straps over her shoulders, down her arms...peeling the satin cups away slowly, Dominique inhaled as cool air ruffled her nipples.

"There's my girl," he joked. Dominique laughed and swatted playfully at his hand.

Leave it to Reese to alleviate some of the tension in the room.

With his eyes on her, she lifted her hips and slid the lace panties down over her ankles and tossed them aside. Reese caught them just before they flew over his head and brought the pink satin to his nose and inhaled.

Oh my, she groaned while her kitty throbbed with want.

"I love the way you smell... the way your pussy tastes." He gazed down at her with hunger so real she began to quiver again. Damn, that man could arouse her with nothing more than the desire in his eyes. Her breasts grew heavy, nipples erect under the intensity of his gaze.

Reese leaned close and forced her to lean back on her elbows as he pressed his hand to her breasts and caressed with his fingertips She cried out and grabbed onto his shoulders, digging her nails in his flesh.

"You like that?" he asked. His hands circled her breasts, molding them, caressing them with his injured hand.

"Oooh," she moaned softly.

"Babe, did you say something?" he coaxed while thumbing her nipples, stealing her breath until she arched her back and leaned closer into his touch.

"Yes, I like that." Her breathing became ragged and her body was burning up with need. She wanted him and she wanted him now.

His lips traveled lower and her breath caught in her throat as he lifted her breast and his lips parted. As soon as he dragged his warm tongue over a nipple she gasped and finally remembered to breathe. He sucked the hard tip into his mouth, a hot wet pull that shot through her like a lightning bolt.

She trembled.

And Reese sucked a little harder.

She writhed, savoring the feel of his mouth on her.

His mouth sucked. His tongue laved. His teeth nipped. She loved the way he nibbled gently before closing his lips around her nipple and suckling hard again. He aroused her until every nerve in her body had come alive beneath his touch.

And when she thought she couldn't possibly take any more, he traveled down her stomach, leaving a trail of wet kisses as he lowered his face between her legs.

"Reese," she moaned cautiously.

"Let me make you feel good," he said softly as he

slipped his strong hands between her knees and parted them until she was spread wide open. And then he knelt before her and skimmed his fingertips along her kitty, not enough to penetrate but enough to separate her throbbing folds in a way that was intensely arousing.

"Quit teasing," she hissed.

"I'm not teasing, I'm just trying to please you…that's all," he said with a wicked smirk.

With his thumb he urged her clit from beneath the hood and caressed it with lazy circles that made her arch off the bed.

"You like that?" he asked as his eyes met her gaze and flashed a lustful grin that sent the blood rushing into her cheeks.

"Yessss," she cried as Reese stroked her again and again.

The feel of his hands aroused her, but his dark gaze staring down at her sex, watching as her body tightened and opened to his touch was almost her undoing. He had made love to her before, but never with such passion and such possession of her mind, body and soul.

And when he leaned forward, she gasped and held her breath waiting for the feel of his mustache tickling between her legs.

Reese drew the little bud in with a soft pull, a move so erotic her entire body melted with a long sigh. Then his tongue joined in with thorough strokes that made her cry out.

"Oh, God!" she cried as he licked. Reese wiggled around on the bed and she brought her hands to his head and held on as wave after wave of overwhelming sensations mounted inside. And just when she felt she couldn't hold on, Reese slipped a finger inside her, a hot stroke that sparked a crackling flame, flaring hot and fast all over. "Reese!" she screamed It was a total consumption that left her thrusting her hips against his hand.

"That's it. Come all over my finger," he said.

Dominique clutched the pillows and held on until her body slowed and her legs collapsed, then she exhaled while her breathing slowed somewhat. Resting his cheek on her thigh, Reese's fingers stroked her through the curls surrounding her sensitive kitty. The touch was light but so intimate. He was driving her crazy and he knew it.

A soft wistful sigh escaped her lips. "Make love to me, Reese."

He gave her a penetrating look. "You sure you're ready?"

"I'm primed and ready," she purred as he rose. Dominique slid up onto the bed and raised up on her elbows as she enjoyed the show. She had watched him undress countless time, yet seeing his naked sculpted body fully aroused turned her on in ways she couldn't have begun to describe.

Suddenly he was climbing onto the bed, positioning himself over her body. He was lying on top and they were face to face, so close she could see the depths of his darks eyes and the thick lashes that ringed them. Dominique draped her leg over his, with her thighs spread wide, and his erection poised at the entrance of her sex.

"You have no idea how much I've missed you all these months," she confessed.

"Probably as much as I was missing you."

"I'd hoped you did, too," she admitted. "I spent months wondering if I mattered to you." She slipped a hand between them and caressed the swollen head of his penis, a tender stroke that made him shudder.

"Dammit..." he groaned. "Yes, you matter."

Lowering her face, she pressed light kisses to his neck

and shoulder. "Oh, yeah? How much?"

"I've never wanted a woman like I want you," Reese admitted, and his muscles flexed as he pushed inside just a bit, causing her to gasp.

"Keep talking," she whispered.

He smiled and pushed a little more. "I used to spend hours dreaming about being inside you."

"Why dream? When all you had to do was call."

He hesitated before saying, "I was an idiot. But never again."

A whimper slipped from her lips as he slid further inside her. Nothing had ever felt so right. It was almost too good to be true.

"Yes! Love me, Reese."

When his gaze met hers, Dominique saw something in his gaze that mirrored everything she was feeling.

Tell me you love me. That's all I need to hear.

Instead, he was positioning himself between her legs. She pressed her lips against the hollow space between his neck and shoulder and kissed him. Then he brought his mouth to hers and their breaths collided as his dick slid further. Arching off the bed, Dominique invited him deeper. He plunged even more and she moaned as her body stretched to accommodate him.

"Oh, yeah," he said with a rumbling groan. Dominique moaned in agreement.

"Baby," he chanted as he drew his hips back and slightly eased out, then slid back in with slow, powerful strokes that were erotically insane.

Reese increased the speed and she got lost in the pleasure of it all.

While he moved inside her he kissed her, and Dominique savored the taste of his tongue sliding around the recesses of her mouth. His hands moved along her waist and hips, then slipped around to grip her ass, holding her in place as he pumped hard and steady with tantalizing force.

"Wrap your legs around me," he ordered.

Dominique raised her legs and Reese spread her wider and quickened his pace. As she moaned, his mouth broke from hers.

"*Yes*, Reese," she whimpered, then begged, "Don't stop," as his lips trailed along her cheek and neck.

"I wouldn't dream of it."

She met his thrusts and brought her hands down along his spine and rested at his ass, where she pushed him even deeper.

Reese raised up and gazed down at her, then planted soft light kisses to her lips. She could see the pleasure building in his eyes, feel it in the power of his thrusts. He drew her hips even closer, until he was up on his elbows, showing her exactly who was in control. Not that she was complaining. Reese drove into her, pulling back to the tip then plunging his entire length into her wet heat, drawing the air from her lungs.

It was so much she was thrashing on the bed beneath him. Climax was so close, and this beautiful man pumping into her body was so overwhelming, she had tears in her eyes.

"I love you," she whispered harshly, then dug her fingers into his butt and arched into his thrusts. Dominique felt the exact moment his magnificent body tensed and together they went sailing over the edge of euphoria.

* * *

Hours later, Dominique woke up to find the moon creeping through the blinds and Reese curled up naked beside her. She was utterly exhausted, but happier than she had been in a long time. Last night they had made love, and it was nothing like it had been before. It was more passionate and tender and filled with even more desire than she thought possible. And when she had briefly glanced into his dark eyes in the moonlight he looked obsessed and in love.

Her heart pounded at the mere thought. Was it possible? She wondered. Reese had said some confusing things about not wanting to let her go, and she just didn't know where she stood. Could she have possibly worked her way into his heart? She wondered if Reese had finally fallen in love with her as well. His eyes said he could love her. His body even said he could love her. But he had yet to say the words to her.

She nibbled on her lips as she remembered uttering those three words in the heat of passionate lovemaking.

Maybe he didn't hear you.

God, I hope so, she thought and suddenly felt embarrassed by the confession. What was even more disheartening was that today was going to be their last day together.

Reese would be leaving in a few hours for Wilmington before heading home to Maryland. And where would that leave them?

Reese shifted and drew her against his body again and wrapped her in his arms. She sighed with contentment, then turned in his arms and faced him. He was staring right at her.

"Good morning, baby," he said, pressing his lips to her cheek.

"Good morning," she said, heart pounding so heavily beneath her breasts she was sure Reese could hear it.

"How long have you been up?" he asked. Reese raked his hands along her back and hips, sending tremors up her spine.

"Just a few minutes. You'll need to be getting ready

soon, right?"

"Yes, but I want to talk to you about something first."

Talk? Dominique's heart was beating so fast she thought it was going to explode. This is it, she thought. This is the moment she had been waiting for all weekend.

Sitting up on the bed, Reese took her hand in his. She could tell by the intensity in his eyes that whatever he was about to say wasn't easy.

"Reese, what is it?"

He paused for a long moment then said, "I want you to take that position in Honolulu."

Stunned, Dominique sucked in her breath. "Excuse me? What do you mean, *you want me to?*" she said with attitude. "Who died and left you in charge?" Angrily, she shook her hand free of his grasp.

"My bad. I said that wrong."

"Damn right you did!"

With a roll of her eyes, Dominique sprang out of bed and rose unsteadily to her feet, then stormed over to the large walk-in closet for her robe. With a sigh, Reese swung his legs out the bed and onto the floor.

"What I'm trying to say, Dom, is that I care about you too much to stand in your way. You have the opportunity of a lifetime, and if you don't do this you'll end up hating me."

She slipped into her robe and swung around as she tied the sash around her waist. "What the hell makes you think you have anything at all to do with my decision?" she lied and felt her heart crack. "This is about me, not you."

"It does have something to do with me," he said confidently and rose from the bed. "You even said so yourself." He closed the distance between them and brought his hands to her shoulders. "I wouldn't be a friend if I didn't want the best for you."

A friend.

There you have it. She was no more than a friend to him. Dominique took a deep breath as tears pricked at her eyes. This couldn't possibility be happening to her, and yet it was.

"You worked your entire life for this day, and I want you to have everything you always wanted," he said huskily, then leaned forward to kiss her.

But all I want is you.

"Don't get me wrong, Dom. I don't want you to leave. I want you to stay here with me, but I don't want you to someday look back with regrets." He kissed her lips and stepped back. His dark eyes were serious, his stare was inciting a warmth that made her shiver.

"How about I come back after the conference and I take you to dinner? I can stay so we can talk some more, then I'll head home in the morning?"

Her entire body trembled. She didn't know what to do or say. Even though he may not have meant them that way, his words were a slap in the face.

Dominique pushed past him, desperate to escape before she collapsed into sobs. "I don't think so."

He turned around and followed her down the stair into the living room. "Why the hell not?"

She didn't bother to turn around as she hurried through the room, padding across plush carpeting. "Because I'm not playing this game with you anymore."

His voice was low. "This is not a game." Reese reached out and grabbed her. "I care about you. More than I've ever cared about any woman. Not that there have ever been *that* many," he added with a smirk, but her heart hurt too much to share in on the joke.

Reese was standing in front of her, naked and beautiful. She looked up into his face, his eyes dark and filled with love and compassion. He cared about her.

There was no doubt in her mind about that.

Why was it so hard for him to love me?

"Sweetheart, I listened to you these last few days and there was no denying the passion I heard in your voice. You might not think so, but this promotion means everything to you, and I want you to have it and everything you've always wanted... even if it isn't with me." His words were soft and she barely heard them over the thundering of her heart.

Unable to speak, she simply nodded.

"Have dinner with me, Dom?" His fingers tightened around hers.

She blinked and stared up at his kind face, and then suddenly asked herself, what reason did she have to be mad at him? He'd never offered her anything. Reese hadn't stuck a gun to her head and instructed her to fall in love with him. Not once had he not been honest with her about his feelings, or what he wanted in their relationship. She had done that all on her own.

"Sure," she choked out as she willed herself not to cry in front of him. "Dinner will be great."

Reese looked relieved as he pulled her into his arms for what she considered a long, final kiss.

An hour later, even before he had pulled his truck away from her condo, Dominique knew what she had to do. Quickly, she locked the door and hurried up to her room to get dressed.

Chapter Twelve

Reese moved through the marbled foyer of the hotel to the main elevators, then rode up to the seventh floor.

The conference had been a huge success, with an amazement turnout that had ended with the auditorium thundering with applause. Afterwards, he met with his colleagues and discussed a rare case that a thoracic surgeon would give anything to be part of, but as much as he loved discussing cardiology, he couldn't wait for the eventful afternoon to end so he could get back to Dominique.

He had spent most of the night thinking about everything that had happened over the course of the weekend, and he knew there was no way he could stand in the way of her promotion. Not if he truly cared about her the way he believed he did.

What he had said that morning was probably the hardest decision he had ever made in his life. Part of him had wanted to be selfish and keep Dominique close and available, but his conscience wouldn't allow it.

He frowned as he thought about how torn he had been, but in the end Sheyna had been right. He needed to let go of his hold on her, and like a robin with her baby birds it was time to push Dominique out into the world to experience everything it had to offer, no matter how much it hurt him to do so.

He had made the right decision, and she might not agree now but he was certain she would thank him later. Besides, it wasn't like they'd never see each other again, he thought reassuringly. Dominique would only be a plane ride or two away. Shaking his head, Reese let out a strangled laugh. Who was he trying to fool? He could stand there in front of an auditorium of people and try all day to convince them that nothing between him and Dominique would change besides her address, but he'd be lying and he knew it.

That's why he needed to see her... touch her... hold her in his arms.

The elevator doors parted and Reese eagerly stepped off onto plush green carpeting. The reception area had been beautifully decorated for the holidays with a large Christmas tree covered with red and white bulbs. An enormous wreath was on the main focal wall. Reese waved at Melanie, the receptionist, who gave him a familiar smile while she finished a call and then waved him on back to the corporate suites. He traveled down the glass-encased elevator and realized he was practically sprinting toward Dominique's office. He wanted to spend the rest of the evening with her, talking about a way to make their relationship, which he still wasn't ready to define, work with the thousands of miles between them. They could make this work. Despite the odds against a long distance relationship, they had been together long enough that it wouldn't be too difficult. He was certain of that.

Grinning, he moved down the long corridor with powerful strides. When he passed Jace's large corner office, he heard him call out to him.

"Reese. Can you step in here a moment?"

He stopped and groaned inwardly at the interruption. He was anxious to make it down to Dominique's office at the other end of the hall.

When he poked his head in, Reese noticed that Jace wasn't alone. He was behind his desk and his wife was draped across his lap. The lipstick smeared on his cheek was evidence of what the couple had been up to.

"Hey, whassup?" Reese said impatiently.

Jace gestured for him to step inside.

As he moved into the large room, Reese didn't miss the look of disapproval Sheyna was sending his way.

"How was the conference?" Jace asked.

"It was great," he said. "Wonderful turnout."

While he talked about the event, Reese noticed Sheyna stealing a glance at Jace. He suddenly got a feeling that there was something going on that they weren't telling him.

"What's wrong?" He directed the question at Jace, but it was Sheyna who answered.

"Dominique came into my office this morning and accepted the position."

So soon. He thought she would have waited until Friday, but then what was the point of waiting when she already knew in her heart what she had wanted to do? And no matter how much she had been straddling the fence, he knew she wanted that job. "I know. We talked about it this morning. That's why I came back so we could have dinner and celebrate," he added for his own benefit.

"You talked? Well, if you'd talked you would have known that Dominique flew out this evening to meet with the staff before Christmas break."

Reese inhaled and felt like someone had just hit him in the chest.

"What?"

Jace's brow arched. "She didn't tell you?"

He shook his head. "Yes...no... I had no idea it was going to be this soon."

"Hmmm, I wonder why," Sheyna mumbled under her breath. Jace placed a hand to her arm, signaling her to behave.

She had left Sheraton Beach without telling him. Why

did he suddenly feel like he had lost her?

"Thanks for letting me know."

Jace looked concerned. "Are you staying at the guesthouse tonight?"

Reese shook his head. "No. I'm on my way back to Maryland."

Jace gave him a solemn look, then nodded in understanding. "Holler at me later."

Reese nodded and was walking toward the door when Sheyna called out to his retreating back. "If you have any sense in that big head of yours you'll go get her!"

He didn't even bother to respond and instead headed toward the elevators, feeling like he was in a daze. Dominique was gone. What had he expected? Somehow he made it down to the lobby and ignored a beautiful woman trying to get his attention. He searched his brain for some sign that Dominique never had any intention of having dinner with him and was planning to immediately fly to Hawaii.

He knew it was for the best. He'd never wanted to stand in the way of her happiness, but he had hoped she would have chosen to have it all—the promotion *and* their relationship.

What relationship?

He frowned at the voice. Had he been assuming too much to think that they could have just finished where they had left off?

I love you.

Last night, when she had made the confession, should he also have said "I love you," when he wasn't sure exactly what that meant? He knew he truly cared about Dominique, and she was the only woman he had ever wanted, but was that love? He wished he knew, or had even lied to her and said he was, anything to keep her in his life.

Shaking his head, he was clearly disappointed at his selfish thoughts, yet he missed her so much. It felt like someone had reached inside his chest and ripped out his heart.

As soon as the valet delivered his truck he handed him a tip and jumped inside, moving toward the highway. The farther he traveled away from the beach town the more it sickened him.

What was he supposed to do now? Chalk it off as a loss and find another woman to satisfy his needs? There was no way. There was only one woman he wanted. One woman he'd always wanted since he'd first started growing hair on his chin.

Thirty miles down the highway he had come to the conclusion that even during the months they were apart, Dominique had still been on his mind. Even in his heart.

Even if he had been too stupid to have realized it.

Ever since he'd first spotted her at the swimming pool in that two-piece bikini that showcased her budding teenage body, he'd known he wanted her. And in fifteen years, nothing had changed.

Except then they were kids with an immature infatuation. But now he was a grown man and Dominique was a beautiful woman who had owned his heart for more than a decade.

Reese whipped around a pokey car and drew in a long breath. Now what? He didn't want to go back to Bowie to his lonely two-bedroom apartment. Even his position at the University meant nothing to him. Not without Dominique.

The woman he loved.

His heart pounded so heavily beneath his chest he was afraid it was going to explode. He loved her. He'd always loved her. Why had it taken him so long to admit that?

He suddenly realized he missed her more than he'd ever imagined. No one had ever come close to her. Why had it taken him so long to discover that Dominique was everything he needed in his life? She knew it and had even told him so, but he had been too stubborn to listen to his own heart or hers.

And now she was gone.

All because he had taken her love and commitment for granted. He shook his head as he stared out into the flow of traffic. As stupid as he'd been, he didn't deserve her or her love.

But despite everything he had done, nothing was going to stop him from talking to Dominique and making her his own. Now he just had to figure out how to get her back. He was sure he could get Sheyna's help if he admitted to her how much he loved Dominique.

Chapter Thirteen

"Everyone, have a fabulous Christmas holiday. I'll see you in two weeks." Dominique waved and exchanged holiday greeting with her staff as they filed out the conference room. As soon as the last member of her team departed and she had shut the door behind her, Dominique swung around and grinned.

Manager, Employee Relations.

"It has a nice ring to it, if I say so myself," she whispered as she gathered her things and stuffed them into a brown leather briefcase.

Dominique had spent the last two days orienting herself to the department and meeting her staff. The time had been well spent. She was scheduled to fly back to Delaware in the morning, in time to pick her sister up from the airport and spend the Christmas holiday with her family. After that she would start packing her bags and start preparing for her new life in Hawaii.

Clutching the bag in her head, she headed out the conference room and down the hallway toward her office, her hunter green pumps clicking with each step. Catching her reflection in a mirror near the bank of elevators, she smoothed out the front of her black pencil skirt.

As she neared her office, a smile curled her lips. While she had been at the staff meeting, her name had been added to the door.

Stepping inside, she moved around her large oak desk and set her briefcase down in her chair. Dominique then moved over and stood in front of the floor-to-ceiling window and stared out at the beautiful ocean view below. Located directly across from world famous Waikiki Beach, the Beaumont Waikiki Hotel enchanted guests with true Hawaiian culture. Since her arrival on the island, Dominique had felt caught up in the aloha spirit that was both warm and inviting. She released a heavily sigh. The place and the job were both everything she had always dreamed of, and more.

So why did she feel empty inside?

Reese.

She missed him like crazy. When she finally decided that crying wasn't the solution, she'd been energized by focusing on her new position. There were a lot of things that needed to be implemented and staff needed to be trained on different aspects of employment laws, but she was definitely the girl for the job. Pouring all her time into the new position gave her something to focus on instead of missing Reese.

And she did miss him.

She couldn't sleep at night because she'd wake up reaching for him. The last few days had been so exciting, she'd caught herself reaching for the phone to share her day with Reese, but then remembered that he was now a closed chapter in her life. The last two days had been difficult, but she was sure that in time things would get easier.

All she had to do was first mend her broken heart.

Dominique removed her purse from the bottom drawer and glanced around the office one more time, making sure she wasn't forgetting anything. If she did forget something it would have to wait until she returned after the first of the year. She turned out the light, locked the door behind her, and headed out through the reception area.

"Milani," she began, addressing the perky Latina woman sitting behind the desk. "You have a wonderful holiday. I'll see you in two weeks."

Milani grinned, flashing dimples on either side of her cheek. "You too, Ms. Wellington. And again, welcome to Waikiki."

"Thank you." She turned on her heels and headed down the hallway onto the shiny marble floor. She was bidding goodbye to the friendly staff at the registration desk when she saw him.

Reese.

Standing at the end of the hall near the exit, dressed in jeans and a long-sleeved red T-shirt. One hand was thrust into a pocket. Her heart did a flying leap and she didn't trust herself to speak. Their eyes met. Held.

He moved toward her with determined steps, separating the space between them and causing her heart to pound uncontrollably. Once they were standing face to face, he stopped. Looking up into his handsome face, she saw something glowing in his sable eyes that she'd never seen before.

"Hello, Dom," he said huskily.

"Hi," she replied barely above a whisper.

Reese gazed fervently into her eyes and reached out, twining their hands together. The moment she felt his warm palm she exhaled and realized she had been holding her breath.

"What are you doing here?" She didn't even want to guess. It was hard enough remembering to breathe.

"I've been thinking about you a lot, and decided I needed to see you." His voice was gentle and soft as cashmere.

"Oh, yeah? What about?"

He lifted her hand to his mouth and kissed the back of it. "You. Us. Dom… I've been a fool. For as long as I can remember all I've cared about was being a surgeon, and nothing or no one was going to stand in the way of my success. Relationships had to take a back seat, and that included you. And then I had the accident, and all I cared about was myself and what I'd lost, and never once did I think about how you might be feeling." He paused and looked deeply into her eyes. "But this last weekend I've had time to realize that nothing in this world matters as much as you do." He shook his head slowly. "As much as I enjoy being a surgeon, it doesn't mean anything if I don't have you in my life."

She searched his face, desperate to understand. "You saying this to me now ... "

"I know, sweetheart, I know," he interrupted. "I have been a fool. Up to now time I just didn't know. I didn't realize I was taking you and your love for granted. But now I know that without you my life is empty. Baby, I need you."

"Reese..." she whispered and tears rushed to her eyes.

"I don't want to be in love without loving you."

Her lips parted. "What... what are you saying?" Because Lord knows she didn't want to get ahead of herself.

"I'm saying I love you. All this time... I have loved you." Reaching up he caressed her chin and tilted it up, and unconsciously she leaned into the warmth of his fingers. "And I don't want to live without you."

It took a moment for his words and their meaning to register. "Did you just say you're in love with me?"

He nodded. "Like a crazy person."

Dominique shook her head as tears spilled from the corners of her eyes. This was the moment she had been waiting for. Reese was finally saying the words she had been waiting more than a decade to hear. And the unmistakable love shimmering in his eyes practically stole her breath away.

"You are the most amazing thing that has ever happened in my life. And I don't want to lose you."

She threw her arms around his neck, pulling him down to her in a passionate kiss. She was lost in his tender mouth before she startled and pulled back from his grasp.

"Reese... I can't leave Waikiki," she replied, and realized how sad that made her feel. She loved him so much, yet there was no way she was turning back now.

He frowned. "I'm not asking you to leave."

"Then what are you saying?" she asked puzzled.

"I resigned my position. I'm sure there's a need for a one-handed cardiologist somewhere on this island," he added with a beautiful smile.

Her breath caught and she shook her head. "But you love that job."

His gaze locked with hers. "I love you more." Sincerity gleamed in his eyes.

A single tear rolled down her cheek. She had finally won the heart of the most stubborn man she'd ever known, and she couldn't be happier.

Reese got down on one knee before her and reached into his pocket. Her heart turned over in her chest. She would know that little blue box anywhere. He raised the lid and she gasped at the beautiful five-carat diamond engagement ring.

"Oh, my God. Reese..."

"Dominique Sierra Wellington, I fell for you the first time I saw your beautiful smile at the swimming pool and I have been crazy about you ever since. Please let me make up for the time we lost and marry me?"

She was stunned beyond words. His dark sable eyes held so much love and uncertainty that fresh tears sprang from her eyes. She heard whispering and looked around in awe, discovering that they had quite an audience in the lobby.

"Sweetheart," he said with a serious expression, drawing her attention. There was no mistaking the suddenly glimpse of uncertainty shadowing his gaze. "Please… I promise to cherish and treat you like the queen that you are every day of our lives together."

There was a collective sigh.

"Honey, if you don't want him, I'll take him!" she heard someone yell. There was laughter and people made other joyful comments, but her eyes were glued to one person. The only man who had ever had her heart. The longer she stared the more she trembled at the raw emotion glittering in his eyes.

Her heart soared. "Yes, Reese Leland Beaumont, I'll marry you."

Reese let out a whoop of joy and slid the ring onto her finger. As soon as he stood he lifted her into his arms, spinning her around while he captured her in a hot searing kiss that she felt all the way down to her toes. Loud applause caused her to suddenly remember where they were. When Reese finally ended the kiss, Dominique pulled back and gazed down adorningly at her ring.

"It fits perfectly," She breathed.

Grinning crookedly, Reese explained, "I had to get Sheyna to give me your ring size. As much as she hates me, she was more than willing to help."

Dominique swatted at his arm playfully. "Sheyna doesn't hate you. She's just protective, that's all."

"Yep, like a barracuda," he joked, then stroked her cheek and pulled her closer into the circle of his arms. "And as much as she irritates me, I'm glad that you have a friend like her who not only has your back but will go to bat for you. You have no idea how many hours she spent grilling me. I had to tell her my intentions."

"And what were they?" she asked staring adoringly

up into his eyes.

"That all I planned on doing is loving you."

"Sweetheart, those words are music to my ears, but I hope you're planning on showing me," she said tenderly.

"Every night, baby," he confirmed. "Every single night."

"Then let's go home, make love, and have some babies," she whispered.

"Dom... you got yourself a deal." Smiling, Reese laced his fingers through hers and led Dominique through the crowd of bystanders and out the hotel doors, anxious to start their new life together.

Other Books by Angie Daniels

ABOUT THE AUTHOR

Angie Daniels has released over two dozen novels. She has won numerous awards including a Romantic Times Reviewers' Choice Award for *When it Rains*, and an Emma Award for Favorite Erotic Romance, for *A Delight Before Christmas*. She began her road to publication in 2001 when she was offered a four-book deal with Genesis Press. In 2002 she signed with BET/Arabesque which was purchased by Harlequin/Kimani Romance in 2005. Angie joined Kensington Publishing in 2003. She has a bachelor's degree in Business Administration from Columbia College. For more information about upcoming releases, and to connect with Angie on facebook, please visit her website at www.angiedaniels.com.

Made in the USA
Middletown, DE
30 June 2015